PALE as
DEATH

* * * * *

Look for Heather Graham's next novel
ECHOES OF EVIL
available soon from MIRA Books.

HEATHER GRAHAM

PALE as DEATH

mira

mira

ISBN-13: 978-0-7783-6873-1

Pale as Death

For questions and comments about the quality of this book, please contact us at
CustomerService@Harlequin.com.

BookClubbish.com

Printed in U.S.A.

To Gail and Kelly Stewart, the amazing parents of Kari Stewart, the beautiful girl—inside and out—who is about to become my daughter-in-law. Knowing them, it's quite easy to see how she grew up to be such a kind, generous and wonderful human being.

To Kari's sister, Jessica; her husband, Adam; and their little ones, Teddy, Olivia and Arthur.

And for Yevgeniya Yerekskaya, Derek's wife, and the mom of Korbin; and Joseph Hunton, Bryee's husband, dad of the little girl who will make her appearance before this book arrives on shelves, and for Zohe and Ellysse.

We are so blessed with the people who have come into our lives!

CAST OF CHARACTERS

The McFadden brothers—Bryan, Bruce and Brodie, all former military,
now registered as private investigators

Jackson Crow—FBI field director, Krewe of Hunters

LAPD

Detective Sophie Manning—a young detective
who keeps catching high-profile and disturbing cases

Detective Grant Vining—a career cop, and Sophie's partner

Captain Lorne Chagall—squad captain

Henry Atkins—police photographer

Lee Underwood—forensic science technician

Dr. Chuck Thompson—medical examiner

Other Players

Kenneth Trent—director of the Hollywood Hooligans

Jace Brown—boyfriend of one of the victims

Ian Sanders—ex-boyfriend of one of the victims

Grace Leon—aspiring actress

Michael Thoreau—reporter from the 1940s
who was covering the original Black Dahlia case

Maeve and Hamish McFadden—celebrated actors of screen and stage,
killed tragically in an accident

PALE as DEATH

CHAPTER ONE

Monday morning

"I thought it was a dummy—I mean, a mannequin. You know, ones they use in store windows. I mean…oh, my God! There's no blood… There's red around the…around the places where she's all chopped up. But still, I mean, this is Hollywood. I thought that someone was making a movie and…then the dog started barking, and I didn't see any movie trailers or signs or… oh, God! She was real. She was once…she still is…like flesh and blood and bone…just…oh, God!"

Detective Sophie Manning could imagine that the woman had thought the corpse was a mannequin, or at the very least, something unreal.

But the dead girl was real. It was only the extreme brutality of her death that made her appear as if she were not, as if she were some creation of the most brilliant and lurid mind working in a Hollywood special effects studio.

Stripped naked. Sliced in half. Slashed. Chunks of flesh… gone. Intestines…under the buttocks.

The woman who had discovered the body—pieces—on South Norton Avenue wavered suddenly, as if she were about to pass out and fall.

The witness was a heavyset woman who was nearly six feet tall; Sophie prided herself on having achieved a full five feet four inches. Luckily, she spent half her life in the gym. Size-wise, she just met police requirements. She didn't have a Napoleon complex—she was simply aware of her size, aware she had to keep up with "the big boys," and was dedicated to her job, determined to be her best.

The woman began to keel over.

Sophie quickly caught her—bracing herself—and steadied her.

"I'm so sorry!" the woman apologized.

The witness was Claudia Cooper, and she lived around the block. Her dog was a teacup Yorkie, and Sophie had to hand it to the little creature—he was small, but he knew a dead body from a mannequin. The Yorkie's name was Tsum-Tsum, and a crime scene tech was checking his tiny paws for blood.

"It's all right. I understand completely," Sophie assured her.

"You must see things like this all the time."

"Not quite like this," Sophie assured her. "You're human. So am I. And this is truly horrible and cruel and tragic. Let's have you sit. Do you mind? There's a patrol car right over there," Sophie said.

As she tried to help the woman, Sophie glanced across the bit of sidewalk and grass. Her partner, Grant Vining, was hunkered down by the body with the medical examiner.

Vining was one of the finest detectives in LA—or anywhere, she thought. She was lucky to be his partner. Captain Lorne Chagall, the supervising officer for their team—an elite unit as it was, handling the most vicious and sometimes *strangest* cases in Tinseltown—had announced Grant Vining as lead detective, with her assisting, from the moment the call had come in.

They'd been specifically handed the case because of their recent involvement in a case where the cast of a cult TV show had been targeted by a killer; Sophie figured they'd handled the high-profile murder without any major gaffes, and this new one was sure to draw media attention. The discovery of the corpse had been a little more than two hours ago, and somehow, reporters were all over it already.

Naturally. The way the body had been found was gruesome, to say the least.

Similarities to the old unsolved murder of Elizabeth Short—aka the Black Dahlia—were obviously intentional. The woman found dead this morning was discovered on South Norton Avenue near the place where the Black Dahlia had been found in a vacant lot. Just like Elizabeth Short, she had been killed elsewhere; she was all but drained of blood. She'd been severed in half, and remained in situ now as the investigation into her death got under way.

Another eerie detail had been included.

The victim's face had been slashed on both sides from the corners of her mouth to the ears—creating a monstrous, Joker-like grin on the dead woman.

It was a case Sophie had studied. Her dad had been a cop; she'd always known that she was going to join the force, too. Cold cases had been bedtime reading.

Even so, the horrible murder of Elizabeth Short was still being pondered and mused on by the best of them—law enforcement and armchair sleuths. While there had been confessions galore, most were easily dismissed as false. No one had ever been able to prove who Elizabeth Short's killer might be.

"Are you all right now? Do you think that you can give your statement to the officer?" Sophie asked Claudia Cooper.

The woman nodded vigorously. "You must catch him—whoever did this!"

"Ma'am, I promise you, we—and every officer in LA—will be doing our best to capture this killer."

No way out of it—this was going to be sensational. Most likely, the killer assumed that he—or she—would get away with the murder. Just as they did back in the 1940s.

Times were different now, Sophie thought. Forensic science had come a long way, for one.

The Yorkie whined suddenly, as if aware of the terrible situation. Afraid. He hadn't minded at all that his paws were under serious scrutiny. He seemed worried about his mistress.

Yes, the whole city would live in fear. Women would be on extra high alert, wondering what they could possibly do to avoid the same horrible fate.

Sophie led Claudia Cooper and her tiny Yorkie over to one of the patrol cars. The young officer quickly leaped to his feet to open the door to the rear for Claudia. He had his work sheet out; he nodded gravely to Sophie. He was ready to take the full statement.

Sophie walked back over to where the pieces of the corpse remained in situ. Henry Atkins, police photographer, looked at her as she approached and shook his head, wincing.

It was one of the worst crime scenes they'd ever seen, and they all knew it.

"Finished. For now," he told her bleakly. Henry had a basset hound look about him. Long jowls, pale blue eyes. He was in his early fifties, and she'd heard he was close to retirement.

She nodded and looked around. Police officers were canvassing the neighborhood. Crime scene techs were busy gathering anything that might be evidence. A lot of what they would find would be chewed gum, bottle caps and smashed fast-food cups, but all of it would be collected. Any tiny piece might be of tremendous help in the investigation.

She almost bumped into one tech, Lee Underwood. Young,

blond, handsome and wire-muscled, he looked more like a surfer dude than a crime scene investigator.

"Sorry," he apologized.

"My fault," she told him.

"I was just getting that butt," he told her, pointing to what remained of someone's cigarette—not more than the filter. "Cigarette butt," he added quickly, as if his intentions might be questioned, even at such a scene. "I don't think that any of this garbage will belong to the killer," he said glumly. "This guy…" He paused, looking over at the body. "This guy went by the book—the Black Dahlia book. And, I think, some kind of forensic book. He won't have made mistakes."

"Everybody makes mistakes," Sophie said.

He shook his head. "Yeah, so we say. But we'll need good luck to find this guy's."

He collected the butt with a gloved hand, smiled grimly, and moved on.

Sophie hunkered down between Vining and Dr. Thompson.

It was a difficult place to be.

The corpse was simply so horrifically displayed.

Just as she had been killed.

Sophie couldn't begin to imagine the terror the woman must have felt as the knife came toward her face. They weren't scratches that created the Joker grin; they were deep gashes. There were so many other cuts on the body, as if chunks of flesh had been cut away.

"Blunt force trauma?" she asked, looking up.

Dr. Chuck Thompson—a big man with iron gray hair and a square ruddy face—nodded gravely. "I'll have to get her to autopsy, of course. She wasn't killed here—that's pretty obvious. I'd say, though, that her head took a good beating. Enough to kill. And the knife wounds…they could have done it, too. I mean, obviously, she's been bisected, but death—mercifully—came first."

Thompson was a dedicated man. He'd never married, and he was always ready to take on a case when others were begging out for one reason or another. He'd been in the county a long time, and stayed stalwart despite the work load. He'd seen a lot, she knew.

He grimaced. "She was alive when the gashes were made," Thompson said quietly.

Death could often be cruel, but this woman had been brutally tortured.

Grant Vining looked resolute. Like Dr. Thompson, he'd been in his job for a long time. Despite the difference in their tenure, Vining always mentored instead of being impatient with Sophie's comparative lack of experience. He also had a great capacity for listening. When other officers discovered something, he was grateful. He worked well with other cops, and with law enforcement officials from other agencies.

"Whatever gets it closed," he often told Sophie.

Right now, he was pensive, and he shook his head and stated the obvious.

"Black Dahlia," he said. "Our officers are canvassing the neighborhood, but until we get something from them or from the forensic team, we're just waving our stuff in the air."

He was right; Sophie knew it.

As she listened to him, she noted that a good-sized crowd had grown around the crime scene tape.

Many of those people were journalists. Some had out notepads; some were with network or cable stations, their microphones and cameras visible. Bystanders were taking pictures with their phones, too.

"Sophie," Vining said, just as the thought came to her that

they'd need to make a statement soon. "They like a young pretty face better than they like mine. Tell them—tell them nothing."

"Gotcha," she murmured, rising. She'd rather be with the press right now than with the corpse. She couldn't help glancing again at the woman's face, at the bizarre grin slashed into it. Once, she thought, judging by her youth and the handsome angles that remained of the face, their victim had been beautiful. Not so long ago, she would have laughed, and her eyes would have sparkled. But now she lay like a broken doll torn apart by a disgruntled and sadistic child.

Did that actually describe the killer?

Sophie walked toward the crowd. People began to bristle like a school of fish eager when a morsel of krill moved by.

She kept her expression neutral.

The press surged forward—with a talent for making their way through the more casual bystanders.

Then Sophie noticed one man.

He was different. It might have been in his curious and determined but unhurried manner, but it was mainly his dress. He was wearing a suit, but it wasn't something many men would have on today—unless they were actors filming a period piece. It was a zoot suit, she thought. The slant of his hat, the cut of his jacket…he appeared to be out of time and out of place. He was in his mid to late thirties, she thought, dark-haired, and with a lean face that was both handsome and engaging.

Argh! she thought. *A new guy.* Maybe he thinks he's going to be quirky and charming and get some kind of scoop from the cops not available to others.

"Hello," Sophie said, addressing the crowd. "I know that rumors are running wild right now, and I can't blame you or anyone for speculating over what you have gleaned about this terrible crime. At this moment, we know that we have a victim who was cruelly murdered. We don't have an identity for the young woman. It will take time for an autopsy. Until then, we ask you to respect—"

"Black Dahlia!"

Sophie broke off. It was the guy in the zoot suit, with his pen raised over his notepad.

"We're not giving this murder any kind of a moniker at this time," she said.

She was surprised when the rest of the people in the crowd looked around at one another—and then at her. They seemed confused.

"As we have information, we'll make sure we get it to you," she said. "We depend on the people of Los Angeles to help us. We are a massive community, a united community in caring for others, and—"

"Black Dahlia!"

The man in the zoot suit had spoken again, cutting Sophie off. The crowd shuffled uneasily. But they weren't looking at him; they were watching Sophie, waiting.

A man in front cleared his throat. "Detective, we heard that she was…displayed. There's been talk. Is this murder reminiscent of that of Elizabeth Short, the Black Dahlia?"

"Yes, of course, you idiot," the man in the zoot suit said.

"There's no need, sir," Sophie said.

"Pardon?" the reporter closest to her said curiously. People were really staring at her now.

She looked back. Even Vining was watching; he seemed concerned that he had given her the responsibility of talking to the press.

But what the hell…?

When she turned back, it was just in time to see him—the man in the zoot suit—walk toward her, right through the crime scene tape, as if it was nonexistent.

She closed her eyes for a moment, and prayed silently.

Not again!

It had happened when she'd been in college, when a fellow student, a wonderful young man with an addiction problem, had died from an overdose. He'd come to her—after his death—and she had nearly had a heart attack herself, and then he'd talked to her and asked her for help with his family.

Not again, not again, not again!

After it all, her father had insisted she go into therapy. The doctor had convinced her that she'd had the information his family needed, somewhere locked inside her, but in order to see that they received it, she'd had to invent his ghost speaking to her so that she could do what she needed to do.

She'd nearly fallen apart. Doubting herself, her senses, in that way had been hard.

But back then, she'd been twenty. She'd been young and impressionable and easily swayed and confused and hurt.

Now...

She was an LAPD detective. Hard-won.

And she was going to solve the murder of the woman who lay so broken on the ground, come hell or high water.

So she ignored the man in the suit.

The instrument of her imagination—or a long dead ghost.

"Please, whatever you're hearing, we ask that you respect the victim. These are the facts that I can give you. At ten this morning, a neighbor here discovered the body of a young woman."

The figment of her imagination was now standing by her side.

"Pieces of her body," he said.

She went on, "At this moment, she has not been identified. When we do know her identity—pending notification of her next of kin—we will let you all know. I can't share details with you right now as we are just beginning our investigation. Thank you for allowing the police to do their work, and thank you for your help. We'll have more information forthcoming soon. Thank you," she said with finality.

She turned around, ready to head back to Vining.

"Ah, ignore me, will you? Good call. But I can help you, I swear."

She lowered her head. She couldn't help asking, "You know who did this?"

"No, but I'm telling you, if you give me a chance—"

"You do not exist," she muttered. "You're in my head, and you're just here because I've gone through a loss of my own, and now...this."

She took a deep breath. She wasn't going to have Grant Vining think that she needed time off. Not now.

"That was fine, Sophie, thank you," Vining said. He was looking at her, though, as if he was worried about her. "A little rocky at the start, but fine."

"We're going to get her out of here now," Chuck Thompson said. "You can meet me at the morgue. Autopsy tomorrow morning, eight o'clock sharp? The mayor...everyone is going to want this done ASAP."

"We'll meet you there," Vining said.

"Yes, we'll meet you there," Sophie said firmly.

Vining looked at her. "It's going to be a hell of a long day," he said. "You all right?"

"Just fine," she assured him, hating the way he was looking at her. "Where do you want me to start?"

Bruce McFadden happened to be at home—his parents' old house in Alexandria—when the news came on covering the murder in Los Angeles.

"Oh, my God," Marnie Davante, his brother Bryan's brand-new fiancée, cried out. Something on the TV had caught her attention.

Bruce and his older brother, Bryan, had been deep in conversation along with their younger brother, Brodie, regarding their futures.

Bryan had made the definite decision to enter the FBI academy. He'd been invited to join what had just been given the official moniker of "FBI Special Assistance Unit" but was known throughout the academy and beyond as the Krewe of Hunters, because of the first case it had taken on in New Orleans, Louisiana. While the unit and the agency never acknowledged that they were also known as the "Ghost-busters," those involved knew the truth: every agent of the group could communicate with the dead. In their recent discussions, the plan between the McFadden brothers had been to create a private investigation firm. To that end, on their exit from the military, each had become licensed as PIs. Bryan had recently been embroiled in a murder case out in Los Angeles—on the request of their mother. An actress, Cara Barton—who was an old friend of their parents—had been killed in a sensational case.

Such things happened. Sons did things for their parents. In their situation, however, it was a bit different. Maeve and Hamish McFadden were dead.

Now discussion stopped. They all stared at the news.

Bryan had risen to walk closer to the wide-screen television on the wall. "Hard to tell much from what the media has so far," he said, "but you can see Vining and Manning caught this."

"Sophie is coming forward to talk to the press," Marnie murmured.

Bruce glanced at Brodie, who gave him a shrug and a look that silently said, "We'll have to wait and see what they're talking about."

Marnie's home had been LA until recently. She and Bryan had met because Marnie had been targeted by the man who'd killed

Cara Barton—and despite the short time of their relationship, it did appear as if they were destined for one another.

"Sophie is behaving so oddly, isn't she?" Marnie said. "Almost as if she's talking to someone else. Ah, she's in control again." Marnie sounded a bit proud—she evidently liked Sophie, who was—Bruce presumed, from her speech and position at the crime scene—a detective with the LAPD.

He realized that he and Brodie had both risen as well, drawing closer to the TV. It was a large set—they could have all seen it just fine from where they'd been. But maybe there was more to their sixth sense. Because he realized that they all knew now that this wasn't a simple case. The body itself was shielded from view, but the questions and the murmurs told them what they needed to know.

A killer had re-created a crime. A horrible and gruesome crime from days gone past.

"There! Look," Marnie said, moving forward to point at the set.

"I see it," Bruce told her, moving forward to point, as well. "As if a little white cloud is next to her."

"Human-shaped," Bryan said.

"She reacted to it—and now she's ignoring it," Marnie noted. "Ah, she's not going to be deterred."

"Where's Vining?" Bryan asked, frowning.

"There, back with the body," Marnie said.

No matter how they might try, no photographer, videographer or cameraman of any kind was going to get a real shot of the body.

But you could see the police and forensic people working the scene.

And then, the entire scene itself was gone. They were looking at an anchor in a news station.

"That's a smart TV—let's roll back," Bruce suggested.

Bryan picked up the remote control. The TV obediently went back to replay the footage they had been watching.

It was strange, what a camera could catch.

There was something there—a shift like fog or misty clouds. It moved. It joined the young woman speaking. And while most people might not have understood her reaction, everyone in that room did.

"There's a ghost there—and she knows it," Brodie said. He might be the youngest in their trio, but he was quickest to state aloud what they were thinking—or fearing.

After their parents' death, when Maeve and Hamish had first begun to visit them, they'd each pretended that they didn't see the ghosts. Until finally Brodie had just shouted it out—they were there! Talking to them. Yes, their parents were dead. But their spirits were there now, and they'd all loved one another, so they needed to embrace this new reality.

Sophie the detective wasn't loving whatever was going on. She was hiding the fact that she was distressed and doing a damned good job of it.

Bruce observed the woman, wondering if she ever had a difficult time being so attractive and garnering respect. She was small, too—maybe five-four, tops, and possibly a hundred-and-ten. She had dark blond hair, reasonably cut to fall around but not into her face. Her features were both delicate and strong, broad cheekbones, wide-set brown eyes, strong jaw.

No doubt, she would have worked hard to get where she was, detective—first grade, he imagined, if she was part of this high-profile situation.

"She never said a word when we were out there," Marnie said softly.

"Maybe she never saw Cara. Remember, none of us can ever explain exactly why we see or hear or sometimes even just feel the dead," Bryan told her.

There was so much affection in Bryan's eyes when he looked at Marnie. Almost more intimate than if he was kissing the hell out of her, right there, in front of them all.

"I'm going to call her," Marnie said. "She was wonderful to me, Bryan. I want to make sure she's all right. I want to see if there's something I can do. A way I can help."

"I'll go back to LA," Bryan told her.

"You can't—you're starting the academy."

"It can wait."

Bruce had no idea whatsoever what suddenly compelled him. Maybe he was curious.

The Black Dahlia. A crime re-created. The ghost of someone—the victim? A victim from the past? Someone else entirely—there, and haunting a detective on the case.

"I'll go," Bruce said.

Bryan, Marnie and Brodie turned to stare at him.

"What?" he said with a shrug. "We're not starting up an agency now. Bryan, you're going to be in the academy, and honestly, I can be just as effective. I'll go," he offered.

Marnie looked at her fiancé, her eyes questioning and anxious.

"He's good," Bryan told her. "He is 'just as effective,'" he added drily.

"Whatever," Brodie said. He shrugged. "I'll go, too."

"You can't go—at least, not just yet. You said that you were going to look into the death of the maintenance man at the theater Adam Harrison owns," Marnie reminded him.

"As head of the Krewe, Adam has a whole crew of agents available to him," Brodie said.

Marnie offered him a beautiful and wry smile. "Yes, but you promised your mother."

Brodie groaned and looked at Bruce. "You're going alone," he said flatly.

Bruce grinned at his youngest brother. Many adults were

plagued by their parents—which was okay. Having loving parents—at any age—was a great thing. Not many, however, were
plagued *and* haunted.

"I'll be fine," Bruce said. He tried to give Marnie his best
reassuring look. "Whoever finishes up first can go and help the
other. Besides, it's a cop you're worried about. She's probably
pretty tough."

"She is—she helped me out incredibly," Marnie said. "But I
didn't know she saw the dead," she added softly. "If it's a new
thing to her…well, it can be a weird time."

"I'll watch out for your friend, Marnie." He looked at Bryan
questioningly. "If she'll let me. I'll try to get out there as quickly
as possible—"

"They're just about magic at Krewe headquarters," Bryan told
him. "If you can be packed in fifteen minutes, I'll bet we can
have you on a plane in two hours."

"I can be ready."

It suddenly seemed as if a door opened and slammed; it didn't,
but it might have. Maeve McFadden—or the ghost thereof—
burst into the room, followed by the ghost of their weary-but-
forever-patient-and-tolerant father, Hamish. Both had been
actors—on stage and screen—in life, and they still carried their
charisma and drama with them.

"Hey, Dad," Bruce said. "Oh, hey, Mom, you're here, too!"

"Don't be a wiseass, my dear boy," his mother said. "Bryan,
Marnie, did you see—"

"We all saw, Mom," Bryan assured her.

"Well, then, you must—"

"We're on it, Mom," Bruce told her. He walked over and
kissed the cold air where her cheek appeared. "I'm heading out
right away. Just as soon as I can get a flight."

"What about…oh, Brodie! You can't go with him now—you
promised you'd help me. I knew Justin Westinghouse for years

and years. I know he was no spring chicken. But… I don't like it. I just don't like it. Bryan is going to be busy running or jumping or learning to shoot—"

"I think he knows how to shoot, Mom," Bruce murmured.

She waved a ghostly hand in the air. "Yes, yes, but he'll be in the academy. Anyway, what matters, Bruce, is that you must go. You must help that poor lovely young woman. Why, she helped watch over Marnie."

"Mom, yeah, I know. I'm going," Bruce said.

He felt the soft, misty touch of her hand.

"I do love you boys," she said, and smiled. "More than life and death," she added.

Maeve could definitely be a bit of a wiseass herself.

CHAPTER TWO

Monday night, late

There was a knock at Sophie's door. It startled her; she'd been online, researching the Black Dahlia case.

It was ridiculously late.

She should have been sleeping.

Hard to sleep, though, after what she'd witnessed today—in many ways.

It made sense to study the Black Dahlia case.

The Black Dahlia—Elizabeth Short—had been from Massachusetts. She had been a struggling actress, like so many a beautiful young woman in LA.

The police at the time had investigated all fifty-plus people who confessed to the crime; they had made comparisons to murders that had occurred in Chicago and in Cleveland.

Sophie believed that when they discovered the identity of their victim, they would find that she had been an aspiring actress, too. Because it appeared that a sick killer was obsessed with the past. If they were going to solve their current murder, she was going to have to know the old case forward and backward.

The murder in 1947 was a long time ago. And yet, there were still writers, film producers and ordinary citizens fascinated by the case, always looking for that one tiny clue that had been overlooked, that might finally give an answer to the question. Far too late, of course, for Elizabeth Short, and for this new victim.

She had to be careful, she knew. The murder of the Black Dahlia—according to most of the credible accounts Sophie was reading, Elizabeth Short had been dubbed the Black Dahlia after her murder, and not before—had received such widespread and almost hectic and desperate press coverage that one had to be careful reading. Much that had been written had been exaggeration or speculation.

Sophie was so deep in thought.

And then...a knock.

Absurd, but the sound sent alarms racing all through her bloodstream.

Normally, she didn't pick up her department-issue firearm just to open her front door. Then again, people weren't usually at her door when it was past midnight.

She saw no one—nothing—through the peephole.

Had she imagined the sound? Or had it just been something from the street?

The knock sounded again.

Again, when she looked outside the front door of her apartment, there was no one there.

She immediately tensed. She'd heard the knock. She held her gun ready, and opened the door. She lived in Los Feliz, which was generally a very good, safe neighborhood, but it didn't hurt to be wary.

He was there. The man in the bizarre 1940s suit, hat pulled in a rakish angle over one eye.

"Well, you could shoot me. But it won't help you any," he told her. "I'm already dead."

Somewhere in her mind, Sophie knew it.

But the truth was too bizarre to accept.

"Who the hell are you?" she demanded, not lowering her weapon.

"All you will do is put a big old bullet hole in your door, miss," he said easily, touching the rim of his hat, "Or worse, you'll fire into the night and hit some poor, hapless soul on their way to the little grocery store on the corner. Dead, Sophie. I'm already dead."

She really couldn't accept it.

"May I? Come in, I mean. Please, honestly, I'm here to help you."

She didn't give him any permission. She just stood there. Somehow, he slipped by her.

"I really suggest you shut the door," he told her, moving easily into the living room and pausing by the sofa. "I'd like to sit, but you know, my mom raised me to be a gentleman. I can't sit while you're standing. And you look silly standing there, pointing a gun into the empty night."

She was imagining him. Maybe she wasn't such a hardened detective. Maybe this was all too much for her.

She found herself moving back in cautiously. She shut the door and locked it, keeping him in front of her—and her gun in her grip. She eased into the armchair facing the sofa. He took a seat across from her, grinning pleasantly.

"First things first—I'm Michael Thoreau. You can look me up. I'm for real. I was murdered while investigating the Black Dahlia case."

He was full of it—but she'd play along.

"You were a cop?"

"Investigative reporter," he said. "I was working hard on the Black Dahlia when some asshole shot me in a dark alley. Whether it was random, or someone associated with the case, I don't know. My murder was never solved, either. I've been hanging around a really long time. Not at all sure why. Then today, I saw you. It's happening all over again. I have been sticking around all this time to help you."

"Unless you were there and saw who did it, I sincerely doubt there is anything you can do to help us. You need to leave— now. And I won't press charges."

"How they will laugh at you when you try to press charges against a dead man," he said.

"Get up. Get out," she said. "I don't know who you really are, or what the hell you're doing. If this is some kind of a prank, it's a dangerous one. You could wind up getting yourself seriously hurt—or killed."

"Oh, Sophie, Sophie. You know that I'm telling the truth. Look me up. Michael Thoreau. Go through the old papers. Everything I'm saying is bona fide. I can be there for you. I can go places you can't go. Hey, I can sift through papers if something is being held from you by anyone just about anywhere. Come on, Sophie."

She didn't blink; she kept the gun aimed at him.

He smiled and rose.

She did the same.

"I'll give you a bit of time. Not too much—we've got to get on this. But I guess this is new to you. Not to worry. I'll be back."

She felt him—*felt him*—as he passed through her.

And then on through the closed and locked door, back into the night.

Sophie's breath left her, and her eyes closed as she sank into darkness.

Tuesday morning, nowhere near dawn

Some called it a "gift." Many called it a "curse." Some pretended to have it, and most often, people just had an inkling of whatever the "sixth" sense was that allowed one to see, hear and communicate with the dead. Those people felt the press of history and the ages seep into them at battlefields such as that at Gettysburg, churches like Westminster Abbey, or old crypts or graveyards, places sacred to the dead, like the Catacombs of Paris or a Capuchin Monastery.

Of course, in one way or another, the dead only communicated when they chose to do so.

Some—like Bruce's parents—seemed to embrace their existence in death with almost as much gusto as they had embraced life.

The thought made Bruce smile. His folks were—beyond a doubt—a *presence*.

Bruce had a tendency to think of his abilities mostly as a curse—but then again, after his parents' deaths, he had sat there and wished that he'd had just one more moment with them... one last time to let them know how much they had been loved, and what great parents they had been.

At that time, he'd never imagined he'd have the opportunity.

Not many people did. Largely, things left unsaid had to stay unsaid, regrets that lingered painfully in the human soul.

The problem for him was that—ever since he and his brothers had been visited by their parents—his gift seemed to have become acute.

He saw the dead far too often. Everywhere. Whether he wanted to or not.

He and his brothers all felt that they needed to use their talents to serve; at first that had meant joining the military, but now, with their unusual skill, it seemed to be pushing them in a different direction.

Bryan was dead set on the FBI and the Krewe of Hunters. Bruce just wasn't sure what he wanted himself. He knew he'd been drifting in the three years since he'd left the marines. Unable to really make a commitment, but restless unless he was working. Tommy Baker—a fellow vet from his corps—had returned to Texas to become a Texas Ranger. When Tommy had called a few months back because of a most peculiar case, Bruce had been glad to go. It had involved kidnapped young women kept in a basement as a harem. He'd been able to help.

The ghost of Gina Patterson—who'd died in the basement due to a miscarriage—had worked with him, helping him find the place where the women were being kept. He could still remember her sweet and beautiful face—her life had been lost, but she didn't want that fate for others.

Then she—unlike his mom and dad—had decided to move on.

Neither he nor his brothers were fools; they didn't explain to others that sometimes the dead came back to help them.

Because of his parents' connection to Adam Harrison, he knew a great deal about the Krewe. The unit had been formed by Harrison, a unique older gentleman whose quiet role in life had seemed to be philanthropy, but also finding people with unique talents.

Bruce would be a liar to say that he hadn't studied many of their cases. They did their work quietly—and kept their methods to themselves. And while others in the Bureau might curiously mock them or tease, the Krewe had the best solve rate of cases among all others. They had earned the respect they were given.

The members came from all walks of life before entering the academy at Quantico—which was required—and becoming Krewe. Some had been in law enforcement previously—cops, US Marshals, military of one type or another. Others came from totally unrelated fields. Will Chan—an agent with the original Krewe—had once been a magician.

While the brothers had all talked about joining the Krewe before—there had never been a determination of "Let's do it!" Or even, from any one of them, "I'm going to do it!" Until Bryan had worked with Field Director Jackson Crow recently and made up his mind.

Bruce did sometimes feel there had to be a greater purpose for the fact that he could see the spirits of those departed.

Even landing at LAX, heading through the terminal, and then out to hop a van to the rental car station, Bruce saw a few of those who had—and still—called LA home even though they were no longer on the earthly plane. Tight curls on the heads of a few ladies who had passed in the forties, bell-bottoms and Nehru jackets on those from the sixties. Sometimes, since it was, after all, something of a permanent fantasyland, Bruce really wasn't sure if he was seeing a ghost, or just someone who had chosen to dress in retro fashion, but since it was after two in the morning, he was pretty sure that most of the people he was seeing were among those who had departed their mortal shells.

From the car rental station, he picked up the 405—the only good thing about the hour was the lighter traffic—and headed downtown; it was kind of a pain to stay downtown, but he figured it would also be central to wherever he might need to be. Marnie was supposed to call Sophie Manning to let her know that he was on his way.

He hoped that the woman really did want some help. Otherwise...

Well, he couldn't just go home.

He checked into his hotel room. It was almost 3:00 a.m. California time—and 6:00 a.m. back East. He was pretty sure that Sophie Manning wouldn't be happy hearing from anyone at this hour, much less a spirit-seeing stranger.

Locking the door, he set his weapon on the bedside table. He was grateful that a contact of his at the DOJ had seen to it that he had a special California permit to carry his weapon as a "security contractor." Set for the night, he stretched out on his bed.

His sleep wasn't haunted; rather his dreams were plagued by the fear that the dead might not appear—and that the living might not have the answers they were so desperately going to need.

Tuesday morning, early

Sophie's alarm rang; it seemed to be coming from far, far away. She woke with a start—and slid off the chair and onto what her parents had always referred to politely as her derriere.

For a moment, she felt as paranoid and vulnerable as a recruit. She had no idea of where she was, or why she was on the floor. Obviously, she'd fallen asleep on the chair.

To her horror, she realized that she'd passed out cold, right onto the big old armchair where she'd been sitting before she'd risen and a ghost had walked right through her.

No. That was far too humiliating. Detectives did not faint.

But there had been a man who claimed to have died in the 1940s, right on the rim of the Black Dahlia case, in her apartment.

Had it been her imagination? She'd seen him at the crime scene. And then he'd knocked at her door.

It seemed she was really good at making up imaginary people.

A psychiatrist had spent months assuring her that she might imagine people so that they could help her deal with whatever was going on in her life.

Yep, that was it: she invented dead people.

She even gave them names. At least, she had done so with this one. Michael Thoreau. She would look him up. Maybe she had read about him at some point—and that's why he was popping up in her subconscious now.

Real—or a product of her imagination—she had to forget about it for the moment. She was due at autopsy. She stood, gave herself a shake. She saw with horror that her Glock 22—the weapon she had received when she had graduated from the police academy—lay on the floor.

With a shudder she picked it up, grateful that the weapon had an automatic safety—and that she hadn't shot up her apartment. Wary—maybe of her own mind—she checked the door. It was locked; she was always careful to lock it. But then again, she had seen her ghost leave by walking through the door.

She went into the bedroom and put the gun away in her bedside table, where it always went once she was home.

She needed a shower. Big-time.

But first…coffee.

She headed to the kitchen to start the brewer. Her apartment was the ground floor of a house. When she'd taken it, she'd loved the fact that it had a front door and a back door—and grass and trees and a little patio out back. Sun was filtering in through the back windows.

She headed to the bathroom, between the two bedrooms—one of which she used for her office.

She had just stripped down, turned on a spray of delightfully hot water and stepped into it, when she heard something.

She froze. It had sounded like a click. Like a door opening. It had been faint, and hard to hear over the water, but there had definitely been a sound.

Her Glock was in the bedroom.

Sophie was careful; she'd been careful all her life.

Her dad being a cop, she'd simply been brought up to be observant—and cautious. The toughest guy out there, the best shot in the world, the toughest damned Ninja warrior, could go down if he—or she—was taken by surprise. Carelessly leaving doors unlocked was one way a lot of smart people wound up dead.

She knew that she had locked the front door; she'd just checked it. Every single day or night when she came in, she checked the locks on her doors.

But that sound.

It was as if someone had come in.

She remained very still and listened. She really couldn't hear over the flow of the water. She moved; she was a cop, for God's sake! She slid silently to the bathroom door and leaned her head against it.

Now she could swear that she heard movement in the office. Someone rustling through papers, moving around her desk.

She grabbed a towel and wrapped it around her, trying all the harder to listen, to hear. She had nothing in the bathroom except for a spray bottle of cleaner. That was something, she told herself. Grabbing it up, she listened again.

Nothing.

Then she heard footsteps.

Were they coming toward the bathroom door?

She wasn't going down without a fight. There was someone out there, and it wasn't her ghost or her imaginary haunt—he had knocked. She had to get to her gun.

With one hand, she threw the door open, the other holding her household bleach cleaner in front of her.

At the same time, she heard, "Detective Manning?"

She raced forward to spray the man, nearly crashing straight into him before thinking *I know this guy!* She stopped dead, all but touching him. *It's Bryan McFadden, the PI who helped catch the killer in her last case, but how the hell was he here?*

Except that it wasn't Bryan. He was someone like Bryan... *but not Bryan.*

And she—an LAPD detective—was standing there, in front of him, in a towel with a bottle of spray cleaner.

Then again...

He was in her apartment.

She got control.

"Who the hell are you and what are you doing in my apartment?" she demanded. He wasn't Bryan, but he had to be related to Bryan to look almost like his clone.

He stared back at her, nonplussed by her fury or the authority and confidence she was certain she had set into her voice.

Then again, he might have measured up her five-four against his six-three. And she was suddenly certain that there was a weapon in a holster somewhere beneath the black jacket he was wearing.

"Why did you break into my apartment? Who the hell are you? What do you want?"

"I didn't break into your apartment, Miss Manning."

"Detective Manning."

"Detective Manning. Your front door was wide-open. I naturally came in as quickly as I saw it—assuming something might be wrong. My name is Bruce McFadden, and you should have known that I was on my way here to help you. Marnie left several messages."

Nothing seemed to be computing. She shook her head.

"The door was locked."

"Not when I got here."

"You were in my office?"

"No. I walked in calling your name, and a second later you burst out with your...spray bottle of bleach."

No way out of it; there was an alarming puzzle.

He reached behind his back; yes, he was armed. He inclined his head, suggesting she get behind him. It made sense. He had a gun. She had cleaner.

"How large is the apartment?" he asked, his voice quieter.

"Two bedrooms, bath between. Living and dining room combo—as we are now. Kitchen—and exit through the back door."

He nodded, backing his way to the front door, closing and locking it. He headed first to her room, cleared it ahead of her, and she slipped in and grabbed her own Glock.

She checked the closet.

They headed into the office.

There were papers on the floor.

"You didn't do that?" he asked her.

"You didn't do it?" she asked him.

He shook his head.

She knew damned well the bathroom was empty. They moved on through the hallway to the kitchen.

The back door wasn't just unlocked. It was open.

"And you didn't do that?" she asked him.

"Nope. Someone was in here, Detective Manning. Gone now, but they were in here. You really do need to learn to lock your doors."

"I always lock my doors!"

"The locks weren't forced."

She stared at him, wondering how Bryan McFadden could have been so wonderful and this almost-clone could be so... judgmental! She studied him. He was different from Bryan. She thought there was more red in his hair and more of a wave to it; he wore it longer than Bryan did, allowing for one of those waves to sit almost arrogantly on his forehead. His eyes had more a myriad cast to them; they weren't really blue, nor green, nor gray, but rather prisms of all three. He had his brother's height, and the same breadth of shoulder. He might have been a little leaner.

And, of course, she was staring at him now, feeling as if a fuse was burning inside of her.

"I locked the doors. I guarantee you. I even checked them before I went to shower."

"Sure. Why didn't you know I was coming?"

"Why would I know you were coming?"

"I told you—Marnie left you several messages."

Sophie hadn't checked her phone. Frankly, she hadn't paid any attention to it; there was a special ring if her partner, Grant Vining, was calling, and if it wasn't him...

She did tend to let it go to messages when she was busy. As in, doing research on the internet.

Or talking to a ghost in her imagination.

Or passed out in an armchair.

"You are Bryan's brother—obviously. I will try to respect that. But if you're not the one who picked the locks, what the hell are you doing here?"

"I'm here to help."

"I don't need help!"

What was happening? This was the second time a person—one living, one dead—suggested that she needed their help.

"You have to get out of here. I have to call in and get a crime scene unit—if it wasn't you, someone was in here. And I have a busy day. Regardless of whatever happened here, I have an autopsy to attend."

"I know."

"You know."

"Yes, of course. I've spoken with Detective Vining. When I couldn't reach you, I called him. He's on his way here, I believe. Worried about you." He stared at her pointedly. "He didn't say as much, but I gathered that he thought you'd behaved a little strangely when you were speaking with the media yesterday.

Also, I'm going to assume you need to get some paperwork done on this—someone did break into your home."

She heard the sound of a car driving up and stopping out on the street.

And the water was still crashing down in the shower.

And she was wearing only a towel.

Sophie ignored him and swore, headed into the bathroom and turned off the shower, and then beat it into her room.

She slammed the door and sank onto the bed for a minute.

She could hear this McFadden—Bruce—opening the door. Then she could hear him speaking to Vining.

Her partner was out there. Her amazing partner—before whom she could not appear to be falling apart or frazzled.

She breathed deeply. She was a cop—a good one. A detective. The entire world seemed puzzling at the moment, but that's what detectives did—they solved the puzzle of a crime.

She gathered herself together and got dressed.

Forget the ghosts.

Forget standing ridiculously in front of stranger in a towel with a spray container of household cleaner.

In five minutes, she was ready.

When she walked out, Vining and McFadden were deep in conversation. Vining stared at her with concern.

"Sophie, someone broke in? Someone who maybe had a key? I've got a unit coming over. They'll dust for prints. You know our crime scene guys—if there's something to find, they'll find it."

"Thanks, Grant."

He was staring at her oddly.

"You're certain you locked your doors."

She prayed for patience.

"Absolutely certain," she assured him.

Be professional, she warned herself. *Be careful not to mention that this ass just walked in and then asked the same damned questions.*

"As soon as they're here, we'll get going," he said. "Mr. Mc-Fadden is going to be joining us."

"What?" she demanded sharply. Too sharply. "But…sir! He isn't LAPD. He isn't—he isn't law enforcement of any kind."

"Licensed PI," Vining said. "And you know me. Help is help—in any form. Hell, Sophie, I'm delighted to have him here. This man is Bryan McFadden's brother. We both know that his folks knew the workings of Hollywood like few others."

"Yes, his parents did," she said.

"Bryan and Marnie sent him. Let's welcome what help he can give, Sophie."

She forced a smile. She was pretty sure that it had to look more like a snarl.

"Welcome, Mr. McFadden, for as long as you'll be around," she said quietly.

He didn't even appear to hear her. He was already talking to Grant Vining again, and more cars were arriving.

The crime scene techs had come.

"You need to fill out a report, as well," Vining said, watching her. "If you know that someone was in your apartment."

"I locked my doors," she said firmly, unflinching confidence and authority in her voice.

Grant Vining nodded. She knew that he did respect her—and her abilities.

She hoped she still felt the same way about herself.

"We'll get the paperwork started," he said.

"And quickly," she added. "We need to be at that autopsy."

"Yes, we need to be at the autopsy."

She turned to greet the officers and crime scene techs who had come. She explained the situation—Bruce McFadden helped, and she should have been grateful. She just found it difficult.

She was glad to see that, among the other techs, Lee Underwood had come. His was a friendly face.

"We'll find out what went on," he assured her.

"Can't believe you're here," she murmured.

"I heard it was you—I asked for the assignment. We all love you, you know, Sophie."

She smiled. "Thank you!"

She admitted to herself she was a bit shaken. There had been a ghost in her house—or in her imagination. Then this morning there had been someone real. Ghosts didn't pick locks and leave doors open. And then, there had been Bruce McFadden.

Way too busy for her little place—and her little, focused-on-work life.

Things moved along, and the head of the unit explained that it was going to be difficult to discover anything—especially if nothing was taken—because, of course, there would be dozens of fingerprints in her home.

She hadn't made an assessment of her belongings; she did that quickly, touring her rooms with an eye for anything out of place.

She found that nothing had been touched in her bedroom. Her computer was fine; her laptop, still in its case, was fine, as well.

She collected the papers on the floor.

Only one thing was missing. It was one of the papers she had printed out on the Black Dahlia case.

"You're sure—just one paper?" Vining asked.

"Yes, I'm sure," she said.

"And you definitely printed out?" he persisted.

"Grant! Yes, I printed it, and it's gone."

She glanced at her watch. The autopsy was due to begin.

"No one has your key?" the head tech asked.

"Yes, my cousin in San Francisco has one," she said.

"Someone could have gotten it—copied it?"

"In San Francisco?" she asked.

"Maybe they copied your key," Bruce McFadden suggested.

"I keep my things with me—or in my locker," she said.

"When there's an unsuspected criminal mind-set," Grant said with a shrug, "anything is possible. I'm going to suggest that you get the locks changed this afternoon," he added.

"I'll call a locksmith while we're on the way to the morgue," she said.

"We've a hell of a day before us," Grant murmured.

"Good thing it's LA," Bruce said. "People work all hours of the day and night."

She looked at him.

Once again, she knew that she should be grateful. Instead, she was still swallowing down her hostility.

Most probably because she'd run almost naked at him and basically straight into his arms.

And because she'd been so...

So vulnerable.

She didn't have a chip on her shoulder—she really didn't.

She'd been raised by a great father who had been certain that a girl or a woman could do anything she chose. She'd hit the academy with a lot of determination to take on whatever challenges came her way, and the humility to accept help when necessary.

She just didn't like the feeling of being so...

Haunted.

They had to work hard to solve a brutal murder. She had to be strong and competent.

And not pass out at the sight of a ghost or the pull of her imagination.

And not go running practically naked into a stranger's arms.

She managed a grim smile for all of them.

"Autopsy," she said flatly. "Let's go."

CHAPTER THREE

Still morning

It was hard to accept that the pieces of body on the gurney in the morgue had ever been a real woman, all in one piece, with no chunks of flesh gone, no bisection, and no horrible gashes in the mouth.

Bruce had seen brutal things done before; he'd been at war. He'd seen men ripped apart by explosions. But the torturous cruelty in this murder seemed above all else.

LA County had a huge morgue—and a constant, exhausting supply of the dead. There were always hundreds of bodies. Not all that long ago, the head of the LA County Department of the Medical Examiner-Coroner had resigned because the backlog of bodies was over two thousand when it came to awaiting certain tests. Budget cuts had made things worse. His resignation had, at the least, amplified the seriousness of the situation and things were getting better.

But often, cops could beg for help until the cows came home—and they'd have to wait.

That wouldn't happen with this case; Dr. Chuck Thompson, one of the top men in his field, had been assigned. An autopsy for this poor woman would be swift.

No one wanted anything but the utmost diligence on this case.

A number of body parts were partially destroyed. The details were explained in a combo of scientific and layman's terms to them by Dr. Thompson. Bruce was impressed by him right away; his dedication in the midst of what seemed to be a sea of death was commendable. He didn't speak to the corpse like a long-lost friend, but he treated the remains with respect. At one point, he glanced up at the assembled investigators—Bruce and Detectives Manning and Vining; he'd been recording his words, but he switched off the recorder for a moment.

"I've read that they sometimes believed that a medical man of some kind might have been the Black Dahlia killer. It had to do with the way she was bisected. This killer has repeated that bisection. He managed to cut with precision at just the right part of the spine."

There was little to say to that. They nodded, and the doctor turned his recorder back on. He went on to use the medical terms to explain the way the body had been cut.

Police photographer Henry Atkins was also there, documenting the autopsy. Atkins kept wincing and shaking his head. He glanced at Bruce apologetically and whispered. "Sorry—I'm so close to retirement. Just a few more months. And somehow… I just had to catch this one!"

Bruce nodded sympathetically. The photographer looked at him curiously. "Your folks were Maeve and Hamish McFadden."

"Yes."

"Shouldn't you be an actor?"

"No."

"You could have been."

Bruce smiled at that. "Probably not—I can't act."

Sophie was watching him as he spoke with Atkins. He wondered what she was thinking. Probably—judging from the attitude she'd given him so far, and the little scowl currently creasing her face—that she wished to hell he had gone into show business instead.

Then Dr. Thompson was speaking again, and they all fell silent; Atkins took more pictures.

They listened to the findings that the medical examiner had for them; not much that he hadn't already believed to be true. The victim had been held for at least a little time. It had to have been somewhere out of the way—otherwise her screams would have been heard when her mouth was gashed to pieces. She was dead before being sawed in half—sawed being a key word; that was the instrument that had been used, evidenced by the raw edges of flesh on each part of the body.

Bruce stayed near the pieces of the corpse. At the same time, he prayed that if the young woman's soul had remained behind, she was not here now.

He listened to the drone of the ME's voice while opening himself to any possibility. He watched Sophie Manning, too, but she stood tall and straight, her expression set and fathomless.

He didn't feel a presence; he was certain that she did not, either.

Nothing. He concentrated more on forensic facts.

There was almost no blood; the body—pieces—had been bathed before she'd been left for discovery.

Displayed.

Too much of too many of the digestive organs were destroyed or gone for analysis of her last meal; from the trace amount of material in what pieces of the digestive tract could be found, she hadn't eaten for many hours before her death.

It was while they all stood stoic—listening to the horrid and grisly details brought down to a clinical dissertation—that Vining received a phone call. One glance at his caller ID caused him to clear his throat, nod at Sophie, and move into the hallway to accept the call.

When he returned, he had all their attention.

"Fingerprints came through. Her name was Lili Montana," he said.

"And she was an aspiring actress?" asked Sophie.

He nodded glumly. "She worked occasionally as a substitute teacher—thus her prints on file. But, yes, she was an actress. She last worked with a group of improv players, the Hollywood Hooligans. I have the director's information. He's expecting us. He's also given me the names of two men Lili had been seeing, one with whom she had a breakup about a month ago, and another she'd been seeing for the past several weeks."

"Has her next of kin been informed?" Bruce asked.

"One of our public relations officers is trying to decide just who that might be—she grew up in the foster system. Anyway, we do have some suspects or at least persons of interest to question." He looked at Bruce. "You have any feeling on this?"

"I have no authority here. I'm at your command."

"If you had authority?"

"I'd say divide and conquer," Bruce said. "Switch around when necessary. If any of the parties come to light as being possible suspects who should be questioned again, it's always good to ask some of the same questions—and compare answers."

"Sounds good. I was thinking you should take on this person named Kenneth Trent," Vining said.

"Who is?" Bruce asked.

"Head honcho—director—for the Hollywood Hooligans," Vining said.

"All right."

"Names for the boyfriend and ex-boyfriend?" Sophie asked.

Vining looked at his phone. "Ex—Ian Sanders. Current—Jace

Brown. I'll start with the current beau and get his alibi. Then try out the ex and find out what his story might be." He hesitated. "Strange that the boyfriend didn't report her missing. She had to have been gone a couple of nights now. We're going to have to establish a time line, too. She was killed at least the night before she was discovered. The condition of her corpse, of course, makes it hard to say, but she was brought there and dumped—or laid out!—in the middle of the night. She had to have been tortured, killed and bathed before then. Somewhere—somewhere where someone could do something like that."

"Outside the city," Sophie murmured.

"Or a room with soundproof walls," Bruce said.

She was staring at him with narrowed eyes. He wondered why he still liked her and found her intriguing.

She was really a bitch.

Yeah, but one who looked pretty good in a towel.

He gave himself a mental shake. Not the time or place to be thinking like that.

"All right, then, I'm off to see the director. I have your numbers. I'll be in touch."

"Oh, don't worry. Sophie will be going with you," Vining said.

"What?" Sophie demanded, sounding shocked.

Bruce had to smile. Inwardly.

"He does need some authority. You are LAPD," Vining said. "Time's a wasting," he added. "And we're nowhere near a suspect. God knows if he'll strike again."

They left the morgue, but they didn't head out to meet up with Kenneth Trent. An urgent call sidetracked their investigation.

A second victim had been found.

The corpse was just behind a cherry hedge on the other side of the park from the place where Lili Montana's body had been displayed.

★ ★ ★

It was uncanny—and terrifying. It was as if the killer had taken a picture of his previous display—he probably had—and then created a mirror image with his second victim.

Just a naked girl. Her face gashed in a horrific grin. Her body torn asunder.

Dr. Thompson and Atkins had followed them; Sophie was grateful. As busy as LA was, it was a great boon to have the same medical examiner working on both victims. It was, of course, pretty obvious that the same killer had struck twice.

Once again, the area was filled with police, with crime scene techs, and with the media—all scrambling to get close.

So far, no one had allowed a civilian with a cell phone to get close enough to snap a shot—it was something that should never pop up on any social media pages. Whoever this young woman was, she had someone out there. Parents. Friends. A lover who cared for her deeply.

They should never see this. Never.

Henry Atkins was busy taking pictures; they might, at some time, help in solving the crime.

The techs were out in force, collecting everything and anything they could find.

Reporters, journalists and the morbid curious were pressing against the police line as Vining, Bruce and Sophie hunkered down by the halves of the ripped body.

"You want to take it again?" Vining asked Sophie.

"What do you want them to know?" she asked wearily. "They know that the last was a copy of the Black Dahlia. I'm sure they know already that this is the same."

"Tell them that you do believe the same killer has struck again, urge them to give us time, to understand that every officer in the region and beyond will be working on this, and that we will find whoever is perpetrating these crimes. It's really important that we don't get people whipped up into a frenzy of panic," Vining said. Then he frowned. He was looking at her a little worriedly. "I mean, if you're all right. You seemed a little off yesterday."

"I'm fine," she assured him.

She felt Bruce looking at her. He evidently thought that there had been something off with her yesterday, too.

Of course. He'd seen the news. He'd seen her stumble when she'd heard Michael Thoreau—or her imagination—talk to her.

"I am absolutely fine," she said assuredly. She walked up to the police line, secured more by a dozen uniformed officers than it was by the yellow crime scene tape.

She was serious and fluid when she spoke. Yes, they were sorry to report that a second victim—most probably attacked by the same killer—had been discovered. The public and the media were begged to understand that, in an active investigation, only so much information could be given out. The public should take extreme care under the circumstances. They should also allow the police and any law enforcement agency all cooperation in the investigation.

"Black Dahlia!"

He was out there again, of course. In his hat and 1940s suspenders and jacket. He had a pen and paper while others held cameras and recorders.

She ignored him, and then another reporter—a real one, she assumed—spoke, "Detective, the rumor is that these victims have been butchered. That the murders are similar to the unsolved Black Dahlia case that occurred here decades ago."

"I'm not making any comparisons right now... Mr. Hampton, right, from the *Herald*? Please, this has just occurred."

"Yeah," someone else shouted. "The police still had the old crime scene tape out when this guy dumped a new body, right?"

There was derision in his tone.

Sophie refused to be angered or swayed to any emotion by him—or by the ghost smirking at his side.

"Our units had scoured this area for hours, sir. This body, we believe, was placed here in the very early hours of the morning. We will keep news coming to you with all possible speed— just as we will catch this killer, with all possible speed. Now, if you'll excuse me…"

They had no intention of excusing her. A barrage of questions followed as she turned away from the line of reporters.

She noticed that Bruce McFadden was watching her. He seemed pensive.

She lifted her chin. She had done well that day, and she knew it. Maybe her imagination, or the real ghost—if there was such a thing as a real ghost—had been out there, active again.

But she had managed to totally ignore it.

She felt something at her side, a brush of chilly air.

Crime scene tape apparently meant nothing to a ghost, created in her mind or otherwise. He was following her over to the body.

Sophie watched as the spirit hunkered down by Vining. She thought that Vining shuddered—like a man who had felt a cold draft.

But he didn't turn or look at Michael Thoreau.

"Poor girl," Thoreau said.

Bruce McFadden showed no sign of seeing or feeling anything.

Just then, someone in the crowd lashed out furiously.

"Two! Two damned corpses in the same damned place in two days. And what the hell has the LAPD done? Nothing, all they do is count the damned corpses."

Sophie froze, her back straight, staring at McFadden.

"Go get 'em," he mouthed. He wasn't being sarcastic or mocking her.

He believed that she could do it.

First, control your temper, she thought to herself. *Spiraling anger in any fight leads to carelessness and poorly aimed blows, be they verbal or physical.*

She strode back to the yellow tape of the police line.

"The vicious brutality of these murders has touched every member of the LAPD, just as they have touched every one of you. We are not seers—we have no way of knowing when a sociopath is going to strike. Such a killer has now seized our city. The LAPD will not rest. We will search out this killer with everything available to us. We will work relentlessly, relying on science and medicine and hours and hours of police work. Rest assured, we will not stop."

"The Black Dahlia killer walked free!"

She didn't think that it was the same man speaking again. This time, the words sounded frightened—and uncertain. Looking out in the crowd, she couldn't be certain who had spoken.

"The Black Dahlia was at work in the 1940s," she said. "Since then, science has advanced greatly. We have DNA profiling— a science no longer in its infancy. Science can match tiny skin cells to a suspect…something so minor as a tossed cigarette or a coffee cup can provide endless clues. Fingerprints can even be found on human flesh. We are no longer living in the 1940s. This killer will make a mistake. And when he does, trust me, the LAPD will be ready."

The crowd had gone silent. She turned and walked back. Dr. Thompson now had his assistants carefully picking up the pieces of the body.

They were even taking chunks of the earth with them.

They needed to know just how much blood—if any—had sunk into the ground. They needed everything.

"Bravo," her ghost—Michael Thoreau—said.

Dr. Thompson and Grant Vining gave no heed.

To Sophie's surprise, Bruce McFadden spoke softly. "Bravo, indeed," he said.

She frowned.

Was he agreeing with a ghost?

Or was "Bravo" a word anyone might say?

She didn't have a chance to find out. There was a commotion at the police line. She heard a young woman crying out. "Please, please... I'm so afraid... I might know her!"

The young woman sitting in Vining's small office was almost as white as snow. She'd cried for over an hour.

They had not let her see the corpse.

Henry Atkins wasn't just a good crime scene photographer—he knew how to clean up a picture. Bruce admired his work.

The man had taken a shot of their new victim's face and used the magic of image editing software to bring her back to her appearance before she'd been so cruelly slashed.

Her name was Brenda Sully. She had been an acting major at a nearby fine arts college.

Her friend was Gwen Grayson. Gwen was not in good shape.

"She was getting some work, even as a student," Gwen said between bouts of sobbing. "She was good, she was really so good. She already got a national commercial. For soap. She did a great dance in the shower."

Her chest heaved.

Brenda wasn't a foster child, but she was an orphan. Her parents had died of separate natural causes soon after she'd gotten into college.

While Bruce might still have been only grudgingly impressed with Sophie, he understood completely how she had come to be so very close to Marnie. Sophie had surely treated Marnie, who had seen a dear friend killed in front of her, with the same empathy she was showing Gwen. She had a way about her.

She managed to soothe Gwen somewhat, and Bruce was certain that Sophie might well be able to get more answers from her than anyone else might.

Sophie encouraged her to talk even when it just had to do with her own life—and with friendship. She was kind. She also managed to get all her questions in.

To the best of Gwen's knowledge, Brenda had never worked with the Hollywood Hooligans—but then, she couldn't be sure.

Gwen was a music major, and while they combined their talents for many projects, she still didn't know every time an acting friend took on a job. The school did not mind if they accepted paying assignments—real work experience meant a hell of a lot more on a résumé than a school play. "Maybe all schools don't feel that way—ours does. Or...mine. Mine does. Brenda can't have anything anymore, can she? She's dead. Oh, God, who would do this to...to anyone?"

Sophie gently brushed back Gwen's hair, telling her again that they were all so, so sorry.

Then she asked if she had any idea if Brenda had known Jace Brown, Kenneth Trent or Ian Sanders. Again, to the best of Gwen's knowledge, she had not. Brenda lived alone, and Gwen wasn't sure who might have seen her last.

Gwen had last met Brenda for breakfast on Monday morning. *Hours after Lili's death, hours before Brenda's own.*

"Did she say where she was going or what she was doing that day?" Sophie asked.

"Oh, yes, she said that she was working on her craft. I remember that she winked at me. She told me that she was going to get places."

"Did she seem excited, as if she had plans to see someone?"

"Maybe. All she said was that if she got a good gig really soon, she'd take a quick break back to Atlanta."

"She seemed to think she was going to land a role?"

"Yes, actually... I think so."

"Did anyone approach you when you were together? Did she say anything about anyone approaching her?"

"No, not specifically."

Sophie gently led the questions in the direction of relationships: Had Brenda been seeing anyone?

Gwen reveled that, no, she definitely had not. At least, no one out here in LA. She'd been with the same boy back in Atlanta since high school. They were still true to one another, deeply in love, despite living on opposite coasts. And, yes, Gwen was sure that Mark was in Atlanta at that moment; she had talked to him because he had called her when Brenda hadn't answered.

"Oh, God, now I have to call Mark," Gwen wailed, her eyes wide.

"Her fiancé?"

Bruce knew that someone in the department would contact the fiancé—and make sure that his alibi was as tight as Gwen believed.

But it wasn't the fiancé in this case. Not unless the man had also somehow known Lili Montana—and all the details of the Black Dahlia case.

Of course, anything was possible.

"You're absolutely sure he has been in Atlanta all this time?"

"Yes, he's a stage manager there. He was working his play. I have to call him, oh, God, he's going to be—devastated."

"We can do it for you," Sophie told her. "In fact, we really need to have someone here for you, a friend, a relative. You really shouldn't have to do this alone."

It was determined that Gwen's aunt, who lived close by in Pasadena, would come. And while they waited for her to arrive, Sophie kept Gwen talking about her friend. No, Brenda was not a fool. She didn't take rides with strangers. She didn't do drugs. She didn't drink a lot. She was focused. If anything, pride might be her downfall.

"She was kind of the way you have to be," Gwen said. "Passionate—and, like I said, focused. She was going to be a star. She worked on all kinds of things—webisodes, theater. Ensemble stuff. But she did want to be in film. And she said that she was happy to start small to go big. She was all into indie films. A friend of ours did a weird student film a few years ago—for just a share of profit if there was a profit—and it was picked up by one of the big companies and now she's on that new sitcom. Brenda was willing to go that route."

"Can you think of anyone else who might have seen her later in the day? She did have classes? Anything?"

"No, she was… I didn't even realize it, but she was kind of secretive. She was excited, vibrant, so alive. But could be a bit private. Oh, I'm not putting her on a pedestal. She was real, flesh and blood real. And, of course, she hated rejection. I know I'd told her that wasn't a good thing—not if she wanted a career in acting," Gwen said. Her eyes started to well up again. "I said that rejection was a lesson she was going to have to learn in Hollywood. Now she'll never get to learn anything else at all!"

She broke into tears. Bruce listened, wanting to do something to ease the girl's pain. Sophie was doing better than he could, he was certain. He kept quiet and kept listening.

And observed.

The ghost plaguing Sophie hadn't come to the station.

Bruce wondered who the man was.

A long-ago detective? Or had he done something else in life?

The day was not going to go as planned; more people were coming into the station. Other detectives were added to the case. Bruce wasn't going to be the one out questioning Kenneth Trent, not unless he headed out right now.

He excused himself while Sophie was greeting Gwen's aunt, who had finally arrived.

Bruce decided it was time to go. They'd had a plan that day;

they'd been going to interview people close to their first victim, Lili Montana.

He'd been assigned Kenneth Trent.

And he was doing no good at the station.

He nodded to Grant Vining through the window of an office where he was taking a statement from another student from the arts school, though it looked like Vining didn't think he was going to get anything useful. Vining nodded in return, and Bruce headed on out.

He knew damned well that Sophie's ghost was in his car, in the back seat, when he slid into the driver's position. He glanced in the rearview mirror. "Okay. Who are you? Why are you haunting Sophie?"

"Hey, you see me!"

"I do. Yep."

"Wow. Amazing." The ghost leaned forward, resting his elbows on the seat back—hands dangling down. "All these years... I've seen the world change so much. I cruise the streets. I go to concerts and shows whenever I feel like it. That part is pretty cool. Hell, I've crashed a few séances, and no one has ever seen me. And now—you. And Sophie, of course. Poor Sophie. She just doesn't really get it yet."

"Maybe you're her first."

"Maybe. Doubtful, though. I think she's maybe twenty-seven or twenty-eight. She should have seen a ghost before me, don't you think?"

"I have no clue how it works. My brothers and I weren't kids when it started for us. Anyway—who the hell are you?"

"Oh, sorry. Michael Thoreau. And you're Bruce McFadden. I know that, because I listened to the gossip about you."

"Yeah?"

"Yes. So, your folks were big-time stars, huh?"

"That seems to have been the consensus."

"Hmm. How was that growing up?"

"It was fine. Thoreau—why are you haunting Sophie? You know something about this case?"

"Tons!"

"Really?"

"Well, no. Not about this case. But the one the killer is copying."

Bruce sighed. "Black Dahlia."

The ghost nodded gravely.

"You know who did it?"

"I had my suspicions."

"So…you had suspicions about an old case, and don't know anything about this case—or now, these cases."

"I can help, and I know it."

"Help? So what were you doing in Sophie Manning's apartment this morning?"

"I wasn't in her apartment this morning," the ghost of Michael Thoreau protested. "I wasn't—I swear it. I saw her last night, but…well, she wanted to shoot me, and I realized I had to let her get used to me being around. I think she's getting there. She ignored me while we were at the second crime scene. Lord, can you believe that? Some psychopath has managed to do this twice?"

It was hard to figure. Did that mean the killer was a social pariah—someone who crept in dark alleys and seized victims from the shadows? Or was it someone who was capable of hiding a complete lack of empathy and emotion behind a façade of pleasantries and charm?

Bruce felt his phone buzzing; his brother Bryan was on the line.

"Saw the news," Bryan said. "Second murder."

"Yep."

"I should just forget this academy thing for the moment and head out—"

"Bryan, I'm good. Grant Vining is fully accepting of my help. Sophie Manning is—a good cop. I've met our ghost. He's in the car with me right now. Michael Thoreau. Good guy," Bruce said, lightly, offering the ghost a quick and wry smile.

"Well, the FBI is coming. Jackson is making arrangements to get out there. He'll be there soon."

"Great," Bruce said, and then hesitated. "Hold your course, Bryan. You and Marnie have a good thing going… Everything here will be looked after."

"Watch out for Sophie."

"I'll guard her with my life. I swear."

He found that he meant it—even if she fought him.

Bruce broke the connection.

"Got a brother, huh?" Thoreau asked.

"Two of them."

"Lucky man."

Bruce nodded slowly. "Yeah, I guess I am. Okay, so I have to drive now. Try not to do anything too startling and cause me to veer into oncoming traffic, huh?"

"Hey, I'm here to help, not get you killed."

Bruce pulled out onto the street.

It had been a while since he'd been in LA. He followed the directions on his GPS and arrived at an office building on Vine. He circled to find parking, and then headed in to Suite 109 in the old thirties-style bungalow where Hollywood Hooligans had their office.

The door to the suite was open; there was a young man sitting behind the desk, maybe about twenty-five or twenty-six years of age, slim, with shaggy blond hair and an easy manner. He was wearing a suit that didn't quite seem to fit his personality.

He stood as Bruce entered. "Hello. Welcome to the offices of Hollywood Hooligans. How can I help you?"

Michael Thoreau had followed Bruce in.

He perched near the door, arms crossed over his chest. He leaned against the wall, ready to just listen. Bruce ignored him.

"My name is Bruce McFadden. I'm working on—"

The young man's face paled. He looked as if he was about to burst into tears. Actually, Bruce realized, he'd clearly been crying before at some point that day.

"Lili," the man said, a catch in his voice. "Lili Montana."

Bruce nodded. "You're Kenneth Trent?"

"Yes."

"Director of the Hollywood Hooligans?"

Kenneth Trent shrugged. "I'm the head. The company was my idea. Director is a title that is shared among us at various times, depending on the event or the project. But..."

"Lili was one of you."

"Yes."

"Tell me about her. And her relationship with you—and the Hollywood Hooligans."

Trent was still standing. Bruce slid easily into the chair before his desk. Trent awkwardly took his chair again.

"You're a cop?"

"A PI."

"Oh."

"Trying to help," Bruce said quietly.

"I loved Lili. Oh, not... I mean, we weren't a duo."

"Of course not."

"My partner, Frank, is with the Hooligans, too. Our company is loosely made up of twelve people." He was quiet a moment. "Eleven, now."

"I'm truly sorry. Please, tell me about Lili. You obviously cared about her."

"Oh, Lili…she wanted it so badly, you know? The fame and the fortune. We went to school together at UCLA. She really was very good. She could be funny—obviously, we're usually working for the laughs with the company. And she could cry on cue. Not that many people can do that well. Not just scrunch up her face—I mean, she could produce real tears. But…"

"But…?"

"She wanted it too badly, you know what I mean?"

"I think. You mean that she was one of those people willing to do anything at all to get where she wanted to be?"

Trent sighed, shaking his head. Bruce wondered if he, too, could cry on cue. He doubted it. The tears dripping down Trent's face seemed real.

"I warned her so many times—this is Hollywood. You have to watch out here. I mean, well you have to watch out any-where, but…here. We both grew up in LA, too, you know? Hollywood calls in the dreamers. And sometimes, people make the dream without the rest of the world having so much as a clue, you know? I can name you dozens of working actors who have names no one would ever recognize, but they work con-stantly. They aren't the stars—they're just the day players, the ones who make everything around the big names appear to be real, you know?"

Bruce nodded.

"Lili… Lili wanted to be the star. Hard to explain to you. I mean, you said you're a PI, right? You wouldn't know about actors."

"Oh, I know a little about them," Bruce said.

Trent barely seemed to hear him. He was drumming his fin-gertips on the desk. "Lili… I talked to her a lot. We all talked to her a lot. She…she was always excited. She went through three agents—not because she wasn't good or because they weren't get-ting her auditions…but she drove them crazy. They couldn't deal with all the times she called, you know. And, then, of course, they'd get angry with her if she went off on something that they didn't think was…legit."

"Like porn? Was she doing pornography?"

"No…and not because she wouldn't. I mean, if she was going to do nudity, it was going to be for HBO or Showtime—someone really legitimate. She wanted fame so badly she wasn't going to do anything that might bite her in the ass in the end."

"But she was working for the Hollywood Hooligans."

Kenneth Trent nodded. "She was. We're just a fledgling group. I am the CEO and the secretary. My partner works construction during the day to keep this all going. We do a play and we make sure people get paid, but…well, we all wind up with a couple of hundred dollars. We do a lot of improv, yes, but we've put together a few really good plays. Well received. Lili even got special notice after our last. It was political. I wrote it. It was good, honestly, even if I do say it myself—but critics said it, too."

"When did the show's run end?"

"The weekend before last—our final performances."

"Have you seen Lili since then? Do you know what she was planning on doing?"

"Oh, yes, of course, I saw her. We had our wrap party, and then…"

He hesitated.

"And then?"

"I saw her the day she must have died. She was with me last Sunday—just a couple of days ago. She came in all excited. She told me that she was sure she was about to get her really big break—but I shouldn't worry, she'd always work with me. And when she was famous, she'd make sure everyone knew that I was brilliant."

"What was her big break?"

Kenneth Trent shook his head. "She was meeting someone

on Sunday afternoon. Someone who could 'rock her world.'"
Kenneth Trent began to cry softly again. "I guess he did. I guess
he rocked her world, all right."

CHAPTER FOUR

Tuesday night

The day had been extremely difficult and exhausting, yet it had seemed almost normal.

Of course, there was nothing normal about the murders. The savagery and brutality—and the display, surely intended to arouse the public and taunt the police—were far from normal. Murder was always heinous.

The very act of taking human life was horrible.

But seldom had Sophie seen such barbaric horror.

Still, working with victims—at the scene of a crime or a dump site—or the friends and family of victims, was something she did often enough. And, so, while the day had seemed beyond hard—an autopsy, a new murder scene, and the suffering of the survivors—it had also kept her from thinking about her own situation.

And the fact that the day had started so bizarrely.

There had been Gwen—Sophie talked to her and the other friends who had come in, as well as the teachers and her landlord and everyone else who had been brought in or called. She had also received and worked through the reports from the other officers who had been out pounding the pavement to see what they could find.

She knew that Bruce McFadden had gone out to conduct interviews.

She chafed that she hadn't been able to be in two places at once.

She was finishing a report when Vining tapped on her door. "Long day," he said. "But time to wrap it up. It's all come down from the top—FBI is getting in on it, and we'll have a task force working with us. Meeting and catch-up and assignments first thing in the morning. For now, Sophie, go home. Dawson and Levy have been given all the info we have so far—they'll be working it overnight."

"There's so much we never got to," Sophie said. "Kenneth Trent and the Hollywood Hooligans. Lili's boyfriends."

"Sophie, you need to get some rest."

"I know. This is just so, so horrible. Two young women. This killer must be stopped. We haven't begun to scratch the surface. I have the reports. I know that our people have been fact gathering—"

"Both girls lived alone. Lili Montana had an apartment in Burbank. Brenda Sully had a studio near the school. No roommates. Landlords checked out—airtight alibis. And your friend—Bruce McFadden—was out to see Kenneth Trent. Naturally, while we were working on the new victim, boyfriends—new and old—were questioned by our officers. We'll double-check their alibis with a fine-tooth comb. I believe that McFadden was also stopping in on Jace Brown. We can question them again, but... well, you know me."

"Yes, I know. The best cops accept help. And I've never cared if we made a collar, Grant. You know that. I just want this man off the street." She smiled at him weakly.

Sophie wasn't sure why she felt so irritated. She was telling the truth—she agreed that they needed every bit of help on this case. It had nothing to do with jurisdiction. She didn't have an egotistical need to be the one who brought down the murderer.

They just needed the murderer brought down. Fast.

She was glad of FBI involvement, and the resources they brought along.

But McFadden...

He wasn't a cop—nor was he FBI. And while his brother had been instrumental in helping them catch a killer just recently, there was something about Bruce that got under her skin.

"Ah, wait a minute. That crime scene tech Lee Underwood called," Vining told Sophie. "He said they gathered a zillion prints at your place. But there was nothing—other than you— that got any hits in the system, and there was no other evidence. Except that one printed page you reported missing. They locked up carefully when they left. Then again, if someone else had your key, that someone can get back in. You did rekey the place when you moved in, right?"

She wondered if there wasn't just a bit of skepticism in his voice. "Grant! Yes, I rekeyed when I moved in. I can call my cousin Lisa right now, but I believe she's traveling. She keeps whatever keys she doesn't need at any one time in a safe. She's a travel writer, Grant, but her dad, like mine, was a cop. She is so far from careless or stupid."

"Then that leaves one thing," he said softly.

"And what's that?"

She realized as she spoke that Bruce McFadden was back from wherever he had been—doing their work.

"Sorry to interrupt," he said.

"You're not interrupting. You heard my question to Sophie. What do you say?"

Bruce turned to Sophie. He was a tall man, good-looking in a rugged way. She doubted he owned a single hair product. Raw soap. Maybe aftershave. "A man's man," some might have called him.

His eyes fell on her.

"Well, if your cousin wasn't careless or stupid..."

"Then I was?" she asked, standing. "Okay, fun and games are over, guys. I am not careless. My purse is in my desk when I'm in the office—oh, yeah, and this is a police station. I like to think that we're competent enough to keep the perps out when I'm moving about. We do have to have some faith in our fellows, right? Otherwise, my belongings are never—and I do mean never—away from me."

"Well, it remains that the locks were not changed today. Lee apologized that he couldn't stay with the team, but he had to head on over to the new crime scene. We're trying to keep a cohesive main unit on this—ME, crime scene and other techs, photographer and cops. Hopefully, we won't miss any little details that way, though, of course, every spare man and woman in the city will be working on this. So Sophie, I don't think you should stay there tonight."

"I'm a cop, Grant."

"Yeah, and a smart one, Sophie. You know enough to know that no man or woman alone can fight off a determined perp—oh, and actually get a night of sleep. That would be important right now."

"I can stand guard, split up the night," McFadden offered.

"Or I can, and will, happily go to a hotel," Sophie said.

Vining waved a hand in the air. "Whichever. Sophie, this case is...what it is. The break-in at your place may or may not be related, but the point is you're valuable. You can't take risks right now."

Bruce McFadden cleared his throat. "Actually, the case is on-going for the moment. I found Jace Brown at his local bar. I brought him in. I thought we might all like to have a chat with him."

"You have Jace Brown here?" Sophie frowned. Maybe she liked him a little better.

"Yes," McFadden said. "The front desk officer escorted him into an interview room. Another officer is watching him until we get there."

Sophie was on her feet. Vining sighed.

"So, the day is going to be just a bit longer...let's get to it!"

Jace Brown was bleary-eyed. He'd evidently been doing a lot of drinking before Bruce McFadden had found him at his water-ing hole. He was sipping coffee now. And maybe his eyes were as red as they were because he'd been crying, too.

He was young, late twenties to thirty. His build was thin but wiry. He was a handsome man, as so many were in LA—land of big-screen dreams.

He tried to rise as the three of them entered the room.

Then he sank back into his chair.

"The cops aren't saying much. And you're not going to say much. But everyone knows. You know, guys, people have eyes. And the talk. And I know that my Lili was cut up like prime beef..." He burst into tears.

In most murder cases, it was true that law enforcement looked close to home for suspects at the beginning of an investigation. Husbands, boyfriends. Lovers.

By the very nature of it, this case was different.

She didn't think that the man's show of wet emotion was crocodile tears.

"You two didn't live together," Sophie said.

He shook his head. "My fault. No, her fault, too. She was… ambitious. I mean, we didn't pretend that we weren't together, but I know she felt that for the time, it seemed important that she appear to be a free agent. You know, she just came off another relationship. Living together is a big step. We were close… I loved her. But we weren't ready for that step."

"When did you last see her?"

He inhaled. "Sunday morning. We had brunch at a café in Studio City. Then she was heading over to Vine to see Kenneth Trent—and then…"

He broke off.

"Then?" Vining prodded gently.

"She was meeting someone."

"But you don't know who?" Bruce asked.

He shook his head. "She—she thought she was meeting someone who was going to give her a great offer. Film. She told me it was going to be a screen test. One that could be a major break in her career."

"But she didn't give you a name, or tell you who she was meeting?" Sophie asked.

Jace Brown shook his head. "No, it was all going to be a big surprise. She said that I wouldn't know the name…new player in town with money, someone who wanted to make her a star. I reminded her that there were all kinds of promises out there, and some weren't true. I told her that she really did have a great opportunity with the Hollywood Hooligans—maybe not big money, but they're gaining more and more respect and critics love them. That's where opportunity lay. But she told me not to worry…"

"You didn't report her missing," Bruce said quietly.

"I didn't know she was missing. We didn't live together. I figured that maybe things were working out for her. Oh, God."

"Where were you after brunch? When your girlfriend was being killed?" Vining asked.

Jace Brown looked at him. "That's right, asshole. Killed. My girlfriend was killed—and now another girl has been killed. Where the hell were you? I played football with friends for the afternoon. Give me a piece of paper. I'll give you all their names. I went back to the home of my buddy, Niall, who lives in Malibu. He still lives with his folks, but hey, if my folks had a three-story house in Malibu, I'd still live there, too. His parents and his sister knew I was there—we had some beer. His mom wasn't about to let me drive. Talk to Kenneth Trent. He saw Lili after I did."

"We will talk to him."

Bruce leaned forward. "Kenneth Trent saw her after you. He told me the same thing, she was excited about a meeting. She was secretive but enthusiastic. Can you think of anything at all she said about the man she was meeting?"

Jace swallowed hard. "She said that…he was young. Wait. Not that he was young. That he was new. I think some rich guy who wanted to use his money to break in to the business, you know. Someone with enough to get going as an indie producer. He'd seen her work—he'd told her that he loved her."

Bruce looked at Vining and Sophie. The man was telling the truth. Of course, they would check out his alibi, but Bruce felt it was going to prove to be good.

"You know anyone else that Lili might have talked to?" Bruce asked. "A girlfriend?"

Jace sighed deeply. He shook his head. "Lili…she wanted this. She—she wouldn't have shared. She had the contact. And—she wanted to be big."

Vining said, "All right, Mr. Brown. We'll let you get on home. Thank you for coming in. You may hear from us again soon."

Jace Brown stood and wavered. Sophie looked as if she would

reach for him. Bruce caught his arm. "You all right? I'm going to see to it that you get home. I brought him here—I'll get him back safe," he told them.

"No, I'll get him home. Sophie—you can stop by your place and get some things. Then check into a hotel. And tomorrow, you'll see about the locks on your place."

Vining didn't ask for anyone's agreement.

"You know," Sophie said, looking at Vining and not at Bruce. "I really can take care of myself. I'm not afraid—"

"And according to you, someone was definitely in your house even though the doors were definitely locked. So someone had a key. We've been through this. You need to be awake, alert—and rested. Spend the night in a hotel. On the department. Where are you staying?" he asked Bruce.

Bruce told him.

"Just check in downtown for the damned night, all right, Sophie?"

"Yes, sir."

"See that she does it," Vining told Bruce.

"No one needs to see that I do anything. I'll check in to Mc-Fadden's hotel," Sophie said.

Bruce shrugged, looking at Sophie.

"I'll get my things," she said simply.

"I'm taking the car. You're with him," Vining said over his shoulder as he walked away, steering Jace Brown toward the exit.

Sophie dashed back to her desk and quickly grabbed her simple carryall bag, slinging it over her shoulder.

"Do you want to stop by your house?" Bruce asked her.

"No. I'm fine. I keep a few things in my locker," she said.

"Just as well. If someone is eyeing you, they won't have a chance to follow."

She glanced at him sideways and spoke emotionlessly. "And if someone wants something in my apartment, we're giving them an open invitation."

"Good point."

Sophie walked off ahead of him and had a quick word with the officer at the front desk. When Bruce caught up, she told him, "We'll have a patrol car go by my place."

"Great."

She was quiet when they reached his car. He started to walk around and open the door to the passenger's seat for her, then changed his mind.

She barely noticed. She wasn't happy. He was trying to be polite; she really didn't care if he did or didn't open the door for her.

She just didn't want to talk. Thankfully, he seemed to figure it out.

They drove in silence.

To Bruce's surprise, as they headed for his hotel, Sophie finally began to speak quietly, almost as if she was musing aloud. "I believed Jace Brown. I think he was really in love with Lili Montana."

"I don't think Kenneth Trent had anything to do with it, either," he said. "Not to mention the fact that there is now a second victim."

"At the moment, we don't have a connection between the victims. Except the one thing. They were both actresses—fledgling or hopeful young actresses—like the Black Dahlia."

"Which makes it appear that we do have a killer who isn't connected—not in a friendly or romantic way. I don't believe, however, that they were chosen randomly. The killer knew them—or knew about them."

"And they each believed that the killer was going to make them famous."

"He has made them famous," Bruce said softly. "Just not in the way they had dreamed."

"Why torture them?" Sophie asked, sounding pained herself.

"Because he takes pleasure in the torture—and in the belief that he can do these things and get away with them."

"Two victims. Two days, two victims."

"Let's pray there isn't a third tomorrow," Bruce said.

"At least we won't find her in the same area," Sophie said, staring out the window. "They've doubled up on the patrols in the area—doubled up over doubling up."

She was thoughtful—and tired. She rested her head against the window as she stared ahead, deep in thought. She was truly beautiful, Bruce thought, her features even more defined now as she leaned there, caught in the strange glow and shadow of the changing light that played upon her as he drove.

To his surprise, she turned to him suddenly.

"I did not leave my doors open this morning."

"I didn't suggest that you did."

She shook her head. "Grant Vining has been the best partner… but I'm not sure that he does believe me. Of course, this making me stay in a hotel is a little ridiculous. I am a crack shot."

"I'm sure you are—when you're awake. He has a point." Bruce hesitated. "Sophie, you said that whoever was in there took a page of paper you had printed while doing research on the Black Dahlia. That could mean that this is all related."

She shook her head. "So—you think he was after me? That would be crazy—trying to kidnap a cop."

He hesitated. She could be damned touchy.

"What?" she demanded.

"Well, you were in the shower."

"Meaning?"

"You came after me with bug spray."

"It wasn't bug spray. It was household cleaner."

"Even less effective," he told her. "Seriously, Detective Manning, what if I hadn't come along? You didn't have your weapon in the shower. What would you have done if it had been someone trying to abduct you at gunpoint?"

"Fought," she said softly.

"You're not that stupid and you are human. You're a cop. You would have tried talking. He might have gotten you away."

"And he knew to target me because?"

"You were the spokesperson on the news. That's why I wound up out here. You did finally get Marnie's messages about me coming to LA, right?"

"Yes," she admitted. Then she said, "So, we've done this wrong. We should have set a trap."

"No. He won't come back. He missed at your apartment."

"Then…why can't I go to my apartment?"

He grinned. "Because Vining doesn't want you to."

She almost cracked a smile at that.

They reached the hotel; he paid the valet but self-parked. She eyed him curiously.

"I like to be able to get my car quickly if I need it."

"Good thinking," she granted him.

Inside, he led her up to the desk. The young woman there greeted him with a smile.

"Hi, Sandra," he said. He hadn't actually remembered her name—it was on her tag. "This young woman needs to register."

"Hi, how are you?" Sandra said cheerfully. "Another key? Are you two together?"

"No, no. Oh, no, no, no. The lady needs her own room," Bruce said.

He realized that his "Oh, no, no, no" had sounded almost insulting. He hadn't meant it that way; he was just beginning to know Sophie Manning.

"Oh, okay, a king will be fine?" Sandra asked.

"A king will be just lovely, thank you so much," Sophie said icily, handing over her credit card.

"Wonderful. I've got you on the same floor, anyway. I always try to put friends together as much as possible," Sandra said.

"Same floor. Lovely, too," Sophie muttered.

There was, beyond a doubt, sarcasm in her tone.

Cheerful Sandra didn't seem to notice. She passed Sophie a key card.

Bruce picked up Sophie's bag for her and led the way across the lobby.

"We're back at the station by seven thirty tomorrow," Sophie said. "There's a meeting on the murders first thing. At least, we'll hope first thing. If there isn't…"

"We won't discover another murder. Not tomorrow," Bruce said.

"And what makes you so certain?" she asked.

"I'm not really certain. I don't believe that there will be another murder. Whatever he's doing has been planned out—a long, long time. And no matter how well you plan, carrying off that kind of a murder and body dump isn't easy. He's beaten the original Black Dahlia killer—two victims. Now he's going to sit back and watch—and assure himself that he was right—and watch for everything the media comes up with and puts out. And if someone is copying the Dahlia case, I believe they'll start following along with a few more elements of the case."

"You mean?"

Bruce shrugged. "I don't know. With the Dahlia, there was just the one victim. But then, about a week after she'd been killed, someone called the paper—worried that police interest was falling off. Soon after that—like the next day, if I remember correctly—items of hers arrived in a packet at the newspaper. Her purse was found later on top of a dumpster. Police never knew what to think because about fifty people confessed to the murder."

"So you think—"

"I think that the paper is going to receive items that belonged to one or both of the victims. Right now, I'm pretty sure the killer is going to sit back and enjoy the sensation of what he's caused."

"But this time, we'll get him," Sophie said.

"Let's hope."

"But that's just it. The police didn't have then the tools we have now. Not even two decades ago, a lot of forensic science was in its infancy. Now...no, the killer won't get away with it."

"We may have to taunt him," Bruce said.

He realized that they had come up the elevator. They were standing in the hall, talking.

"Taunt him?" Sophie asked.

"Well, he's not actually being perfect."

"He's pretty damned close. Have you seen the 'then' and 'now' photo comparisons?"

"But there was a bag found near Elizabeth Short. A bag for concrete—filled with watery blood. Obviously, what the killer used to transport his body pieces. I shouldn't say obviously— that was what the police thought at the time. There was no bag this time."

She looked at him curiously. "I grew up here. The Black Dahlia story is one of LA's most famous cold cases, and I always knew I was going to be a cop. How is it that you know so much about it?"

"I read."

"And..."

"It was a five-hour trip out to LA. Lots of time for focused reading. There have been, literally, hundreds of suspects over time. There have been maybe ten or so who really might have been the killer. I picked up every book I could, and from what I've read… I still don't know. Some even suspected one of the main detectives on the case—Hansen. I'd rule him out. There was a connection to the gangster—later murdered himself—Bugsy Siegel." He shrugged. "It's all possible. One of his henchmen later claimed that the murder wasn't hands-on, but that Siegel had ordered it. He had massive Hollywood parties—he was major league crime all the way round."

"Do you think that's the answer?"

"No. I read and read and read—and think a number of theories are good."

"I see."

He shook his head. "I don't think we'll ever know all the facts. It's like a Jack-the-Ripper case. We can have our theories. But unless science comes up with something we can't even imagine yet, we'll all be speculating. Anyway… I think we need to figure out a way to let the killer know that he's not as perfect as he thinks."

"What if it causes him to find another victim?"

"I think it will cause him to try to fix his mistakes."

"Interesting," she murmured.

Then she yawned. Instantly she looked flushed and embarrassed, and, once again, beautiful and even oddly charming.

"Sorry! Well, I'm here to sleep. So I'm going to go to bed. Double bolts on the door. Good choice of hotel—only Spider-Man could possibly reach a window."

"Or a window washer, but there's no scaffolding of any kind," Bruce assured her. "Okay, I know you're a cop and all, but while my dad might have been a renowned actor, he was a Virginia gentleman first. Please—let me see you into your room, door locked."

She smiled. It was a real smile.

"Yes, of course—that's my room right there. And, uh, thanks.

I'm sorry. I have been a bit of an ass. I know that your brother and Marnie made you come out here. This is…well, I'm not sure it can be worse, but it's at least as bad a situation as the Blood-bone killer. Thanks for coming out. Thanks for being here."

She hurried past him, slipping into room 2011. He walked closer to the door, listening for the bolts to slide into place.

"Good night, all locked in," she said, as if aware he'd followed her.

He smiled. "Good night, Detective Manning," he told her.

He headed to his own room.

Yes, she'd been an ass.

But there was something about her that captivated him. She was tough. He liked tough. She could smile and laugh, and there was something so appealing to him about her size, her movement, her bone structure…

He tried to get to sleep; morning was going to come early.

He lay awake, though. On the one hand, remembering the crime scene. And then he'd think about his arrival at Sophie's apartment. Something was wrong; that had been evident. The door hadn't just been unlocked, it had been open.

He remembered her, tearing out of the shower, hair wild, eyes huge, manner that of a cornered lioness…

The more he thought about it, the more the open doors and the fact that a paper was missing from her apartment bothered him.

Was it connected to the murders? He thought about the victim from that morning again. Brenda Sully.

The killer might have been after Sophie. But maybe not…

Happenstance?

Now, happenstance was something that he didn't believe in.

It was really late. He had to quit ruminating. Vining was right about one thing—they needed sleep if they were going to be any use. And morning was now just hours away.

He stared at the ceiling for a minute, and then closed his eyes.

Sophie still didn't know that he was well aware that she saw ghosts.

Michael Thoreau was a ghost convinced that he could help. How?

Morning could provide so many answers.

He wanted to sleep. He kept picturing her…running out, sleek and wet, in just a towel, hair wild…household cleaner raised high for the attack!

He smiled. She'd been an ass. A jerk with a chip on her shoulder.

But really, she wasn't quite so bad.

At least she was a really striking jerk with a chip on her shoulder.

Sophie had to admit that curling into the cool, clean sheets at the hotel did not feel so bad.

She wasn't afraid. She could look after herself.

But it was even oddly comforting to know that Bruce Mc-Fadden was down the hall.

Idiot that he was. He'd walked right into her house. If she'd had her gun, she might have shot him. No, she wasn't trigger-happy. She'd have definitely leveled it at him.

Still…

She was a trained professional. She didn't need to feel comforted.

But Bruce seemed to know, and Grant Vining definitely knew that no man could be an island. Vining wasn't afraid of backup.

Yet sometimes, she did feel that she needed to be stronger, more confident, more…

More of an island.

Just to prove herself.

Maybe, for the first time in a very, very long time, she had actually found someone who was...interesting.

He was definitely an attractive man. He just had all the right stuff. And where she could be so tense—so damned certain that she wouldn't hold her own if she gave an inch—he was relaxed and confident without having to prove a thing.

That made him so damned annoying.

She'd almost drifted to sleep. Her eyes flew wide-open.

Annoying, yes.

But attractive. And she had almost...almost...drifted off into a light sleep and dreamed...

About touching him.

CHAPTER FIVE

Wednesday, morning

The current murders were even more sensational than the original Black Dahlia.

In the 1940s, there had been no internet.

News didn't travel with the speed of light.

It was the crack of dawn when Sophie rose and showered and prepared for the day; every channel she hit on the TV was telling the tale.

Just like Elizabeth Short, the original Black Dahlia, Lili Montana and Brenda Sully had become far more famous in death than they might have dreamed they could be in life.

The media, of course, had little care for the fact that the first body had just been found on Monday morning, the second just twenty-four hours after. The coverage didn't seem to be concerned with helping the police, but in sensationalizing that two young women had been savagely slain, and noting that the original killer had never been caught—and this copycat might well be about to get away with murder, as well.

She had just finished dressing when her phone rang; it was Bruce McFadden.

"Ready to head out?" he asked.

"I am."

"We have some new support," he told her.

"Oh?" She wondered if it was his brother Bryan.

"Jackson Crow, FBI, he's with a special circumstances unit—"

"I know Special Agent Crow," she said. She'd worked with Jackson and Bryan not so very long ago. Bryan McFadden was, she now knew through Marnie's messages, in the FBI academy in order to become a part of Crow's unit.

"He's here. He's going to go with you to your house to get the place rekeyed. After the meeting, of course."

"Why?"

"Why?" he asked, his tone surprised.

"How did he get here so fast? And if he's here, why would he spend his time on something so trivial as getting my apartment rekeyed."

"I thought you were a detective."

Just when she was beginning to like him a little better.

"I am a detective, Mr. McFadden. Which is why I believe I should be detecting."

"Okay. You want to stay in a hotel forever, fine. This isn't me—Vining isn't going to let you go back to your place."

"He can't exactly stop me—it's my call, in my mind. But I'm not even sure he believes me," she murmured.

"Sophie," he said patiently, and she was irritated just to hear the easy, almost gentle way, her name sounded on his tongue. "Sophie, you know as well as I do that we could spend weeks—months—on this case and get nowhere."

"No, there's too much riding on this. We need to keep working our leads."

She was silent for a long moment. "Do we have an alibi yet for

Kenneth Trent? As of now, he's the last one to see Lili Montana alive. And while Brenda Sully might not have been a member of the Hollywood Hooligans, she was a young actress, and she might well have gone to an audition or into the office, or—"

"Wait until we get to the meeting."

"Why? What has happened?"

It was still just 7:00 a.m., but she'd been watching nothing but the case since she woke up. "Have you talked to Vining or the captain or—"

"Jackson has been in touch with the station. There have been so many calls with suspected sightings of both women that it's going to take an army just to track them all down. I'm in the hall. Jackson is downstairs. We'll go into the meeting together."

"I'm ready. I'm coming out now."

She met Bruce at the elevator. She kept silent, wondering why she resented him so very much, as they stepped into the elevator together. She was determined, however, not to show how she was feeling.

Then, just as the door closed, the ghost of Michael Thoreau stepped in with them. She deliberately looked past him and ignored him.

"It's all right, Sophie, he sees me," Thoreau said.

She didn't respond in the least. She was getting better at this.

"Sophie?" Bruce said.

"What?" she snapped.

"I do see him."

She was so startled that she stared at Bruce—and then at the ghost.

She wondered if her imagination was so strong that she could create a delusion witnessed by others, as well.

Bruce was looking at her with very gentle, sympathetic eyes.

Pitying eyes?

"You see—him. Him who?"

"Michael Thoreau. His ghost, that is."

"Yep, he sees me!" Thoreau said happily. "Amazing. So cool."

"Did they say things like that in the forties?" Bruce McFadden asked him.

Thoreau shrugged. "To be absolutely honest, I'm not sure. I've been hanging around forever, so I've picked stuff up. For instance, I still love 'groovy.'"

"Groovy," Bruce said.

"This can't be happening," Sophie said.

The elevator was descending to the lobby. She was startled when Bruce McFadden took her by the shoulders. "Okay, this is new for you, I guess. But, Sophie, it's real, and there are others in the world who see the dead. When the dead wish to be seen. It can be alarming. I can't tell you how freaked out I was the first time—it was my mom! She figured she'd raised three sons who could handle anything. Sophie, you're tough as nails. You will handle it."

His eyes were intense. Something inside her was still fighting. It couldn't be real. Was he trying to help, or feeding into the insanity?

"Sophie, please," Michael Thoreau said.

The elevator door opened.

Jackson Crow was waiting for them. To Sophie's astonishment, it seemed that he nodded to the ghost of Thoreau.

"Three of you! This is heaven!" Thoreau said. "Well, not literally, of course. I am looking forward to that, but first, this copycat killer."

Jackson shook hands with Sophie. "Nice to see you, Sophie."

"You, too, sir. I'm glad you're going to be the FBI liaison— but there is an LA field office."

"Yes, I'm here as a special consultant. Area FBI will also be on the case. You'll meet some of them at the station now."

"And you'll let me help?" Thoreau asked.

"We'll take all the help we can get," Crow said.

So he was real. Her ghost was real.

And suddenly she liked Crow—and even McFadden—all the more. They were on her team.

It was just the way she had first met McFadden. Maybe she'd never recovered from being caught so off guard.

She turned on Michael Thoreau suddenly. "Were you in my apartment yesterday morning? If so, you will not be welcome in any way—"

"I wasn't in your apartment," Thoreau said indignantly. "I knock. You know that. I would never be so rude."

"Shall we get going? People are coming into the lobby," Bruce noted.

Thankfully, Sophie realized, no one had been there when she'd turned on Thoreau. To anyone watching, it would have appeared she was talking to thin air.

"Yes, for God's sake, let's get going."

On the way to the station, Jackson Crow filled them in. "Our unit has our own jet, Sophie, that's how we move when we choose," he told her. "And as to what I know…nothing yet. Just that the tip lines went crazy after they were posted in the news."

"Did they check out Kenneth Trent yet?" Sophie asked. "As to where he might have been on Sunday night?"

"According to him, he didn't leave his office until about five that afternoon," Bruce said. "This morning, I spoke with his partner. They were both at a movie Sunday night. They have the ticket stubs. We'll go by and hope that someone remembers the two of them at the concession stand."

"And there are two victims now," Jackson Crow said.

"So now we find out where Brenda was on Monday night. I spent a lot of yesterday with her friends."

"We have the same story from everyone associated with both women," Bruce said. "Each was excited. They were both scheduled to meet with someone who was going to change their world—make them famous."

"That's what you see a lot of with the original Black Dahlia," Sophie murmured. "That she wanted to be a star."

"Elizabeth Short had a mom and a family in Massachusetts," Bruce said. "One of the papers brought the mom out here— they were really using her to keep up the numbers for the paper. Some of the news sources tried to blast Short as a call girl or a prostitute—or at least someone willing to sleep with anyone to get where she wanted to go. But according to reliable sources, that just wasn't true. She had been in love with a serviceman. He was killed. She was out here like other women were out here— chasing the elusive dream."

"But neither of these girls really had family—friends who love them, yes, but no family," Sophie mused. "Surely, women would be smart enough these days not to go with someone… someone they don't know, someone who could be dangerous," Sophie said.

"The lure of stardom is huge—worth a lot of risks—to many people, men and women. But he may change up his game," Bruce said. "Playing the big producer worked at first. Maybe now—now that we're going to make sure the public knows what was going on with Lili and Brenda—they won't be so foolish."

Michael Thoreau piped up. "I still say it's going to help to figure out just who killed Elizabeth Short!"

"Police then and now have gone over the case for decades," Sophie reminded him. "There was still no proof."

"Maybe we can't prove it. But maybe we can know," Thoreau said.

When they reached the station, the ghost followed them in.

Sophie and Grant and a squad of eight officers worked directly beneath Captain Lorne Chagall. He was an experienced man with thirty years in the force—he'd made his way up from

patrol officer. He was usually in his office at the station, jug-
gling the cases handled by his squad. They all just called him
Captain, something that worked well since he spent his leisure
time out on his little fishing boat.

He was a great superior, a man who never micromanaged,
but listened intently and gravely, and he imparted wisdom with
his years of on-the-street savvy behind him.

He nodded at them all when they came in.

"Captain, you're taking lead on this?"

"No, Sophie. Grant Vining is lead. He'll get what he needs
from me. And the two of you have any other officers or anything else required as you go along. Anything you want to say
or add in, just speak up.

"Bruce McFadden?" he asked then, reaching across to shake
Bruce's hand.

"Yes, sir, Captain, glad to meet you," Bruce said.

"Glad to have you here. I understand you're a consultant, but
we know about Special Agent Crow and his unique unit. I sup-
pose this case could use all hands on deck."

Sophie kept a forced expression of calm as Bruce thanked the
captain. She hadn't actually realized how warm and chummy it
had all become between law enforcement agencies—and "con-
sultants" like Bruce McFadden. She was pretty sure that the
captain had no real idea that members of the Krewe spoke with
the dead, but she had learned that the Krewe had an incredible
record for closing cases, and figured the captain was glad to be
working with such a unit.

There was barely time for them to grab paper cups of coffee before the meeting began, headed—as Captain had said it
would be—by Detective Grant Vining. He welcomed Jackson
and other members of the FBI, and the dozen other officers from
their major crime divisions, along with state police and a forensic psychiatrist named Bobby Dougherty.

Grant Vining went through the discovery of the bodies, including time lines. Dr. Thompson, the medical examiner, was there and reported on the state of the bodies.

An officer from the hotline reported on the number of tips they had received. They would be doled out to patrolmen who would follow up. While Vining would remain lead detective on the case, they were asking for help from everywhere.

Henry Atkins was there; his crime scene photos blazed large on a pull-down screen. Henry had gone a step further; he showed the similarity to photos from the original crime scene—that of the Black Dahlia.

The similarity to their new murders—down to detail—was remarkable.

"The bag," Sophie murmured. "He didn't leave a bag."

"No," Henry agreed. "I was among the first responders. Our man may know that such a thing might have led to some kind of forensic discovery."

"And we're still doing all kinds of tests," Lee Underwood put in. "But so far, we've got cigarette butts that match nothing we have. We haven't found a thing that would give us any help. We checked Lili Montana's body for prints, but he was careful. He wore gloves the whole time."

Media attention was getting out of hand. Following the meeting, Vining was going to give a press conference, and among what information they did intend to hand out, he would warn young women about being anywhere alone with a stranger. Especially if that stranger promised to be a producer who would help them reach the big time in Hollywood.

A young officer entered the room, wincing at the sight of the crime scene photos, and went over to Detective Vining. He spoke in a low, urgent voice.

"Well, we have another similarity," Vining said to the room. "Lili Montana's driver's license just appeared on the desk of a reporter at the newspaper. The Black Dahlia killer, as we all know, sent the paper items belonging to Elizabeth Short, as well. We sent a team to collect the license and the envelope—forensics will get on it right away."

"Do we know where it was mailed from?" Sophie asked.

"Yeah," Vining said drily. "The mailbox on the corner down the street from this station."

The room was silent for a second; they all knew that the killer was taunting them.

Vining ended the meeting by assigning tasks, and the officers headed out—vigilant, but with little more to go on.

There would be another door-to-door bout of questioning in the area where the bodies had been found—both sides of the park and beyond. Apartments would be searched in the hopes that there had been some small clue one of the young women had left behind.

The killer had dropped an envelope within blocks of the police station. They could hope that he had licked the envelope.

He most probably had not.

They could hope for fingerprints.

They would probably find those belonging to the postal employees and workers at the newspaper.

But somewhere out there, both girls had been seen by others. And Sophie was anxious to follow up—hours of treading the streets didn't matter—and find out just which of the hundreds of callers had really had something of substance to report.

"We need to go through the leads," Sophie said.

"There are hundreds. It will take our entire team days to follow them through," Grant told her. "Yes, you can get on them. But you need to get your place fixed."

"I will, but please, Grant, let's get on this now, while the leads are hot. Please. I'll stay at the hotel another night."

"Sophie, we're cops. There are hundreds of law enforcement

people now working this case," Grant reminded her. "Look, I'm
not trying to be an ass, I swear it. You can't let a case become
so much of an obsession—"

"Another night. Maybe there is something hot," Bruce said.

She glanced at him; he was supporting her. She really needed
to be grateful.

Vining shook his head. "All right. But, Sophie—we both want
to stay on the force, right? So let's remember that this is a career
choice, yes, but that we're human beings, too, right?"

She nodded. "Please, let's see the leads."

As they went through the hundreds of notes taken, Vining
glanced at her occasionally to see if there was anything that
spurred her. She listened patiently as he went through them, including those that had come in from psychics who had seen Lili
or Brenda in their minds, or in a crystal ball.

"Psychics have helped on other cases, you know," Vining
said grimly.

"I'm not discounting them. You just haven't got anything from
a psychic that rings true to me yet," Sophie told him.

Grant excused himself and began to dole out some of the help
line info to others.

"I'll follow up on Kenneth Trent's alibi," Jackson Crow said.

"I think he's innocent," Bruce said. He looked at Sophie,
awaiting her opinion. She didn't know why, but she trusted his
instincts.

"Maybe you can find out if he had any connection with
Brenda, too," she said. "We do know that he saw Lili the afternoon before her murder."

"Right. Thing is, we're looking for someone who could pull
this all off," Bruce said. "I talked to Kenneth. I just didn't get
that he'd even begin to know how to…to kill so brutally."

Sophie continued to leaf through the reports. There had been sightings of Lili Montana and Brenda Sully all over Los Angeles, but finally, one in particular struck Sophie.

The tip had come from a young woman at a coffee shop. She had spoken to Lili Montana, she claimed, at seven on Sunday night—just hours before she had been killed. Lili had been about to meet a producer, she had said.

"I think this is for real," Sophie said.

"Here's another tip from a dog walker," Vining told her. "He claimed to have seen her near where her body was found."

Sophie shook her head. "We should see him, yes. But I just don't think that this perp does his killing near his dump sites."

"I can't figure where—not by where they were found. But think of our geography. God knows where he might have a lair. This city is all mountains, hills and valleys. There are basements, foundations, old maintenance tunnels—just about everywhere."

"Still, we'll talk to the dog walker," Sophie said. "If he lives nearby, he might have seen a vehicle or something else unusual for the neighborhood."

Vining looked especially tired. "Pick out the ones you want, but take a handful. Try to go geographically, save yourself time."

"I do want to check out the waitress who called in. I know that people may not become instant best friends with waiters and waitresses, but they often chat," Sophie said. "And this café where she works—it's near Olvera Street, the oldest section of the city."

"All right," Vining said. "And here's another in which the officer on the tip line thought the person sounded both sane and sure—this one is from a convenience store clerk who said that a girl matching Brenda's description bought a pack of gum from him on Monday. The store is also near Olvera Street."

"I'll like to take these for a start," Sophie said. "From what I've heard from friends and coworkers about both the victims, they would have loved history and the city and..." She shook her head.

"What's wrong?" Bruce asked.

"I talked to Brenda's friends. She seems like a really nice girl. And I was thinking, from what I know about both women, that the area would have appealed to them—lots of history and fun Hollywood. And, I'm willing to bet, old secrets. But I don't think it's so much that the area appealed to them. I think, possibly, that there is something in the area that appeals to the killer."

Vining frowned. "I don't know. It's also high traffic. Filled with restaurants and museums."

"And near a few places where there might well be deep basements and other areas to carry out torture and murder," Sophie said flatly.

"I'll go with Sophie," Bruce offered.

Sophie wanted to deny him; she thought she should be working the case with her actual partner.

But she realized Vining was going to be at the station for a while, going over every tip and clue—no matter how misguided or bizarre— and handing out assignments. There would be endless legwork involved with this case, and as lead detective, it was his responsibility to see that nothing slipped through the cracks.

Vining was a good partner, and she was grateful to work with him. But she was glad that he hadn't suggested that she remain at the station with him, trying to read between the lines of every tip.

Sophie just had a feeling about the old section of LA.

And if she was stuck with McFadden... Well, with or without him, she was eager to start the hunt.

"Let's go," she told Bruce.

"I'll be in touch, if I find anything else in this massive pile of communication... I'll get the info to you. And if our men on the street get anything, I'll reach you. Keep me informed."

"Yes, sir," Sophie said.

"I like your Olvera Street, too," he said. "So, two there…let's start with the dog walker and head on over to the other section of town. I've got the rental car. We'll use that?" he asked Vining.

"Blends right in. Yes."

Vining gave Bruce a sticker for his vehicle so that he could easily park wherever.

Bruce McFadden seemed glad of it as they left the station. "Hey, I can even leave the car in the middle of the road, if I need to, with this!"

"Yep. Great."

They had reached his car when he stopped, not opening the door for her—not even unlocking it. He stared at her over the roof.

"Get over it," he said. His voice was rock hard.

"What?" Sophie demanded.

"Your attitude."

She naturally wanted to deny that she had an attitude.

"I'm over it," she said.

"You're not—but you need to be. Sophie, I came out here to help you because Bryan couldn't come—and because we both have training and because we all see the dead. Jackson is here for that reason, too. We can use Thoreau. Yeah, it's a lot to take in. We've all been through it. Speaking with the dead goes against everything you've learned or been taught your entire life. Accepting it is hard."

"I've accepted it."

"Just not me."

"Don't be ridiculous. I don't know you well enough to like you or dislike you. You're just not a cop—you're not even from LA."

"Vining and your captain are just fine with me. You know what your problem is?"

"I'd like to get going."

"I saw you shaking—in a towel. You're just so damned determined that you're an invincible cop that you can't bear anything that suggests you might have a weakness."

She felt her anger rising.

"Maybe I... I just don't know your real qualifications."

"Maybe I make you feel vulnerable. Whatever it is, Sophie—"

"I don't have to prove anything," she snapped.

He stared at her, looking hard, cold and very fierce for a moment. She thought that maybe he'd missed his calling—if he'd been an attorney, he could have probably made mincemeat of a perp in a courtroom in seconds flat.

Then, suddenly, his demeanor changed.

"Marnie said you were the best," he said softly. "And, hey, we could work on this thing investigating together, you know. I like you."

She grimaced. "I... I'm over it. Whatever it is you think I'm not over. I am. I swear."

"You're shaken about speaking to the dead."

She was quiet for an instant, and she swallowed hard.

"Maybe. I think I saw the dead once before. And I was ridiculed and sent to a shrink for it."

He nodded slowly. "You're not crazy. It's real."

"That's just as crazy—as being crazy!"

"But real. And it has its benefits, really," he said, and added softly, "Please, just accept Michael Thoreau. Seriously, we can use him."

She didn't have to answer. She was startled by another voice.

The ghost of Michael Thoreau had been coming down the walk; he was by the car when he spoke with a cheerful note in his voice.

"You can indeed use me."

"Lovely," Sophie said.

"If it helps at all, I think you're right," Bruce said. "There's something about old LA that just might appeal to this killer."

"Old LA?" Thoreau asked. "Ah, yes, because he's imitating an old murder. But hey, that area is way older than Hollywood. You know, back in 1908, this was all real new. The big 'film' production—what there was!—was happening in NYC. And France. Before Hollywood, France had it all over us. By 1918, Hollywood was already the hot spot. Founding fathers, corruption, bootlegging. Great stuff."

"Pre-Dahlia," Bruce reminded him.

"Yep. But cool."

"Yes, there's so much out here that's so beautiful—and so much that's so ugly right now," Sophie said. "My instincts—and your instincts—might be wrong. And it might take forever to follow them all through."

"You're a good detective, Sophie. You have people skills, which are important as all hell, too. So I trust your instincts."

"You may not be a cop, but you've obviously been around law enforcement—and very bad things. We'll be damned lucky if our first instincts panned out."

"We won't know if we stand here talking about it," he said.

"You need to unlock the door. I—unlike Mr. Michael Thoreau—need to enter a car properly."

"She is a wiseass, isn't she?" Thoreau asked.

"Attitude," Bruce said.

"Hey! I'm right here," she said.

Bruce clicked the car open.

The dog walker was a Mr. Milton Nguyen. He had a gray terrier mix named Scamp. He had been certain that he'd seen Lili Montana walking down the street the day she was killed. "Pretty girl, dark hair, wearing jeans and a T-shirt," he told them.

"Where was she going?" Bruce asked.

"Um—I don't know. She was just—she was walking that way."
He pointed north.

"Did she seem to have a car...did she appear to be heading toward anyone or anything specific?" Sophie asked him. She pulled out her phone and found a photo of Lili—alive—that the police had been using. "Do you really think that you saw this young woman?" she asked.

He studied the pictures. "I think, yes. But I could be wrong."

Sophie thanked him for his help, and gave him one of her cards, asking him to call if he saw anything else that might be suspicious, or if he thought of anything else.

"This is a nice neighborhood. To have bodies dumped in our park... You will catch this killer, right?"

"We're doing everything humanly possible," Sophie assured him. She stooped down to pet the little dog.

"You walk this little guy a lot, right?" Bruce asked him.

"I do. He's my best friend."

"Have you seen any unusual vehicles around—maybe even around a few times?" Sophie asked.

He was thoughtful. "Well, you know, there's some idiot with a souped-up dragster who goes by now and then with rap music blaring."

"Anything else?" Bruce pressed.

"Maybe. A sedan. Black or dark blue. Yeah, I've see it a couple of times," he said excitedly. "No music—goes slow. Real slow, just driving around. First time I saw it, I thought maybe they were lost."

"You don't happen to know the make of the car, do you?"

He shook his head. "No hood ornament...and I wasn't really looking. I just watch for speeders sometimes. Lots of dogs—and kids—around here. A dark sedan. That's all that I can tell you."

"If, by any chance, you see that car again, can you let us know right away? Don't endanger yourself in any way, but if you can see what kind of car it is—" Sophie said.

"Or see the tag," Bruce added.

"Can you call us right away?" Sophie asked.

"Yes, yes, of course."

Sophie and Bruce thanked him again and headed back to the car.

"What do you think?" Bruce asked Sophie.

"I think he's a really nice man trying to do his civic duty," she said.

"It's possible he saw Lili," Bruce said.

"Or just an unfamiliar car," Sophie said.

"The killer checking out the neighborhood?"

"Could be," Sophie said. "But a dark sedan isn't much to go on."

"There are hundreds, if not thousands, of dark sedans in LA."

"I know. And still… Bruce, do you think—"

"Yes. Whoever did this has a fantasy going—a fantasy of re-creating the past, and getting away with murder, as well. Times changed, the neighborhood changed. The killer—even if he grew up here—would have to see just how the terrain had changed."

Sophie was quiet for a minute and then said, "You're right. The whole Black Dahlia thing is the killer's hang-up—or fantasy. Lili and Brenda might have never heard of the Black Dahlia. Or they might have heard of the case in passing. They were just trying to get famous. The killer is playing a savage role."

"Let's go see what the convenience store clerk knows," Bruce said.

The clerk was a young man with deep dark eyes and brown skin and a pleasant manner. His father owned the franchise on the store. His name was Amal, and he left another young girl at the counter while he brought them into the office.

"I know that I saw the young woman—the second young woman killed, Brenda Sully. I know that it was her. She was so pretty, dressed up, and so pleasant. She just wanted gum. She said that she needed good breath. She had an extremely important meeting with a producer. She was very chatty. She said it was 'a little weird, but hey, this is movie land.' I remember because I thought she would be famous someday. She was so beautiful."

"What time was it when you saw her?" Sophie said.

"Right about 7:00 p.m. I know, because I was leaving right after," he said, and grimaced. "I had a hot date. Suzie—the girl out there now—was taking over for me. And right after Miss Sully left, Suzie showed up. She teased me a minute, and then I left, and when I walked out, I checked my watch. It was just about seven fifteen then."

"Did you see where she went? Was she driving?"

"If she had a car, I didn't see it. I don't know. Maybe she came in a taxi, maybe she used one of the apps people now call for rides."

"Maybe," Bruce said, "she was picked up out front here?"

"She was gone when I came out."

"Did she say anything else about where she was going—or why the meeting would be weird?" Sophie asked.

He was thoughtful. "We were talking about summer. She asked if I'd ever seen a movie at Hollywood Forever. I have—it's really cool. If you've never been, they show classic movies on the big mausoleum wall. People bring blankets and ice chests and…it's cool. Kind of like the real old Victorian concept of a cemetery, the living honoring the dead in an odd way—kind of like they keep including the dead in life."

"I've been to the movies at Hollywood Forever," Sophie assured him. "And I've been to a concert there, too. But did she say she was going to the cemetery?"

"Oh, no, she wasn't. She was just saying that maybe, only in LA, could you do so many weird things—and have film involved with weird things. She was going somewhere else. I don't remember her exact words, but I know that she wasn't heading there."

They talked a while longer. Sophie thanked him sincerely and gave him her card, asking if he would please call if he thought of anything else at all.

"That's it!"

The ghost of Michael Thoreau had been very quiet so far, but he spoke now before the door to the convenience store had closed behind them.

"She was going somewhere weird," Sophie said.

"In Los Angeles. Sadly, somewhere weird in LA is almost like a dark sedan in LA," Bruce added.

"No, but she was talking about movies at a cemetery," Sophie said.

"And she wasn't heading there," Bruce put in.

"But—" Michael Thoreau said.

"Somewhere weird that has to do with those already dead?" Sophie said. "Catacombs, an old church—"

"Deconsecrated church, maybe," Bruce said. "Or—"

"Graveyard, mortuary," Sophie said. "Deep underground, away from the living who can hear—"

"Yes," Bruce added, "where blood could flow and a woman could scream forever..."

"And only those already dead would know!" Michael Thoreau put in. "See? I told you I could really help. Let's talk to that waitress—and then, my friends, I'm going party hopping. I'll go haunt some cemeteries!"

CHAPTER SIX

Wednesday afternoon/evening

Kenneth Trent had been seen at the concession stand with his partner, Frank Oliver. The two had even seen friends in front of the theater—they had been there talking until probably around midnight. Jackson had checked out and confirmed Kenneth Trent's alibi.

"One man telling the truth. I'm going to question the boyfriends again—past and present," Jackson told Bruce over the phone.

"We think we're onto something here." Bruce went on to tell him about their conversation with Amal, and that they were now off to the see the waitress.

"The women were both seen in this area, a day apart. If we get a similar story at the café… I'll really believe we might catch a break. The thing is, if we can find his murder room or hole or whatever it is, we'll have a good shot at finding the killer. At least, we may have a real shot at finding some forensic clues."

Bruce ended his call, and got into the car where Sophie and

Michael were waiting. Sophie ended her own call; she'd given Vining a quick update.

Michael Thoreau spoke up as Sophie steered the car out into traffic. "This is different from the original. Some people think that the killer was angry with the entire Hollywood studio system. And the pornography filmed out here. And the auditions that turned into exploitation, if you know what I mean. Elizabeth Short did want fame—so did these girls. Back in my day, there were all kinds of suspects. The LAPD originally thought they had about twenty-five viable suspects. Some were cleared, and some new ones popped up on the radar. Her father lived out in Vallejo, but he was just about worthless. Let's see, she really did love men in uniform, so any guy in the military was of interest. One suspect—one I followed up on—was Dr. Walter Bayley. He was a surgeon, he and his wife had a painful divorce—and his wife still lived in the family home, just about a block from the Dahlia's dump site. His daughter had been friends with Elizabeth's sister, Virginia. Bayley died in 1948, and his autopsy showed that he was suffering from degenerative brain disease. A few detectives believed that it was definitely him."

"I've read up about the Dahlia case," Bruce said. "But as you said, this is different."

"The thing is figuring out how it's different. A surgeon makes sense—Elizabeth was so cleanly dissected, her organs...removed. So a surgeon makes sense."

"But," Sophie said, "someone studying the case now has easy access to the old crime scene photos, autopsy reports and more. So would someone need to know what they were doing—anatomically—or could they pull this off by imitation?"

"They'd likely have to know *something*," Bruce said.

"But I don't believe that the killer had to have been a surgeon or even a doctor," Sophie said.

"Agreed."

"Well, in the original case, there was Leslie Dillon as a viable suspect—he was a bellhop who had once been a mortuary assistant. He left LA, and wrote in to a police psychiatrist, de River, saying that his friend did it. He wound up being arrested, but nothing could be proven, not even that he was in the city at the time of the murder. His friend turned out to be a man named Artie Lane, though Leslie Dillon had called him Connors. Artie Lane was a maintenance man for Columbia Studios—one of Elizabeth's favorite places. Again, nothing could be proven."

"I've got pages and pages on the original crime. I think I've ordered every book written," Sophie told him. "I always thought that Leslie Dillon was a sound suspect. Then again, with degenerative brain disease, the surgeon made a good suspect, too."

"Ah, but could he carry out that kind of murder—with his disease?" Bruce asked.

"A former cop, Steve Hodel, wrote a book, and he's certain that his own father, Dr. George Hodel, did it. Dr. Hodel's daughter accused him of molestation. There were other factors, and some circumstantial evidence. Then again, Hodel himself wrote that nothing could ever be proven. Janice Knowlton, whose father—another George—was a suspect, also wrote a book. She claimed that her father was the Black Dahlia killer—and she knew that because of hypnosis to recover 'repressed' memories," Sophie said. "The problem with LA is…"

"There are a lot of people willing to confess to a horrible murder—or to blame it on a parent or relative?" Bruce asked.

"Go figure," Michael said.

"Geography," Sophie murmured. She glanced at Bruce briefly and smiled. "First European settlement was mid-eighteenth century. The Spanish found about 300,000 Gabrielinos and Fernandinos—as they came to call them, and as they were associated with their missions. Captain Juan Rodríguez Cabrillo and Sebastian Vizcaino—they came in 1542 and then 1602, but the first

person to really make a dent in the Spanish presence here was
Felipe de Neve, early governor of California. He wanted pueb-
los to support the presidios and the military. The city was officially founded in 1781. In 1821, Mexico gained independence,
and California celebrated, but fast-forward to the Mexican War,
and the Treaty of Guadalupe Hidalgo ceded California to the
US—officially—in 1848."

She thought that Bruce was staring at her blankly, wondering
why they all needed a history lesson.

But he was actually watching her with interest, she realized.

He looked over at Michael Thoreau. "We are in an old section of the city," he said.

"Right—where people have knocked down and rebuilt over
and over again," Michael said. "We're not really known—as
human beings—for ever being bright enough to really appreciate our pasts."

"Still...we're looking for something weird. And maybe old,"
Bruce said. "And," he added, looking at Michael Thoreau, "no
one knew where the Dahlia was murdered, either. They knew
where her body was dumped, and that it was drained of blood
and mutilated, but—they never found the place where the killer
carried out the deed."

"Could be the same," Michael said softly.

"Could be," Sophie agreed. "Michael, when you were investigating—doing your investigative reporter stint—what did you
believe?" Sophie asked him.

"Well, that's just it," Michael said. "That's why I was bringing all this up—now." He was quiet for a minute, and then said,
"This is the area where I was shot and killed. There is an area just
a bit out—all this is now part of El Pueblo de Los Angeles Historic Monument. All kinds of buildings are part of it, but head
a little out and you have alleys and smaller buildings and farther
out you even have the remnants of old churches and mansions

and more." He paused and pointed. "See those thirties build-ings? I was killed late one night, 1948. I was following a lead that there was a producer out in this area that Elizabeth Short had said sounded a little sketchy but might just be the man she was looking for."

"Let's go," Sophie said. They had reached the café—The Very Old Old-Town Café.

Michael Thoreau fell into step with them as they exited the car. He continued musing. "You know that the police inves-tigated the Cleveland torso murders, too. Although—never proven—a lot of people think that killer was Frank Dolezal, who died mysteriously in police custody at the Cuyahoga jail. An autopsy revealed a bunch of broken ribs, so…it looks as if the cops thought he was guilty, whether justly or not."

A historical marker told them that the foundations for the building dated back to the late 1700s, and, in one form or an-other, it had been serving up delicious food to the residents of the area for, literally, hundreds of years.

"So, it has been The Very Old Old-Town Café all these years?" Sophie murmured.

"Well, when you're new, you can't be old," Bruce said.

"But it was here in 1948," Michael said. "I had coffee at the café the day that I died."

He seemed very somber and morose. Bruce glanced at So-phie, who was then looking at Michael as if she wished she could give him a hug.

"I'm so sorry, Michael," she said softly. She glanced at Bruce, wanting him to do or say something gentle and kind, as well.

"You must have been a damned cool dude," Bruce said. "And I, too, am so sorry."

Michael brightened. "Well, at least I'm here with you two," he said, sliding between them and setting his ghostly arms around their shoulders. "Let's do it."

"What's the waitress's name?" Bruce asked Sophie.

He watched Sophie as she consulted her cell phone for her notes. "Gina Wyler. And she's at the café until eight."

"Let's get on in," Bruce said.

He opened the door. An old-fashioned little bell tinkled.

The café was obviously a popular place; the tables were filled except one, and every stool at the counter was taken.

Sophie walked up to the register and showed her ID and asked the tall man in an apron there if it was possible for them to see Gina Wyler. He was immediately helpful. "Yes, I'm Xander Young. I own the café now. And I'm glad you're here. Gina is quite certain we saw that woman. If we can help, we want to do so."

"Mr. Young, thank you," Sophie said. "The LAPD is grateful, of course. Did you see Lili Montana, too?"

He nodded. "I saw her. I didn't get to speak with her the way that Gina did." The man pointed to the empty table. "I'll send Gina right over."

Sophie and Bruce took seats across from one another in the booth.

Gina Wyler was tiny—it was easy to see since she was wearing sneakers for her job. She was about five-one or five-two, pleasingly plump—as Sophie's mom would have said—and possessing a beautiful smile, even when it was punctuated with a worried furrow of the brows.

She slid into the booth next to Bruce. A good thing since Michael Thoreau was next to Sophie.

If Gina had taken that seat, she might have received a startling little chill.

Bruce had become so accustomed to Michael Thoreau following them around that he almost introduced the ghost to Gina.

He managed not to—these days, he seldom gave himself away with the least movement, word or even whisper.

Sophie seemed to quickly have gotten the hang of having a ghost around, as well.

She welcomed Gina with a firm handshake and an expression of gratitude. The girl—Gina couldn't possibly be more than in her very early twenties—seemed very quickly at ease with the two of them.

"I was so stunned when I saw the news…and when I saw her picture. It was Lili Montana who came in here. I never asked her what her name was, and I should have, because we really did chat," Gina said. "She was so pretty…and nice. And nervous. She was going for an audition."

"She told you she was actually going to audition?" Bruce asked.

"Yes. I always ask customers how they're doing, what they're up to, and she said she had an audition that day."

"For—who? Or what?" Sophie pressed.

"She didn't name a name. She said the whole thing sounded a little odd. It was all going to start off as theater that would be filmed. You know what I mean—a play that's filmed. Anyway, sounded even odder to me that they intended to film it, because it wasn't going to be usual theater."

Bruce and Sophie glanced at each other.

"Did she ever use the word 'weird' in your conversation?" Bruce asked.

"Yes! Exactly! The show was going to be weird. We started talking about *Sleep No More*. That's a play that showed in New York City. It was very cool—you follow certain performers around. It's a different experience for whoever sees it. The performers make use of different floors of the hotel…you're just not sure where you're going to end up. I saw it when I went back home to see my brother—he had just finished his enlistment with the military. My mom took us all to the show. I loved it. And that's how Lili and I started talking."

"Is there going to be a performance here? Was she trying out for it?"

"No. I mean, there might be a show out here—but not that I know about. Although then, we started talking about *The Johnny Cycle—III*. That was done not far at all from here in a mausoleum. It was fabulous. Same thing—you followed different performers around, only out here, it was a mausoleum. Not at all strange for LA County, I guess. The Speakeasy Society is great for doing amazing new theater," Gina told them.

"So, was she going to audition for them?" Bruce asked.

"No, no—if only she had been going out for something they were doing. No, the guy was brand-new in the game, she said. She had the chance to get in with him from the get-go. And if she was one of his major players and it all came out right— she'd be set."

"She never mentioned a man's name or the name of the production house he'd formed—or where she was going at all?" Sophie asked.

"All she said was 'weird.'"

"Weird?" Bruce repeated softly.

"She was going somewhere 'weird.' No, she wouldn't say where. She didn't want to jinx herself."

"But it was near here?" Bruce asked.

"I think...because we talked until about a quarter of eight— and she was supposed to meet him at eight."

"Did you see where she went when she left here?" Sophie asked.

Of course not, Bruce thought.

That would be too damned easy.

"When she left the café, she headed away from downtown— toward the west."

"Walking?" Bruce asked.

"She came here by something—taxi, Uber, Lyft. When she left the café, she was walking."

There wasn't much else Gina could tell them. "I wish I could help you more. She was just so sweet. So pretty and natural and... I didn't meet the other girl. And to think...this horrible person killed Lili, and then went on to kill again—just a day later. God knows, he might have another victim right now. He's going for the hopefuls, you know. The girls who come out here just hoping... Hollywood can be such a dream. And it can be such a killer, too." She was silent a minute. "Literally," she said drily.

"Gina, you've been incredibly helpful. Thank you so much," Sophie told her. Gina's hand lay on the table; Sophie squeezed it.

"Yes, thank you so much," Bruce echoed. He and Sophie handed her their contact cards. "If you need us for anything—anything at all—call. If by any chance you think anyone even remotely dangerous is hanging around here, you call us. Don't ever be hesitant, okay?"

Gina smiled and nodded. "I'm not a Hollywood hopeful. I was born here, but I never wanted to be in the movies. Yep, I know that most of the waiters and waitresses out here want to be actors. Not me. I'm in nursing school. I love medicine. I've thought about going into it full blast—to be a doctor, you know. But I like people. And people who are hurt or sick need compassion. I want to be the person who really helps them feel better."

"That's commendable," Sophie told her.

"I guess I should get back to work." She smiled grimly and rose. "Thank you—for not just putting us off. I know you must have received a thousand tips. I do pray that you find whoever killed those young women."

"We intend to," Bruce assured her.

She left the table. Sophie already had her phone out to report to Grant Vining.

He called Jackson Crow.

"We believe Lili Montana met her killer within fifteen minutes of this café—on foot."

"I'll call the home office and get Angela started on possibilities."

"You'll call Angela—at headquarters? In Virginia?"

Jackson laughed softly. "Don't ever underestimate my wife. She can pull up any old plans you might imagine. She'll find everything in the near vicinity with a foundation, basement—or anything that might have been an old soundproof studio."

"That's great. I guess we'll keep searching the general area. Two sightings of the victims in the same area."

"Go to it. I'll meet you down there in an hour or so."

He hung up; Sophie had just done the same.

"Vining is on his way down."

"Jackson is coming, too. My suggestion is that we go out—and walk west and see what we see."

She smiled. "I like that suggestion."

"Brilliant," Michael Thoreau's ghost agreed.

They started down the street. Sophie started telling Bruce why she loved California—and even Los Angeles—so much. She pointed out the various historic buildings near them, and told him that he really should see the many old missions that were on the historic register. "These buildings, though," she said, "are filled with tourists daily. All kinds of historic boards work with and on them. I can't imagine that anyone could do anything secret with them. They'd have been discovered by now. I'm almost positive."

"We're looking for something that might be private. And while we're in an old section of the city, it might not be that old. But Jackson has an agent searching old maps and plans."

"I know that it's near here," Michael said. "We're about two blocks from the alley...where I was shot and killed. In fact..."

"Don't go there, Michael!" Sophie said. "It will just make you…"

"Sad," Bruce said for her.

"So follow me," he said. "Be there for me."

He turned to head for his alley.

"Michael—it might not even be an alley anymore," Sophie called.

"It's an alley," Michael said with assurance.

"It's a secluded place—and it's in the area of interest," Bruce said to Sophie.

She nodded with a slight shrug and started off after Michael.

To his surprise, she then stopped and looked at him seriously. "I'm sorry," she said.

"About what?"

"I have had an attitude."

He smiled. "Thank you."

"I actually rather like you."

"And I like and admire you."

She looked embarrassed and uncomfortable then. She started walking again.

He reached out and stopped her. "You're so dedicated, but… Do you have a life?" he asked her. "I mean—any kind of social life?"

She blushed furiously. "Yes. No. I'm going to find one," she admitted on a quick breath. "I thought I was going to start having one. And then…this case. And Michael."

"Did someone convince you that you were crazy when you first saw a ghost?" he asked her softly.

"Yes."

"It's happened to many people," he assured her. "I don't know what it is… Adam Harrison—he's the head of the Krewe of Hunters—has a knack for finding such people. It's maybe one or two percent of the population. And some never do accept it. Obviously—we could be ridiculed for it."

She nodded. "Yeah. So Bryan sees ghosts, too?"

"And my younger brother, Brodie. For us, it started with our parents."

She smiled. "Your famous parents, right?"

"They were actors—well-known in their day—yes."

"I think I have accepted Michael. But…isn't it…weird, even for you, when they first show up?"

"Sometimes so weird that I have to figure out if they are the living or the dead," he assured her. "But, Sophie, honestly, they help. I just found a missing woman, because a ghost helped. And Cara Barton helped solved her own murder—the ghost of Cara Barton. I know it's strange, but it really is a gift—and we are able to do some amazing things because of this gift."

"So you think that Michael can really help?"

"I'm not sure how yet, but yes."

She smiled, but then she gasped. "There he goes—down that little alley. I wouldn't have even looked for an alley there…it seems to be set there between a building from the late 1800s and one from maybe 1930 or so."

"We said we'd follow."

"And we will!"

She started off again, but he caught her arm and pulled her back. "Sophie, you said that you almost had a life."

She nodded. "I was being a caregiver. To an old friend."

"And old lover?" he asked softly, thinking that she'd probably tell him that it was none of his business.

"Not recently—way back in high school. But we were still friends, and he didn't have the help that he should have had… so basically, I had work, and I had him."

"I'm sorry. I'm so truly sorry."

"We all lose in life, don't we?"

"We do. But to honor those we lost, Sophie, we keep living."

"We're going to lose Michael," she said.

"Nope, we're going to catch up to him," he told her, and they hurried down the street.

The alley was a very narrow strip between the two buildings. Bruce didn't see Michael as they first started down it—it was riddled with trash cans, empty boxes and, he discovered, stepping around one of the old boxes, two homeless men sleeping in makeshift "housing" created from some more empty boxes.

He caught sight of Michael down at the end of the alley, looking at a door into the late 1800s building. But he didn't walk to him quickly as he might have done; the homeless men were sitting up, looking at the two of them with surprise.

"Hey, hey...we're not hurting anyone!" the older of the two, a man of about sixty with a full gray beard and headful of long gray hair said.

"It's good here, please, hey—we even got blankets here," the younger said.

"We haven't come to roust you," Bruce assured him.

"You're not cops?" the younger man asked.

"Well, Detective Manning is a cop—but not here to bother you in any way," Bruce assured them both.

"No, but I'd love to speak with you," Sophie said.

"We don't trust cops," the older one said.

"Nope. Can't trust cops. They want to shake you down," the younger one said.

Sophie squatted next to them. "I wanted to ask you if you'd see any young women around here."

The older one laughed. "I haven't really seen a young woman in a long, long time."

"Girls like guys with money," the younger man said.

"There were two women brutally murdered, and we think it happened somewhere near here," Sophie said.

The older one immediately looked suspicious.

"I never hurt anyone in my life!" he said.

"No, no—I was hoping desperately that you might help, that you might have seen something," Sophie told him.

The old one looked at the young one. He stood up, and the younger man did the same. Sophie rose with them.

"I'm Tom. This is Billy," he said. And he smiled sheepishly. "You're the prettiest young thing I've seen in a long, long time. Maybe even forever."

"Yeah," Billy agreed. "You don't happen to be pretty—and have a pack of cigarettes on you, do you?"

"No, I'm so sorry. I don't smoke."

"Pretty—and smart," Tom said. He let out a long breath, looking over at Billy. "There was…someone."

"An attractive young woman? Dark-haired?" Bruce asked.

"She might have been," Tom said.

"We didn't really see her. She ran by us," Bill said. "She was trying to get somewhere…but the building here…on the side. It was a studio. Guess it was an independent kind of place. It shut down about a month or so ago."

"Really? So there's no one there?" Bruce asked.

"People come and go. Guess whoever went down is getting the last of their stuff. Some kid gave us the blankets," Tom said.

"A kid? How young?" Bruce asked.

"Oh, he thinks everyone is young," Bill told him. "Kid as in…maybe thirty or so."

"But was he here when the girl was here? Did you talk to her?" Sophie asked excitedly.

"No, no… I think that the company had already cleared out whatever it was they were going to clear out," Tom said. "And we didn't really see her because…"

"Because some idiot dropped a whole bottle of whiskey out

on the corner, and Tom and I figured we might enjoy it—rather than let it go to waste, you know," Billy told them.

Tom sighed. "Okay, okay, so we were pretty blitzed. She went by. She disappeared. Maybe through that door down there."

"Thank you," Sophie told him. "Hey, what do you smoke? I'll get you a pack of cigarettes."

"Nice! Thank you—anything," Billy said.

"We may need you again. Not to bother you in any way. But…if this proves to be anything, would you help again?" Bruce asked.

"We don't like cops," Billy said.

"But she's kind of all right. For a cop," Tom said.

"Let's get down to the door—and see what we see," Bruce said to Sophie.

"I'm going to have to get a search warrant if we want to get inside," Sophie said.

"Hey, I'm not a cop," Bruce reminded her. He was already walking away.

Michael Thoreau stood at the end of the alley, looking at the door speculatively.

"Bruce, stop," Sophie called. "Let me get ahold of Vining. We don't know who owns the place now. If there is something…"

Bruce startled Michael Thoreau—almost walking right through him.

He tried the old metal door with the simple metal knob.

Locked.

Bruce jiggled it roughly, but the door held fast. He sighed in frustration.

"Wait!" Michael said, "I'll go. Ghosts are good for something."

He stepped through the sheet of metal.

Sophie reached Bruce just as Michael Thoreau stepped back into the dim light of the alley.

"Call a judge," he said. "You're going to need that warrant."

CHAPTER SEVEN

Wednesday night

Sophie was grateful that Bruce had stopped cold when he'd opened the door and looked into the now-empty studio.

Because she was convinced that they'd found a lead. Maybe the studio wouldn't prove to be the place where the murders had been committed, but it was starting to seem likely that it was the place where Lili Montana and Brenda Sully had first met their killer.

It was Hollywood—studios of some kind or another were just about everywhere. If the young women had believed they were going to an audition, they might have easily accepted the address, and it might not have seemed odd if they had been asked to come by the alley door.

Sophie wasn't sure what was "weird" or "odd" about the studio yet—but it might well have been the meeting point, or the gateway to wherever "weird" place their killer had convinced them he intended to film their auditions.

The place had been cleaned out—and then set up.

The law was tricky; while never perfect, American laws had been created by the Founding Fathers who didn't want to see illegal searches and detainments, and in the end—even when it made it hard on law enforcement—civil rights were of utmost importance in the "land of the free," and upholding the law meant just about everything to Sophie.

Once Bruce—and then she—had looked inside, they both believed that they were looking at a scene that had been staged. Just for Lili, and then, most likely, Brenda, as well.

It meant that they had to wait.

Wait for Vining and other cops.

And for a forensic team.

Because, as Tom and Billy had told them, the studio people had cleared out.

But then, someone else had gone in. With just one private and intimate setting.

It wasn't easy, waiting.

Sophie covered part of the time by leaving Bruce McFadden with their new friends—Tom and Billy—so that she could run over to a gas station and buy them cigarettes. Billy had admitted to breaking a drug problem a year ago, and so, since they seemed to be helping him stay off anything harder, buying cigarettes for him didn't seem like such a bad thing in comparison.

Tom's wife had died three years ago, Sophie learned. They'd never had children. He'd tried to keep his job and take care of her—cancer had been the culprit stealing a bit of her life day after day. The amount of work he'd missed had caused him to be laid off. Then he'd gone through his savings.

Bill's story was a bit different. He'd come home from serving in the Middle East to wake in the middle of the night with violent nightmares. Then he'd started having them during the day.

He was a pilot; he'd been working for a major airline at the time.

He was never fired—he quit. He'd fought a war to save people; he wasn't going to lose his mind in the air and kill hundreds.

When Sophie came back from buying the cigarettes, Billy
and Bruce had been comparing service stories.

"The homeless…we're not disposable people," Billy said.
"We've just had some hard breaks."

Bruce, sitting with the two of them and leaning against the
wall as they did, spoke up.

"I think I've talked them into coming down to the station
to tell their stories. Jackson is on his way here. What the LAPD
can't handle, not to worry, Jackson Crow will."

"I know they'll be grateful for statements at the station," Sophie said.

"My colleague Jackson will accompany you," Bruce said to the
two men. "And, for tonight, he'll see to it that you have a room
and a shower—and breakfast wherever you like in the morning."

"On the taxpayer's dime?" Tom asked him bleakly. "Well, at
least I did always pay my taxes."

"Not taxpayer money," Bruce said. "My friend's boss is just a
really rich guy who likes people—and is happy to pitch in when
they need a break."

"And these are really good guys," the ghost of Michael Thoreau piped up.

He, like Bruce, was leaning against the wall with the two men.

Finally Grant Vining arrived with a forensic unit right behind
him. Sophie felt that she was on pins and needles, watching as
everyone put on gloves and booties over their shoes as they prepared to enter the studio.

As they had noted—and as Sophie had told Vining—the place
had been cleared out. What had seemed to point to young actresses being lured to the address was the fact that there was a
single camera set on a tripod in the middle of the floor. One
chair was by it—as if for an interviewer or cameraman. Another

chair faced the camera in what appeared to be the place where an actor might sit while answering questions or giving a bit of a performance.

A switch on the wall turned on floodlights that illuminated the cavernous room, revealing a great deal of empty space—but also the reason they needed a search warrant.

There was a small teddy bear seated on the "audition" chair. It was like…a talisman. Or a good-luck charm. Something that a young actress might have brought with her to an audition, especially if she had been asked to talk about herself, her hopes and dreams, and her background.

"We're not sure yet about the full story on this place," Grant Vining told them, surveying the room as the forensic team of four headed in. "It had been leased by Silvertone Productions. They are a new indie company, but responsible for two recent documentaries that were highly acclaimed. Anyway, they didn't go broke and abandon the place. Their lease was up and they were moving out of the downtown area—out of the congestion to where they could get a really big studio for half the price. You know how things go. Landlords increase rents. Anyway, Silvertone has been gone completely for at least a week now, but their lease actually ends Sunday night. The building's owner is one Ralph Haver, who currently lives in New York City."

"Did you get a warrant—or speak with this Ralph Haver?" Sophie asked him.

"I have a man still trying to reach him. We didn't have a problem in the world getting a search warrant once the judge knew that Lili Montana had possibly been seen going into the building," Vining told her.

"What do you think?" Sophie asked him.

"I don't know how you did it, Manning, but you and McFadden might have found the first real lead in the case," he told her.

Michael Thoreau came here, and we followed. He said that he could help, and it appears that he may well be helping.

She smiled grimly at Vining. "If he's playing out the whole Hollywood scenario, he would have convinced his victims that they needed to read for him."

"I don't think they were killed here," Vining said. "We haven't searched that far, but how could he have carried out such gruesome murders—and not left blood?"

"I don't think that he did murder them here. I think they met here, and he talked them into going somewhere else."

"Hey, Manning," someone said. She looked over. Henry Atkins was there, camera in hand.

"Hey, Henry."

Henry looked around at the almost-empty studio and nodded grimly at Vining. "This place is still listed as a working studio. Easy enough to lure someone here. Thing is, with those two homeless guys out there…if he killed the women here, how did he get by those guys?"

"Well, the one night, they'd found a bottle of whiskey," Sophie said. "They might have been passed out."

"One night. What about the other?" Vining asked.

Bruce came striding toward them from the back area. "We found a sparse worker's kitchen and a bathroom. There's no shower or tub, though, just a commode and a sink. I don't think that anyone would be able to mutilate a body here—and not leave a speck of blood. You had to have someplace big enough to have cleaned the corpses of the women the way that he did. Your people are working to see if there is any sign whatsoever of blood."

One of the members of the forensic team walked over to them. "Don't worry, sir!" she said to Bruce. "We will find it—if it's here."

"Of course," Bruce said.

The young woman nodded and headed over to join the others in her team.

"She's new?" Sophie asked.

"I've been trying to keep the same group working," Vining said. "That's Shelby. We had Morton. But Morton's wife is having a baby. Right now. Can't fault him for calling in. But Lee Underwood is here, and the other two who have consistently worked the sites. I have clearance right from the chief and the mayor. God help us, we have to hope there aren't any more murders, but we get the same ME, same photographer and same forensic team. We all know what we're looking for—and willing to find what we didn't know we were looking for. This one has to be solved."

"What about the teddy bear? Do you think it belonged to one of the women?" Sophie asked. "I have numbers for Brenda's friends. And I know that Jackson Crow is interviewing Lili's boyfriends."

"I'll call Kenneth Trent," Bruce said. "Find out if he knew anything about a teddy bear."

"I'll make some calls, too," Sophie said.

As she pulled out her phone, she saw the number that she had most recently entered.

That of the waitress, Gina Wyler. She dialed the young woman, who answered immediately.

"Detective Manning?" Gina said.

"Yes, it's me. I'm sorry to bother you—"

"No bother!"

"Did you happen to notice or see—did Lili Montana have anything with her?"

"Her purse."

"Anything else?"

Sophie had to stifle her gasp at Gina's reply. She was beyond eager to relay the news to Bruce and Vining, but quickly regained her composure.

"We're investigating. I can't really say more right now, but again, we do appreciate your help, " Sophie told Gina and ended the call.

She saw that Vining and Henry Atkins were staring at her.

"Sophie?" Vining asked.

"Lili Montana, at least, was here," she said. "Gina Wyler, the waitress, just confirmed that Lili had a small stuffed bear with her, about five inches high. Lili called it Jasper." She paused, inhaling deeply. "It was supposed to be her good-luck charm."

Vining nodded grimly. "We've found the way in to this case. Now we keep going." He turned to Sophie. "Except for you. Go home. No. Go to the hotel. Call it a night and get some sleep. Do you understand me? If I didn't know you so well, I'd actually tell you to go to a club and drink too much or do something—anything—fun."

"I'm really fine—"

Vining turned to Bruce.

"McFadden, can you please get her the hell out of here?" Vining asked. "Back to that hotel. Sophie, get some sleep." He looked at her and then lightened his tone. "I swear, if we make any kind of headway, I will call you immediately."

She nodded. As far as the investigation went, the day had been a good one. Michael Thoreau had led them to the alley where he'd been killed. How he might have known it could have been related to the murders, she didn't really understand.

Maybe he hadn't known. Maybe he had been drawn.

And maybe the studio had been used before—when the Black Dahlia had been killed in the 1940s. And maybe Thoreau had been shot because he'd been so close…

They weren't really close to figuring this out yet, but it was a good day's work.

Part of being a cop was learning to work with others—other cops, other departments. No man was an island. She really did need to let it go, to let others do their jobs, as well. It was arrogance—something that did no one any good—to assume that she needed to be there.

"Fine," she said softly. She turned to Bruce.

"Let's go," he said.

"What about Jackson?" she asked. "Wasn't he supposed to have met you here?"

"He's come and gone. He took Tom and Bill down to the station. They're telling what they've seen and what they might know. And then he'll see to it that they get a bit of a break."

She nodded and took one final look around the studio.

The alley was empty. She realized that she hadn't seen the ghost of Michael Thoreau inside; he was out in the alley. He fell in step behind Sophie and Bruce.

"So that's it!" he said. "I was killed because I was close. I mean, what do you think? Way back when—whoever the Dahlia killer might have been—they knew that I was getting close."

Sophie was careful not to answer him until they had cleared the alley, which had a couple cops and forensic investigators lingering about.

"Who were you after? Why were you in that alley?"

"That's the oddest thing," he told her.

"What's that?" Bruce asked.

"I was working that night. There was a bum in the alley. I could see him from the sidewalk. He had a sign…just by his side. And a dog. I'm a sucker for a dog. So I went to put some coins in the old army hat he had out and…he thanked me. I thanked him—for serving, you know. He was grateful. He had a bum leg—it was keeping him from getting work. So, later, I talked to some friends when I was at the bar down the street and we took up a little collection for him. I went back to give it him, and he was gone, and while I was walking up and down the alley seeing if he'd fallen asleep somewhere... I was shot and killed."

Michael fell silent. Sophie wanted to touch him—to say or do something that could somehow ease his pain. She felt that she had said "I'm so sorry" so many times that it was meaningless.

"Michael," she murmured.

"It's all right," he said. "You see, I am a lot of talk. I said that I could help you, and I wasn't even sure how. But this is right. I blindly helped you. This is good. I feel...well, not good. I won't feel good until a killer is caught this time. I was murdered *here*. Is it just Fate? Anyway, here we are again. I felt I'd been just drifting and wandering for so long, but there must be a reason...a real reason." He stopped as he reached the car, and gave them a grin. "See you guys."

"Where are you going?" Bruce asked him.

"I'm going to go be a fly on the wall. Oh, and, by the way— my mama taught me right. I will never just show up anywhere— as in anywhere private—without knocking. So...go have fun. And don't worry about being interrupted."

Sophie felt a flush rise to her cheeks.

"Thoreau," Bruce said. "We're working a case here!"

Michael was already walking away. He lifted a hand and kept going. Sophie watched him, wondering why her face was so hot, and why she felt so acutely uncomfortable. People joked all the time. It was certainly not the first time someone had suggested she should hook up with someone else.

She worked in a male-dominated field, had always been "one of the guys," and she could slough off almost anything. And she usually gave as good as she got.

But looking at Bruce across the car, it seemed that more than her face was burning. She realized, it was because it was the first time that a teasing comment seemed to reach in deep and find home.

She was attracted to the man.

She'd been working so hard, and giving whatever else she had to being a caretaker, that she'd almost forgotten about living outside the job.

She had a feeling about Bruce. Something about him. He was decent. He didn't condescend, and yet he stood his own ground.

But, yes, somewhere deep in her psyche, she knew that she had noticed his evocatively clean and ruggedly male scent. And the energy that hung about him, he was like walking with or touching fire: vital, so alive, so in possession of his sensuality and sexuality…a handsome piece of blithely walking seduction.

She gave herself a mental shake. Bruce was out here because Marnie had asked him to come. Her friends Marnie and Bryan were just looking out for her.

She was no one's charity case, she determined.

"Don't," he warned her.

"Pardon? Don't what?"

"Get all defensive on me."

"I'm not defensive."

"You are."

She waved a hand in the air, choosing to ignore his words. "I'm not defensive. I'm long past that kind of thing. I'm thinking."

She was lying.

But as she slid into the car, she did have an idea.

"I'd like to stop by my house."

"I thought you promised Vining you'd go to the hotel."

"I will go back with you to the hotel. I just want to stop by my house first. One page of my research was missing. I want to find out what page that was. If I have them all and retrace my steps on the computer, I should be able to figure it out. At the very least, figure out what was taken—and that could be a clue."

"You think it was the killer who was in your house?"

"It wasn't the ghost—and anyway, I don't think that ghosts steal papers, do they?"

"Not that I know about," Bruce admitted.

They drove in silence for a minute, and then she asked him, "So, where is home for you?"

He shrugged. "Here and there. We have a cabin up near the Blue Ridge, and a place in Virginia—my parents' place. Who knows? Bryan is in the FBI academy now, and Marnie is going to open a children's program at Adam's theater. Maybe they'll take over the old homestead—our parents left it to all of us, naturally."

"And you guys all get along?" she asked.

He laughed softly. "As kids? Not so much. Yeah, like siblings get along. You know, we'd fight with each other, but tear anyone else apart if they had anything nasty to say. Not literally—you know, just whatever the hell you do, don't bad-mouth my brother in front of me. Then, of course, we have our parents back, haunting us all. Guess they really do want to watch over us. We don't make it easy for them. We all went into the service, and knew we're all interested in investigation and law enforcement. How two actors had the three of us as children, I don't know."

"But…you just came out to LA, with no notice," she said.

"We were kicking around the idea of opening our own firm for private investigation. Seemed a good idea. We've helped out—mostly unofficially—in a number of cases, in Virginia, and elsewhere. Anyway, trying to make a long story short—too late, I know—my parents were friends with Adam Harrison. And Adam has a touch…he can find people to help out at the right time in the right place, and he turned that into the Krewe of Hunters. Jackson Crow was his first recruit. Jackson met his wife, Angela, through that first investigation. I don't know all the legal and jurisdictional procedures, but the Krewe of Hunters works as a separate and elite unit. After the investigation on the Blood-bone killer out here—as you know now—Bryan decided that he was going to try to join the FBI."

"So what about you and Brodie?"

"Not sure. This all just came up. But, hey, Brodie and I might stick with the original plan, and then again, we may not." He glanced her way and shrugged. "I've considered the Krewe. Jackson has convinced me that it's a good place to be. And, hey, there are medical benefits and a retirement plan."

She smiled.

"And you?" he asked her.

"I always knew I wanted to be a cop."

"You have to be a hell of a good one—to have gotten where you are."

"Well, thanks. I've had Grant's support, too. Not many people luck out and come up with a man like him to be a mentor and a partner."

"Your dad was a cop?"

"Yep."

"And you grew up in LA?"

"I did."

He grinned. "And you never wanted to be in the movies?"

She laughed. "Not once. Over the years, I've met the good, the bad and the ugly. Some of the nicest people I've ever met are performers. And, of course, I've seen the ones who strike out, get crazy with the money and attention, and go the other way. And I know the average working Joes—the guys working behind the scenes on every movie known to man, but they'll never be household names."

They'd reached her house; she realized that they'd gone a full twenty minutes without talking about the case. She wasn't sure if that was good or bad.

They headed up to the house. She slid her key into the lock with Bruce right behind her.

She realized that they both stepped in carefully, listening, looking around. But they could also both *feel* the emptiness.

No one was there.

"I'll just gather up what I have," Sophie said. "There's water, sodas, iced tea, in the refrigerator."

"You want something?"

"A bottle of tea, thanks."

"We should probably eat something."

"Food. Hmm. Not so sure about that," Sophie admitted. "I mean, I really haven't been here—"

He laughed. "And grocery shopping isn't high on your 'to-do' list."

"No," she admitted, ducking into her office.

In a few minutes, she had gathered up everything she had printed off. Bruce was in the kitchen; he had a bottle of tea for her and one for himself.

"Ready?" he asked her.

They went out again, with her locking up.

"I like your place," he told her. "Lots of pictures of your parents. No siblings?"

"No."

"Parents gone?" he asked.

She looked his way and offered him a sad smile. "Really gone. They don't come back to haunt me."

He nodded. "And you were just taking care of an old, dear friend—who just passed away."

"Yes."

He fell silent. When they reached the lobby of the hotel, she turned to him. "Well, thank you. And if I've had a bad attitude, I'm truly sorry."

"Not so fast. I ordered dinner to the room. One chicken, one beef. You take your pick. Oh, this is California. Just in case you're a vegetarian, I ordered some fruit and spinach salad and—I think—asparagus and bread."

She smiled. "I'm not a vegetarian. But I do like vegetables. And fruit. And…"

"And?"

"You're right," she admitted. "I hadn't thought about food, and I am starving."

"Good."

She felt a little odd, heading up to his room. They passed a bellboy who just said nothing but "good evening" to the two of them.

Not so odd.

There was a table in the room, and their food had arrived.

"I really wasn't being presumptuous—ordering for you, I mean. I just knew that room service was going to close."

"It's okay."

There was one chair at the little work table where room service had set their tray; Bruce dragged another from the dresser area and they both sat and lifted the covers that had been keeping the food warm. One plate had a nicely broiled chicken breast and the other a really nice and thick steak.

She looked at him.

"Whatever you like."

"Let's split them both."

"All right!"

She wondered for a minute—as they divided chicken and steak—if this wasn't something like a date.

She couldn't remember being on her last date.

The thought made her a little nervous, so she went and collected her papers, going through them. "Okay, suspects in the original case…they talked to Elizabeth Short's father, who lived out here, but he was quickly eliminated. Then, of course, they asked him about her dates, and he was pretty callous—he seemed to believe that she'd go with anyone in a uniform. She was supposed to have been or gotten engaged at one point, but that fiancé was killed in the military. The police decided that it wasn't someone she was dating. Obviously, this was a pretty sick individual." She looked up at him suddenly. "What's missing is a page I'd printed about the police and forensics at the time."

"That's interesting. But I'm not at all sure what it says. Spinach?"

"Um, yes, sure."

He reached over and took the papers from her hand.

"I've been thinking about poor Michael Thoreau. Have you ever been shot at?" he asked her.

She nodded. "Twice. Caught in the upper arm...we'd been called to a domestic. Sad case."

"A man shot his wife?"

"No, actually. The wife shot up the husband. He'd been cheating—with her best friend. She decided to end the affair."

"Did she kill him?"

"He survived. And he married the best friend. She's still in jail."

"Weird justice—that goes to show you that you just can't... well, divorce would have been a much better option."

"Yep. It's sad, but you're right. You just can't shoot people. Anyway, she got a round off at me. I was working patrol at the time. We were called in because the neighbors heard shots. She caught me blindly, but I got the gun from her."

"And the second time?"

"The second time... A little boy had his dad's gun. He didn't hit me or his father on purpose. He had found the gun. He was sitting there crying with his dad on the floor, and he was talking to me and...dropped the gun. Got me in the foot. But...that was patrol, too. Patrol is the most dangerous job in the police, really."

He nodded. "The patrol officer never knows when a routine

traffic stop may get him shot. Patrol officers really do have their lives on the line all the time."

"And you?" Sophie asked.

"Wanna see my scars?"

She laughed. "Depends on where they are!"

He grimaced and drew off his T-shirt in one smooth motion, revealing a scar across his chest.

"And you were working?"

"Navy. Iraq." He was quiet a minute. "I was trying to get a gun from a ten-year-old. We got the gun—and we even got the kid into a good home and a school and...it was worth it."

"When something goes right, it's all worth it." She didn't mean to, but she was staring at his chest. He was bronzed, his muscles finely honed. And she was shaken to realize just how much she wanted to stretch out her fingers and touch him.

"You going to show me yours?" he asked, and then laughed suddenly.

"Hey," she said with a shrug. "You are more than welcome to see my foot." She pulled off both boots and her socks and wiggled her toes before him. "Left side, left foot. Oh, and on my arm. It's just a nick there—right arm, biceps, toward the back of the muscle area."

"Ah, poor foot!" he said, and gently ran a finger along the thick red line.

She almost jumped out of her seat. He didn't hurt her, he didn't tickle...

It was a touch she felt through to the core.

"It wasn't that big a deal, honestly."

"Had to have hurt."

"Like a mother."

He grinned at her, easing her foot down. He leaned closer. "Just when is the last time you had sex?"

"What?"

"Honestly, that isn't a bad opening line. I can't help but be really curious."

"I… Okay, it's been a while. When I say I took care of a friend, he was a friend. That is not a fair question!"

"I'm not trying to be fair—I'm trying to figure you out."

"Fine. A while. Over a year. Now I'm also intrigued—what about you?"

"It's been a bit," he admitted. "I was in a relationship for a while…it kind of fizzled. I think I'm just too tightly wound for most people."

She understood that. Some guys were afraid of a woman who was a cop; some wanted to know things they shouldn't want to know about. And some wanted to prove that they were stronger and smarter than everyone else.

And for him…

Having dead parents around couldn't help.

"You?" he repeated.

She inhaled a deep breath. She'd known him a matter of days. She wasn't sure when she'd felt so intimate with someone.

"About five years," she admitted.

"Five years?" he demanded, incredulous.

"I've been busy!"

He looked at her with amusement, but also something more. And she realized suddenly that he wouldn't push anything.

To her own astonishment, she murmured, "We could fix that, tonight, I mean, if you're at all interested."

CHAPTER EIGHT

Wednesday, late night

Bruce wasn't at all sure he had heard her correctly. But just what he *thought* he heard her say seemed to awaken his desire like a bolt of pure, hot lightning shot down right into his gut. And lower.

He was dead still for a minute, looking at her.

Now she was flushing again.

It was extremely attractive, somehow both very sweet and vulnerable—and sexy as all hell.

"Oh, God!" She covered her face with her hands. "I don't believe I just said any of that. I didn't mean... I mean...oh! Seriously, I don't need..."

Bruce found himself up from the table, then down on his knees by her. "Hey!"

"I—" she began.

He leaned to her, cupped her face into his hands and kissed her. He realized that whatever it was about her, he'd felt the draw since he'd first seen her on television—shaken but determined, brusque and yet graceful. Whatever it was about her...

she seemed to beckon to him and enchant him in a way that was unique and absolutely charming.

Her lips gave beneath his and he tasted a sweet liquid heat that seemed to catch swift fire and burn between them. Her fingers fell on his naked chest. Her touch was featherlight, both natural and ridiculously erotic.

He stood, drawing her to her feet. They started to kiss again, tongues both dancing and dueling, as if neither could taste enough of, or draw deeply enough from, the other. Their lips were still all but glued together as they shed their clothing, pulling at their own, helping and hindering one another.

They wound up pushing away from the table. At some point—maybe when he shed his shoes—they crashed down on the bed together, and there was laughter. And then a very still moment when they paused, and he looked into her eyes, and he was amazed by not just the sense of desire he felt, but tenderness for her, a need to protect and cherish, even though he knew she was so capable and fine and...

Maybe cherish and protect was something you felt whether you were tough or not. He didn't know, and he sure as hell didn't understand, because it seemed that everything in him caught fire, and he was desperate to remember to be a courteous lover, because the desire in him seemed to be sparking out of control.

She was as lovely as a little sylph, tiny but finely muscled, her form exceptionally fit. He realized Sophie would be in great shape not for her ego, but out of determination to be as physically capable as possible.

Of course, he had to admit, it did work in bed.

She touched him, and it was a jolt of magic; she moved beneath him and he was on fire. He kissed her flesh, moved against her and then moved within her. And he wondered, feared, that he had not given enough, but she was with him, eager, sweetly, wickedly moving...against him...with him...

They rolled and moved, and every motion was electric.

She climaxed first; he followed in moments. And when he lay by her side and could breathe again, he spoke to her softly.

"Wow. Um, forgive me—"

"Forgive you?" She leaned her hands on his chest and arose to accost him, a frown furrowing her forehead. "For...?"

"Oh, babe. Five years." He grinned, drawing her back down to lie atop him. "There should have been... I mean really...a lot more foreplay. Five years!"

She flushed, grimaced and fell by his side.

"I thought it was great."

"Ah, well, thanks, but honestly, I can do much better."

"Hard to believe. But hey, you're definitely more of an expert."

He laughed. "I sure as hell didn't say there was anything wrong with it." He pulled her close to him. "It was just a bit spontaneous..."

"Well, it was a long day. I mean, actually, I would love a shower."

"A shower," he repeated. "Great idea."

He leaped up, bowing slightly as he reached out a hand to her. "Seriously. I can't be remiss. If I mess up too badly, you may let it all go another five years."

"Oh, I rather think that you've piqued my memory quite well," she assured him.

"But a shower..." he said, letting the word trail and then shaking his head. "I really have to show you what the shower is all about. Got to make absolutely sure that you don't fall back into your old, lonely habits."

He pulled her with him, laughing.

He started the shower, telling her how they needed the perfect water. And then he let it run, and found the soap, telling her it would be absolutely delightful to help her wash away the day.

He loved touching her.

Loved the way she felt as his hands moved over her.

And then she took the soap from him.

And did amazing things.

"I'm a fast learner," she whispered to him.

She was.

He wanted to give so much. Wanted to see that he gave her perfect moments, perfect sensations.

Five years without a loving touch. Other women might lie about something like that…or exaggerate. Not Sophie. Success at her chosen field had meant too much to her. Caring for a friend had meant even more. She'd put a lot of other things ahead of her own happiness.

He wanted the night to be…magic.

But they reached a point where the heat and the water and the steam and suds and their hands on one another became more than he could bear.

He managed to turn the water off, lift her out of the shower, pull her against him, and then back toward the bed, grabbing towels as he did so. She was still sleek and clean and she smelled amazing, and while he'd thought he was being driven insane with desire, he still managed to wait, kissing her, because the sweetness of her taste was something that he could not ignore.

She tugged him down to the crisp sheets, and made love to him. Later, they lay together, exhausted, catching their breath. And he was holding her, teasing her about something, when he realized that she was asleep.

He lay awake a while, grinning to himself, and then he slept, too.

Thursday morning

It was almost impossible to believe the way that she had behaved, Sophie thought vaguely, waking up with a smile. On several levels, it was all so wrong. They barely knew one another. They were working together. Okay, so he wasn't a cop, but...

Then, of course, she just wasn't sure that rational, career-driven, respectable young women were supposed to behave in such a way. Her folks had really taught her manners and courtesy...

Well, hopefully, she'd been polite!

She rolled slightly, curling more tightly against his bare chest, delighted by the warmth there, loving the feel of his breathing.

His arm came around her, moving her even more closely to him.

"Hey," he murmured.

"Hey," she said.

"You good?" He sounded a little anxious. "You good with everything?"

"Excellent," she said softly.

"I'm glad. I was afraid that you'd wake up..."

"Embarrassed? Yeah, well, there is a bit of that."

"Don't be," he said firmly. "Don't be...and please don't let another five years go by."

"I shouldn't have told you that."

"Well, you won't have to worry about that now... I mean, I'm not leaving town anytime soon."

She smiled.

He was gazing warmly at her. But then he asked softly, "So... what's been keeping you so busy?"

She blew out a breath, and then admitted. "Well, first it was my dad. I lost my mom when I was young, and I guess, I kind of hero-worshipped him. He taught me about being a good cop. He was the best... He got to see me make it through college, and graduate the academy. But there was also a friend..."

"Your old flame."

She nodded. "Andrew. We were together in high school, then

we were off. Then we were together at UCLA...then we were off. Then he got sick. We had just gone to lunch, and talked as old friends, and then, the next week, he got the diagnosis. We never got back together, so to speak. But he lost his job, he was so ill so often from chemo... Anyway, he needed help. So, I was there for him. And then, there was work..."

"Sophie, Sophie," he said softly. "Life can't just be work."

"I didn't mean to make it that way."

"And no one asked you out? I don't believe that."

"No one who I wanted to go out with," she whispered.

He smoothed back her hair, pulled her closer.

"Sophie," he whispered again.

They started to move toward one another.

But suddenly, both their phones were ringing.

Sophie leaped up, with him now far too intimate to worry about her nudity, and made a dive for her handbag over by the table where they'd eaten dinner.

It was LAPD photographer Henry Atkins on the other end of the line. "Sophie, the captain asked me to call you."

She was confused. If something was up, Grant Vining would have called her. And if Grant had been hurt or injured, Captain Chagall should have called.

Unless he wanted to be as delicate as possible.

"Oh, God, what's happened?" she asked. "Grant—what's happened to Grant?"

"He's alive, Sophie," Henry assured her. "But he was shot."

"Where? When? Where is he now?"

"The hospital. He asked that no one call you until he was out of surgery. He came through fine. He's in recovery—"

"I'm on my way," Sophie said.

She broke the call and looked at Bruce. She saw that he'd received the same information, and she assumed that he'd been talking to Jackson Crow.

"Let's go," he said simply.

She nodded.

Two seconds in the shower; neither of them joked that they should join one another.

They were dressed and out of the hotel in a matter of minutes.

She was glad that Bruce was driving. She realized that she was shaky. He was okay. Grant would be okay. But she couldn't help but feel guilty; she'd been having the time of her life while her partner had been in danger.

Bruce didn't say anything at all, and she was relieved. He didn't try to tell her that she deserved what little happiness she could grab.

As he quickly found parking at the hospital, he spoke at last and said simply, "Jackson assured me that Vining is going to be fine. The bullet caught him on the side of his chest. They had to extract it. Apparently he was sure at first that he could simply pluck it out himself."

"That would be just like Grant."

"That would be just like you!" Bruce said, offering her a bit of a smile.

Sophie looked at Bruce. "I didn't even ask where it happened, if they caught the person who shot him, if it was random, if…"

"He was shot just outside the alley when he reached the street. Long-range rifle. Cops have been combing over the streets."

"In the alley… Right where…"

"Yeah. Near where Michael Thoreau was killed."

They hurried in. There were a number of officers around, sitting or standing politely in the waiting room. Henry Atkins hurried over to see Sophie as she and Bruce came in. "It's all good. One person can see him at a time, so we all waited for you."

"Thank you!"

She glanced at Bruce.

"Go," he told her.

A nurse showed her the way.

Grant Vining looked thin and somewhat haggard in his hospital bed. She must have made a distressed sound when she entered, because he immediately shook his head and said, "Sophie, Sophie, honestly, I'm fine, they all made a big deal out of a scratch."

"It wasn't a scratch. You had a bullet in your body."

He shrugged. "Well, thankfully, our guy was a lousy shot."

"Or," she murmured, "a good shot—a good shot that he was able to catch you at all. I heard that—while I was back at the hotel—cops were out combing the neighborhood."

He laughed softly and then quickly stopped; laughing must have hurt. "Sophie, they did a good job. I know that our guys did a good job. The shooter was far away. How far, I don't know. He didn't get me until I was out on the street."

She hesitated and then said, "You know that I've been looking into the Dahlia case—"

"As have we all."

"And there was a reporter—an investigative reporter named Michael Thoreau—who was killed in that alley."

"Okay, that I didn't know."

"It's possible his killer might have thought that he was getting too close. Maybe Elizabeth Short was lured to the same studio."

"We've checked everything. The renters were out—completely gone. The owner was in Europe. Whoever got in had to know. And how the hell did he know what studio the Dahlia went to—and how the hell could he know that it was going to be empty?"

Sophie murmured, "Hmm," and then said, "Grant, what do you think? Maybe this killer was biding his time?"

"Well, we've figured we're looking for a home-grown killer," Grant mused.

"This isn't someone those girls knew—not someone they had dated casually. This is someone who can present himself as a young producer—and lure them in." She was thoughtful again a minute, thinking about the prowler in her apartment.

Because she was not careless with her keys, and she didn't go into the shower without seeing to it that the doors were locked.

"It's a cop," she said aloud.

"Not a cop, not a cop we work with," Grant argued. "Come on, Sophie. When you think about it, we've made remarkable progress on this case. We found our first victim Monday, second on Tuesday. This is Thursday. We can't just make assumptions."

"No assumptions," she assured him. "Just an idea."

"You got some sleep?" he asked her.

"I got some sleep," she assured him. *And a hell of a lot more.*

A nurse popped her head into the room. She was young and smiling and seemed very nice, but she said to Sophie, "I told him he had five minutes. I'd really like to get him to rest for a bit. Doctor's orders."

"I'm leaving," Sophie said. She was suddenly worried, though. *What if she was right? What if a cop was involved?*

"Sophie!" Grant Vining had caught her arm.

She looked at him, her brow arching slowly.

"You behave while I'm in here. You call for backup. You either keep that FBI consultant with you—and swear that you will— or I'll call Captain and tell him that you need a new partner."

"I am not going to try to work this with a new partner—"

"Then you stick with that consultant and his coworker, that Jackson Crow. They know what they're doing. No bullshit, no heroics, but straightforward investigation."

"I will stay with Bruce McFadden."

"Promise me."

"I promise."

He released her arm. "Okay, then, get out of here. I do need some sleep."

They had always been friends—partners who obviously cared

about one another. But their relationship was also professional. She hesitated. She'd never thought of Grant as a father—no one would ever be like her father, and she wouldn't think of anyone else in that light.

But he was a mentor—like the world's best uncle.

"You get well."

"Of course." He tried a smile again. "Don't know when the feds and that PI boy are going to bag out of here, and I sure can't leave you alone on the street."

She smiled and kissed him on the forehead.

"Wow," he murmured, smiling—and frowning with confusion at the same time. "You do care."

"Look after yourself," Sophie said and hurried out. As she walked to the exit, she took a close look at the officers standing around, the forensic people, even the techs who were civilians. They weren't there because they had to be. They were there because they were, definitely, in their way, a brotherhood or a family. They weren't being paid; they just cared.

Bruce was waiting for her, looking at her expectantly. She tried to smile at him, but he could obviously tell that she was worried.

"What's wrong?" he quickly asked her.

"I can't help thinking about that page missing from my research. It was about the suspects the cops thought most likely—and about the fear that it might have been a cop. Bruce, I'm worried about Grant being in the hospital. Yes, they'll have a police guard watching over him, but..."

"I have an idea," he said. He turned and left her, heading out to the hallway where he could make a call in private.

Henry Atkins—looking hangdog and weary—came over to her.

"See? He's really going to be all right."

"He's really going to be fine," Sophie said.

"I wouldn't have lied to you."

"I know that, Henry." She gave him a reassuring hand squeeze. "Hey, can you do me a favor? I know that they're available at the station, but could you see to it that you email all the pictures you've taken of the bodies and all the pictures of the Dahlia you were using for comparison?"

"Sure. Of course."

"Thanks, Henry."

"I'll head back in soon."

"Did you go home last night?"

"No."

"Then go home."

"Sure. I'll go to the station, and then go home."

As they stood there, Lee Underwood came striding through the door to the waiting room. He saw Sophie and let out a breath of relief.

"Sophie, I thought I should call you. Everyone said no, and then Vining made a big deal about you not being told, that you'd wind up going crazy all night and that wouldn't help the case or anything. Vining said you needed sleep badly and..."

"It's all good. I saw Grant." She looked at him. "You haven't slept, have you?"

He shook his head. "No, I've been at the studio all night. We went over and over the place. No blood anywhere, and we went through a hell of a lot of luminol. The big guys never thought that our girls were murdered there, but still...you have to eliminate."

"Yes," she agreed. "You have to eliminate."

Bruce came walking back in from the hallway. He greeted Lee.

"Nothing," Lee told him.

"I don't think that we were expecting anything. You must have hundreds upon hundreds of fingerprints."

"Yep," Lee agreed, letting out a sigh. "We were trying something with the teddy bear, but…so far, I'm afraid, nothing."

"I don't think that we'd find fingerprints even if we did find exactly where the girls were murdered," Sophie said. "He's smart. He wears gloves."

"Yeah, he's clever. Like he knows everything we're going to look for," Lee said. He made a face. "Too much TV. Perps are learning from shows. Of course, cops never get you in an hour. And most of the time, even today…we're waiting and waiting for results. Oh, well, better than before, huh?"

"Better than before," Sophie agreed.

As they stood there, Captain came in—along with Dr. Thompson. Seeing the medical examiner made Sophie's heart turn over.

But he apparently saw her face and hurried on over. "Don't look like that," he begged her. "I'm here as a friend. Grant and I go way back."

"He's doing well," she said, smiling at Captain, too.

"You got some sleep?" Captain asked her.

"Yes, sir. Ready to work."

Captain nodded.

Jackson Crow strode up to the group and spoke quickly. "I went back to the alleyway, searching the streets with a few fellow feds. We think we've found the shooter's spot—down the block, top of the roof of the Dontcha Wanna Donut shop. Scuff marks, like someone was up there. Forensics has gone on over."

"I should be there," Lee said.

"Absolutely, I want the same crews working so similarities or differences aren't missed," Captain said. "But I don't want my people keeling over. We'll get another crew in for now. Sleep— then you can all get back to it, okay? You, too, Atkins," Captain said. He turned to Jackson. "We are grateful for the federal assistance on this, Agent Crow."

"It's what we do, sir," Jackson said. "I'll be hanging around here, Captain, if you don't mind. Keep an eye on Vining?"

"Of course. We'll have some patrol officers on duty, too," Captain said.

Jackson nodded. Sophie thought that he looked at Bruce, and while he said nothing, they'd somehow had some kind of communication. Jackson gave her an almost imperceptible nod, and she knew that he'd silently let her know that she didn't need to worry; he would be guarding Grant Vining and no one—cop, friend, relative—would get by him.

Bruce turned to her.

"Sophie, you good?" he asked.

"Yes, of course. I need to move. Um, we need to move. I have some reading, some street work, some interviews," Sophie said.

"If you need help—" Lee began.

She smiled at him. "Hey, I went to sleep, as ordered. You go do the same."

"I'll be happy to get some sleep," Dr. Chuck Thompson said. "You all may have to work hard to wake me up, if you need me." The laughter left his face. "I'm going to pray that we don't have another victim."

Sophie and Bruce turned together and headed out. She didn't look at him or speak until they had cleared the hospital.

"Thank you for calling Jackson... I trust him. Seriously—I don't know what I'd be doing if you and he weren't out here. But of course, Jackson can't stay endlessly. And I'm really concerned while Grant is in here—there are just things that can happen in a hospital."

"Sophie, it's all right."

"But—"

"Sophie, I have another brother."

She stared at him and slowly smiled. "Oh…"

"Brodie. He was working on a case for Adam's theater, but as it happened, a maintenance man did die of natural causes. Brodie will be here in five or so hours, and then Jackson will be free."

"Thank you. And thank Brodie."

"He's glad to come. You haven't met my parents yet. If we don't help out where my mother thinks we should…"

"So coming out here is better than torture, right?" Sophie asked, smiling.

"Something like that. Okay, so…you said a few things in there. I'd been thinking we should try to find out more about Grant's shooter, but Jackson already found the final firing position, so…"

"The papers. Whatever is happening, this killer wants to reproduce the past. I want to get the old newspapers. Atkins is going to email me all the photos he's taken, and all the photos from the past. Let's study what we have. Let's go back and repeat everything, and see if we've missed anything."

He was thoughtful a minute. They'd reached the car and he hesitated, his hand on the door as he looked over the car at her. "How about the big screen in the conference room at the station? We'll put all our information up on the projection screen—including any of the websites you'd been visiting. It'll help to get an overview."

"It's a plan."

When they reached the station, Sophie gathered up her computer and hooked up the feed to the large screen in the conference room.

An image flew up to the screen. It was from the past—a picture taken at the site when Elizabeth Short had been killed.

"There's the bag—the canvas bag with the bloody water in it," Bruce pointed out. "And there wasn't such a bag when Lili was found, or when Brenda was found."

"Among the many theories back then, some wondered if Elizabeth Short had been cut in half because the killer was small—

either a woman, or a weakened man—and just couldn't carry
the weight of an entire body at one time."

"Only one bag," Bruce said.

"You mean—"

"I mean, there was one bag. The killer didn't put two body
halves in two different bags. I know that it was suggested that
one suspect, the surgeon Walter Alonzo Bayley, didn't have the
mental or physical capacity at the time to carry a body, and thus
the two pieces. At his autopsy, it was diagnosed that he had a
neurological disease. The authors Larry Harnisch and James Ell-
roy looked into such a theory. Bayley must have been a horrible
person—with what came out about the abuse of his daughter
during his later life. And he did live in the neighborhood where
Short's body was found—until his wife kicked him out. His
daughter was best friends with Short's sister. His disease might
have made him exceptionally violent. I don't think that cutting
the body in half had anything to do with strength—I think it
was some kind of a sick and twisted ritual."

Sophie clicked to the next picture.

At first, it appeared to be exactly the same. It was black and
white. The hue, contrast, saturation…everything seemed to be
identical.

"The police must have taken the bag up before this—" she
began.

She broke off.

"No," Bruce said quietly. "That's one of the first shots taken
by Henry Atkins when Lili Montana's body was found. Why
in hell…"

"Henry?" Sophie whispered. "Oh, God, no. Henry could
never, never do anything like this."

And yet…

The pictures…two distant decades…two different girls.

The images were almost exactly the same.

CHAPTER NINE

Thursday afternoon

So many images…so grotesque that none of them seemed real.

And yet they were.

"He is a police photographer," Sophie said, her voice toneless.

"Yes, a photographer who has worked for years and years—and who probably wants to make something more of his work than just images for a police file. How well do you know Henry Atkins?" Bruce asked her. He could see that the very idea that someone she knew and worked with could even begin to think about perpetrating such a crime was disturbing to her. He wanted to tell her that it was still—despite the photos—most unlikely that Henry Atkins might have had anything to do with the crimes.

But he really couldn't tell her anything. He just didn't know.

She shrugged. "We've worked together a long time. He's with the forensic team. He's not LAPD. He's a civilian employee. He is called in on major cases—obviously—and he's also asked to work as a sketch artist. He's enhanced photos for us—he's aged them for us. He's good."

"Does he do other work? I mean, with his photography."

"I know that he photographed a friend's wedding," Sophie said. "And birds—he loves to take pictures of birds."

Bruce drummed his fingers on the conference table and looked at her thoughtfully. She didn't want a friend to be guilty, but she had independently come up with the idea that it might be a cop. Or, someone connected to the cops.

It was more than possible. The similarities to the old case were amazing. The present killer's ability to avoid forensic clues seemed pretty remarkable, too. But was that from close proximity to law enforcement? Or research?

"Henry doesn't look much like a young and upcoming producer," he said. "And he sent you these quickly and willingly. He might be doing the same thing—trying to find exactly what the similarities and differences were in the killing."

Sophie nodded. "Of course. Can we…"

"Have him tailed?" Bruce asked her.

She nodded.

"I'll have to talk to Jackson. I mean, I assume you want someone not associated with LAPD."

"Right." She sighed. "You know, this department has gone through so much with so many sensational cases. And a lot of times, the cops have come out not looking so good. But it is a good department now, honestly."

"I believe you. And if we're looking back, two of the primary suspects were surgeons, not cops."

Sophie sat silently. Then she sighed. "About sixty people confessed to the Black Dahlia killing. Sixty! We barely even have one lead."

"Sophie, it's considered the most sensational unsolved murder on the LAPD books. Armchair sleuths across the country have studied it for years. But here's the thing. Our case is fresh. Let's go over what we know now. We know that the girls were fed a line about auditioning. We know where they met with the 'producer' who was going to make them rich and famous."

"This guy is pretending to be the kind of player who could change the industry—and that would lean toward the Bugsy Siegel/Norman Chandler theory—which some believe, and some discount." Norman Chandler had followed in his father's footsteps and become editor of the *LA Times*—and he and his wife had also been high in society. Chandler had been the money behind the Hollywood Palladium—a very important man.

"So, on that end, from what I've read, the idea is that Bugsy Siegel was hired to killed the Dahlia, and bisected her because she was pregnant with Chandler's illegitimate heir."

"We can go crazy on theories."

"But you're right. There's something we're not seeing."

"Let's shake it off. We need to head out."

"Yes, you do," Michael Thoreau suddenly interjected.

Bruce had been so focused on Sophie that he hadn't seen their ghost arrive. But there he was—looking despondent—seated at the end of the conference table. He said bleakly to Sophie, "I really meant to help you. I didn't mean for your partner to get shot, you know."

"Michael, you did help us," Sophie assured him. "Because of you, we know where the girls were lured. You've given us a start like no other."

He seemed to perk up a bit, then he asked, "But at what cost?"

"Grant Vining is going to be fine," she told him.

Bruce stood with purpose. "One of them—either Lili or Brenda—had to have said something to someone that will give us more of a clue. I want to see Kenneth Trent again—with you, this time, Sophie. We'll try him, and then we'll go back to Lili's boyfriend, and the ex-boyfriend, and then any friend of Brenda's."

"They've all been questioned," Michael said.

"But not by the super-trio of Michael, Bruce, Sophie," Bruce said. "Let's go."

Their first call was Kenneth Trent. He was easy to find—usually in his office, unless he was rehearsing, and he didn't call his rehearsals until night.

It was nearly 5:00 p.m. when they arrived, but they could hear someone talking inside the office. For a moment, it sounded like a fierce argument. Sophie rapped on the door, and the voices stopped abruptly.

Bruce and Sophie looked at one another.

Bruce was just about to bust the door in.

"Wait," Michael said. "It's just a scene from something... they're reading or rehearsing something."

A minute later, the door opened. Kenneth Trent stood there, and looked curiously out.

At first, he saw just Sophie. "Hello. I don't have an appointment for you... Are you here to audition?"

Bruce realized he wasn't so sure he liked working in Hollywood. Law enforcement had to be damned difficult.

"Who the hell ever knows what's real out here?" he whispered to Sophie.

"Or anywhere?" she whispered back quickly. Then she raised her voice pleasantly and spoke to Kenneth Trent. "No, I'm afraid that I'm not here to audition, Mr. Trent."

"Oh, well, I have an actress with me now, but you're more than welcome to leave your information, to come back..." He stopped speaking, finally noticing Bruce. "Oh...hey. It's um, it's you, Mr. McFadden."

"Yes, it's me," Bruce said.

"This is Detective Manning."

"Sophie." Politely offering Kenneth a hand, she suggested he use her first name.

"Come in, come in!" he said. "Grace and I were just rehearsing."

Bruce was startled by the resemblance to Lili Montana, Brenda Sully—and the Black Dahlia—that he saw in the pretty, curly headed brunette in the seat before Kenneth's desk.

She stood when they walked in.

"This is Grace Leon," Kenneth said, introducing the young woman. "She's just done an audition for the Hollywood Hooligans."

"Great," Sophie said. "I understand Kenneth has created a really talented troop of players doing all kinds of interesting things."

"Yes!" Grace said enthusiastically. "One of his actors just landed a major role on a cable show."

"Sloan Johnson," Kenneth said. "We're really so proud of her."

Bruce wasn't sure why, but he was pretty certain that Sloan Johnson just might have curly dark hair, too.

"Her opportunity gave me my opportunity," Grace said. She let out a soft sigh. "This just isn't an easy town…or an easy dream."

"No, not at all," Sophie said, looking at Kenneth. "You're sure that this cable show thing is totally legitimate? I'm assuming you've seen the news. Young women are urged to be extremely cautious when attending interviews or auditions."

"No, no, it was legit," Kenneth said. "I drove her to the audition myself."

"We're hungry for success—but not stupid," Grace assured them. "We've all been watching the news. Lili was a friend. But… Do the police have something? Any suspects?"

"Well, you know," Sophie said lightly, "contrary to what you see on TV, it's not all that easy. But in this case, no matter how many times we have to go back to the same friends, family, witnesses and even casual acquaintances, we will get our guy. And, of course, that's why we're back. Hoping, Kenneth, that you might have something…anything…else that might help us."

Bruce thought that Kenneth would give off a weary sigh, shake his head, and swear that he didn't know anything more.

But Kenneth glanced at Grace Leon, and she looked down at her hands.

"He does know something," the ghost of Michael stage-whispered from behind them.

"Wow, I am so sorry," Kenneth began.

"You're going to be sorry," Sophie interrupted sweetly, "if you don't tell me what it is you're hiding."

"I—I no, no—"

"Come on, Kenneth," Bruce said.

"We can go back to the station," Sophie said. "In fact, we should do that."

"Oh, crap, I think I need a lawyer. I can't afford a lawyer," Kenneth said bleakly.

"Why would you need a lawyer? Did you have anything to do with—"

"God, no! I loved Lili—I didn't know Brenda…"

His voice trailed. Bruce knew the sound of his voice—and his expression. There was something that he wasn't saying. Maybe nothing important in the end, maybe something. He tried to home in on what the truth might be.

"You didn't know Brenda well. But you did know her. At the very least, you met her. Or you saw her—somewhere."

Kenneth turned the color of pale white chalk. His mouth worked.

"Oh!" Grace Leon urged him to take her chair. She stared at Bruce. "Kenneth is a good man," she said.

"We believe that," Sophie said. "But…"

Kenneth took the chair.

Sophie hunkered down by him. "Look, Kenneth, I just met you, but I'm a cop and I've been one for a while, and I'm getting to know people. I don't believe for a minute that you killed anyone. But there is something that you're holding back. You do know Brenda Sully, too. Or, at the very least, you met her."

Kenneth looked at the two of them. "I swear to you, I didn't even realize it at first."

"He's telling the truth," Grace said quickly. "I told you, Kenneth is one of the good guys, working hard for everyone. And that's why... I know what he knows—and doesn't know and didn't know. Until he figured it out. We—were just talking about it."

"Talk to us," Sophie suggested softly.

"I swear, I didn't even know her name," Kenneth said. "But I met the young woman I now know to be Brenda Sully when she came here to audition. It's not like actors flock here, but I get a fair amount of interest. Because I pay people. And the thing is, a lot of our talent does go on to be seen by the right people, picked up by good agents. We have a good reputation."

"Why didn't you say before that you knew Brenda, too?" Bruce asked him.

Kenneth looked at him with wide eyes. "I swear to you, I didn't even realize that I knew her at first—like I said, she just came by. She didn't have a scheduled appointment. I had a group in here doing reading. I had them keep going and I went to the door. When I told her we were busy, she promised to come back in a few days. Like I said—I never even knew her name. But just today I found her head shot and résumé on my desk."

"When was this, that she stopped by?" Sophie asked him.

"I guess about a week before she was killed." He paused and took in a deep breath. "About a week before Lili was killed, too."

Bruce looked at Sophie. He believed the man.

He believed that Sophie did, too.

"I would have brought it up if I had thought that it could have helped…but honestly, she was just another pretty girl with dark, wavy, swinging hair, and…" He paused for a minute, wincing as he looked at Grace Leon. "I'm so sorry. I wasn't sure. I kept looking at the picture on the news. She did seem familiar. And then when I was sorting papers on my desk I realized that Brenda Sully did come here. But not the day she died! Lili was here that day, and she left. I swear it. But I didn't see Brenda that day—just before."

"It was at least a week before. Kenneth is a really good guy," Grace said. "I mean, it can't be important, right? The news is all over the fact that a studio was found and that the girls were last seen there. There were bums in the alley. Darned bums probably did it!" Grace said.

Grace seemed to be getting on Sophie's nerves. "How long have you been with the Hollywood Hooligans?" she asked her. "Were you friends with Lili Montana? Or are you here to take her place?"

The young woman was suddenly and acutely uncomfortable. "No, I'm, uh…if I'm taking anyone's place, it's Sloan Johnson's. Except people don't take other people's places here. It's an ensemble, right, Kenneth?"

"I see. And let me ask you this—how long have you known Kenneth?" Sophie asked.

"Well…we met years ago."

"At an audition," Kenneth explained.

"And you've stayed close since then, have you?" Sophie asked.

"Once friends, always friends," Grace said, squeezing Kenneth's hand.

Bruce couldn't judge the young woman's acting skills. Though, with his folks, he'd had a certain amount of experience with all levels of talent.

But one thing he was certain of. Whether she could or couldn't act, she was quick to find the right words to create a truth out of what she wanted to be true—even if it included a great deal of exaggeration.

Kenneth, on the other hand, just didn't seem to be much of a liar.

"We, uh, met up again this week," he admitted.

"So I figured," Sophie said.

"How the hell could you know that?" Grace demanded, irritated.

Bruce laughed. "She is a detective."

"Well, then, she ought to be finding the damned murderer, right, and not tormenting people like Kenneth!" Grace announced. "Some detective! Letting murderers get away and harassing good people."

Sophie's stiffening was barely perceptible. She was furious, of course. Bruce thought she was also just a slight bit drily amused by Grace's naïveté.

He was ready to step in, but Sophie just looked at her and said softly, "We do hope to find this killer, Miss Leon. Before he strikes again. And harassing good people, as you say, often helps us in our search. We are afraid—and perhaps you should be, too. You see, despite our warnings, LA is filled with dreamers—not a bad thing—but of course, dreamers who might be thinking the bad couldn't possibly happen to them, so if something was offered to *them*, it would naturally be legitimate. Everything helps, Miss Leon. Everything. Our knowing that there is a link—that both women had been here—may be incredibly important. It could be where this killer first saw his victims. Where he's searching for more."

Sophie turned away from her and focused on Kenneth. "Mr. Trent, we do hope that you'll be here, ready to help us again if we need to speak with you."

"Yes, for sure," Kenneth told her. "I'm not going anywhere."

"Be seeing you," Bruce told Kenneth, nodding to Grace Leon.

When they were out the door, Bruce turned to Sophie with admiration. "Wow. Good job."

"I'm not sure where we've gotten, so I don't really know what you mean."

"Well, let's see—you didn't crack Grace Leon in the jaw after her wiseass comments," he said.

Michael Thoreau's ghost had followed them out. "I'd have decked her. No, no, I was taught never to hit a woman. But, hey, I would have been tempted to deck her."

"It's okay—I've met with worse," Sophie assured them.

"So, both victims…" Bruce said.

"I'm going to stick around here tonight, see what I see. If nothing else, I'll be a fly on the wall and see what Kenneth's new girl is up to," Michael said.

"That would be helpful," Sophie said. "I don't believe that Kenneth Trent is guilty of anything—other than being a good guy who likes to give actors work—but maybe you'll see or hear something that might be useful." Michael nodded at her and she smiled. Then she grew thoughtful. "I've got to call Captain—now we know that both young women have been in this building, trying to become part of the Hollywood Hooligans. We need to start running the names of others involved with the troupe of performers. Venues where they've performed, professional suppliers, costumers, whoever else." She took her phone out as she spoke.

Bruce nodded. "I'll let Jackson know, too."

They were both on their phones as they said goodbye to Michael and left the building. When they reached the street, Bruce checked his watch.

"I want to speak with Lili's boyfriend again. Jace Brown has a job at a bar just around the corner, and he comes on at seven, so he's just gotten in."

"Let's go see him."

The bar where Jace worked had a handsome facade of glass and chrome and pretty paint-scrolled writing on the window that advertised it as "Pasquale's."

There was an attractive young hostess at the door. Sophie explained who she was and asked if they might see Jace for a moment.

The girl immediately turned white and tears popped up in her eyes.

"Has he taken time off?" Sophie asked.

"He's working...he needs the money. But..." The young woman indicated toward the bar.

Jace Brown was a handsome guy, about six feet tall, with a swatch of ink-dark hair that fell devilishly over his forehead.

But staring at them, he looked stricken.

"Thank you," Bruce told the girl. He and Sophie walked across the little room between the few scattered tables in the front.

"You're that cop, the main cop," he said. "I saw you on TV."

"My partner is the main cop. And we met at the station the other day," Sophie told him, settling on a barstool in front of him. "I am so sorry. We know you loved Lili. We just hope you might be able to help us. As you probably heard, Lili and the other woman, Brenda, were both lured to meet someone out at an abandoned studio."

Jace nodded gravely. Tears rolled down his cheek.

"Lili wanted it all. She'd perform anywhere for anyone. She— she took chances. But she told me that this was so aboveboard, I wouldn't be worried in the least. She could just tell the guy was a straight shooter."

"We think he might have found the girls through the Hollywood Hooligans. We've recently discovered that Brenda Sully was going to audition there. Can you think of anyone who was at all their performances, or who seemed too interested?"

Jace Brown almost smiled. "Sure. Several of the moms. And, yeah, the Hooligans have a fan base. They're good, you know?"

"If you were to think about it, do you think you could recall a man who might have been watching—maybe several times?" Bruce asked.

Jace Brown wiped his face and glanced down the bar. A young couple had just taken two of the stools. "I gotta work," he said. "The owner here...he knew Lili. He'd have given me time off, but... I gotta pay the rent." He paused and frowned, looking from Bruce to Sophie. "I have pictures from the performances. You can see a lot of people standing around. When I'm home, I can email you everything—all digital. I'm not sure I'd know a suspicious character...but I don't know, I'd do anything to help... I loved her," he said, ending with a whisper.

"That would be deeply appreciated," Sophie said, producing her card. He quickly put it in his pocket.

"I'm off days," he said. "So I could do auditions with Lili, when something came up. Kenneth is great like that—he wanted people to succeed. If you need me tomorrow, just let me know."

They both thanked him and headed out.

On the street, Sophie consulted her case notes again. "The ex, Ian Sanders, lives in Burbank. The detective who questioned him said that he had an airtight alibi. He's a guitarist—he was playing up in San Francisco over the weekend and didn't even get back into town until Monday morning."

"You still want to see him?"

Sophie sighed. "You'll probably think I'm obsessive."

"We can all be that way on a case."

He realized that her quirks—and dedication—were part of

what made her so fascinating to him. Beyond the obvious—
she was a compact design of fitness and perfection, with a killer
smile, gorgeous eyes and a sweet sensuality that haunted a man,
no matter how cool and professional her demeanor—she simply
had a mind that was equally as stunning. She cared. She loved
her work, served justice and was determined to be a good cop—
not for the accolades, but for people.

"After Burbank, we call it a night. Yeah, the powers that be
have put the FBI in on this, but I'm not even FBI—I'm a consultant. And I'm not having Vining kicking me off the case, okay?"

She nodded. "No, we won't have Vining kick you off the case.
I'll act like a normal cop and go to sleep at night."

Ian Sanders lived in a garage apartment at a house on Burbank Road. It was about eight when they arrived—not that late.

The apartment was dark.

Sophie looked at Bruce, and Bruce shrugged and knocked.

Nothing.

He knocked harder.

A woman with wild blond hair answered the door, barely clad
in a bright green kimono. She stared at them balefully.

"What? Who are you? What the hell do you want?" she demanded.

Sophie introduced herself and Bruce, producing her creden-
tials. "We need to speak with Ian Sanders. Is he here?"

"No! And I'm sick of this shit—cops have already been all
over us because of that whore he was dating."

"Allison!"

The woman's name was called sharply by a male voice.

Ian Sanders appeared at the door in briefs; it was apparent that
the two had been in bed. Sleeping or not, Bruce wasn't sure.

But he didn't like Allison, so he didn't care much if they had
been sleeping or not.

"I believe you're referring to Lili Montana, who was brutally murdered, miss, and liked and admired a great deal by everyone else we've spoken to," Bruce said pleasantly. He looked at the man then. "Ian Sanders, our apologies."

"But we do need to speak with you," Sophie said.

"Of course. Anything," he said softly.

He stepped outside.

Allison slammed the door behind him.

"I'm sorry. This has unsettled Allison."

"So we see," Bruce said.

"I'm sorry," Ian Sanders repeated. He was tall and blond—a beach-boy type. "Lili… I still love Lili," he said softly. "Always will." He inhaled. "I never thought that we'd stay split up. We had one of those fights about the future. I—I wanted marriage. She wanted a little more time. I supported her in the Hooligans. Lili wanted more. I went away one weekend—we weren't living together, but we were still talking. She didn't cheat on me or anything. We were technically split up. But…when I came back, she'd found a new guy, and…well, I admit, I spied on them. And they were happy. And I…" He glanced toward his door. "I don't guess this will last."

"Sorry," Sophie murmured.

"How can I help you? I spoke with detectives right after… right after they discovered it was Lili. I…wasn't here when she was…killed."

"We know that. We're hoping that you might know something about the person she was supposed to meet, or how she might have met him. Frankly, we're hoping for anything. We have discovered a studio where she was the night she died, but we're falling short on leads from there."

"I…wow. We've been split up a couple months, you know. I don't think that…" He paused, thinking again. Then he frowned and said, "She did tell me once…ah, man, had to have been about eight or nine weeks or so ago now…"

"That's okay, tell us, please," Bruce said.

"Well, she did tell me that she might have finally made a great connection at…at…"

"At?" Sophie pressed gently.

"Sorry, I'm trying to remember. Oh, yeah! They did a performance in a cemetery—the Hollywood Hooligans did. It was really cool. You know, some people think all that is disrespectful, but I like it. It means that we remember and honor the dead while we're living, and with happiness."

"I understand that," Sophie assured him with a smile. She glanced at Bruce.

Somewhere "weird."

"Well, this is an old, old place near downtown," Ian said. "The property is privately owned by some company that specializes in preserving old churches and cemeteries. I don't remember the name, but I know you can find it. Once you're on Olvera Street, you just head south and then west…" Ian drew them a map in the air. "There was an old church there and an old burial ground. Started with the Spaniards, and then the Mexicans, and then…well, I don't know, but it's old. And the Hollywood Hooligans did a special Saturday night performance there for one of those service clubs. I was actually there, and I didn't see who she was talking about, but when we came home that night, she was revved. He'd said that he wasn't quite ready yet, but that he'd find her when he was—he said he grew up here and wanted to be independent. He was coming into some money and had an amazing indie project and she just might be perfect for it."

"We'll find the place," Sophie assured him. She handed him a card. "Call if you think of anything. I'm so sorry to have bothered you this late."

Ian Sanders shook his head.

"No, it's fine," he said. "A part of me will always love Lili. Please, get this bastard…"

"We will find him," Bruce said firmly.

Ian went back in. Sophie and Bruce headed to the car.

"It's a bit awkward, interrupting someone like that," Sophie murmured.

"I think we did him a favor. I'm betting that he got himself involved with the kind of woman who would not be his usual mate, and that we might have let him know tonight just how hard a person she might be."

Sophie glanced at him and grinned. "You mean he's going to ditch that bitch now."

"Something like that," he said, grinning, too.

"Cemetery, burial ground, old church…"

"By daylight," Bruce said.

"But what if he has another woman there? He killed two people in two days…"

"And now he's lying low."

"We have to go see it."

"We'll drive by."

Bruce drove; Sophie had her phone out.

"It's called St. Augustus of the Lambs…according to this, it's owned by a company called 'Everlasting.' They specialize in saving old things, just as Ian told us. For the upkeep, they rent out churches, burial grounds and other 'salvaged' places and institutions by renting out for parties, theatricals, and—get this— even weddings."

"And the exact address? I'm trying to follow Ian's finger map, but…"

She laughed and read off the street address.

Traffic was heavy; the highway was jammed. Bruce pulled off to weave his way through the streets.

Eventually, south side of downtown, he found the address. Sophie quickly hopped out of the car.

She was looking up at the old iron and stone archway that announced the church and the burial ground.

She rushed to the gate.

"Locked," she said. "Padlocked. Look, Bruce, you can see the old church just down that path. And the family vaults and mausoleums...it looks like there are a ton of them, like something you might see in New Orleans..."

"I think that was a Spanish style," Bruce said. "If I remember right, Spain was in charge when the old St. Louis Cathedral was built in New Orleans...and this would have been a Spanish mission originally here."

"There are a few floodlights on," she murmured.

He read off the sign on the gate. "It's open from 10:00 a.m. to 6:00 p.m."

She looked at him. "Let's climb over the fence."

"Sophie! You're the cop. If we don't have a warrant..."

She cupped a hand to her ear. "I really might hear screaming."

He groaned.

But he was coming to know Sophie.

"Let me go first. I'm taller. I'll get better leverage. Not at the gate—not at that arch. I can hop up on the wall, and get over, and pull you up."

She smiled widely.

"Let's go!"

He didn't feel good about what they were doing; he prayed this wouldn't come back to haunt them.

Then again...

It was a graveyard.

Who might just have hung around here after death...

And who, among the dead, might have something to say?

CHAPTER TEN

Thursday night

The place might have been less eerie, Sophie thought, if it weren't for the floodlights.

They created little spits of light...surrounded by fields of looming dark shadows.

Some of the graves were ancient—whatever had once been etched into the stones that marked them had long ago worn away.

Some—for instance, a small but very old vault—had evidently been researched, and a plaque in front told them that the man interred there had been a farmer, beloved by his wife and children. His wife, and many of those children, now lay with him in the vault.

There were carvings of angels and cherubs. Some broken, some weeping, and in the strange light, it looked as if they mourned time itself—time, and all those forgotten as it swiftly passed on by.

No grave with readable stones or plaques seemed to be less than a hundred years old, making the burial ground feel like a museum of funerary art. There were stacked graves, one stone or concrete sarcophagus atop another, mausoleums, vaults, plain markers for soldiers lost in World War I, and tombstones depicting death memorials in styles ranging from old Spanish to Victorian.

Bruce stood amidst a row of sculptured lambs, a field where children had been buried. Spanish names blended with English and other European names.

From where they were, they looked up at the old church.

"What do you think?" Sophie asked him.

He turned and looked at her. "No ghosts."

She arched a brow. She hadn't been looking for ghosts.

The whole thing about ghosts being real to her was far too new.

"The church...might have catacombs. What do you think?" she asked him.

He answered by walking to the church door. He tried it. It was double-padlocked.

"I think you need a search warrant," he told her.

She nodded, admitting the truth. Yes, she would need a search warrant. They were on private property. A lie about hearing screams might not stand up in court, and if they were to find something, a good attorney could have it all thrown out.

"I think there's something here," she said.

"Can you get a search warrant?" he asked.

She shrugged. "We can just ask the owners, too. We'll get a hold of Kenneth and find out about his contacts with them... They'll probably let us search. And the burial ground is open by day. It's small and compact, and honestly, I didn't even know it existed, but others apparently do."

"Then we need to get started on the proper channels," he told her.

"We could check for an open window," she said.

He smiled slowly. "Meet you around the other side."

"Right," she said.

She had to admit, as she walked around the far side of the building, where the floodlights provided little glow, that she felt chilled.

Chilled—and frightened.

And she wondered why a dark graveyard—with its old, broken, moss-covered and decaying stones—could create such an unease in her heart.

She jumped, certain that she had heard something out of place. A strange sound, like a swift whispering, with a rush of air. And then a small crack, like a step on gravel.

She froze, listening. It didn't come again. There seemed to be some commotion from the other side of the enclosing stone wall, but she couldn't see over it.

Teenagers?

She kept studying the windows on the church—many of them very beautiful and old, but covered over with more protective glass and securely locked.

And then—just as she was about to come around the other side—she stopped dead, something like terror suddenly filling her heart.

Someone was there.

Someone in a white gown that seemed to catch the slight breeze and move.

Sophie almost reached for her gun. She remembered Michael Thoreau's words. She could shoot him, but he was already dead.

"Hello," the vision said softly.

Sophie wasn't sure how she managed to speak. "Hello."

"You see me. You hear me."

"I do."

"You can't stay. It's very dangerous here," the image said.

Somehow, Sophie made herself move closer. Her vision was

that of a very pretty young woman. The flowing white gown was of a long-gone age.

Sophie swallowed and spoke softly, "Why? And can you tell me…"

"I'm Ann Marie. I'm waiting… I try so hard…"

Bruce came hurrying around from the other side. The ghost swirled around. Bruce saw her; he went still.

"I'm Ann Marie. I'm waiting," she said. "You must go. Please, take this lady. Take her…and leave."

"But we fear for someone else," Bruce said.

"There is no one here tonight. Leave…wait for the light!"

With those words, the image faded away.

Sophie stared at Bruce.

"There's no entry. We're getting out of here now. We'll come back by the daylight—with permission to search."

"But—"

"You heard Ann Marie. There is no one here now."

"But—"

"She won't be back tonight to help us anymore, Sophie. We'll come back. By day—legally."

She nodded. He was right.

He caught her hand and they continued around the church, through the stones and the vaults and the cherubs and the angels to the spot where the wall was low.

Bruce paused for a minute. She knew that he was much more experienced with the dead than she was. He waited. Was he… waiting to see if anyone—unseen—might be there?

Then, he hefted himself up, and then reached back for her. They got back into the car and Bruce drove.

Sophie started to call the station and then decided to call Kenneth Trent instead, and he was quick to give her what he could about the old place.

Then she immediately called the contact number he had given her.

Unsurprisingly, she reached voice mail.

She hesitated, and then identified herself, and said that they'd like to search the premises.

"Recording?" Bruce asked.

"Yep."

"They'll call back."

"I hope so."

"Waiting is hard, I know."

To her amazement, her phone rang.

"This is Detective Manning."

"I'm Sabrina Hayes. I manage the old church and burial grounds."

"And I'm so sorry to bother you, but—"

"No bother! I'll be happy to meet you there first thing in the morning. If our property is being transgressed in any way, we want it stopped immediately!"

"Well, thank you—"

"Delinquents! They like to come in and put graffiti on graves and drink in the church—I thank you so much! Eight a.m.?"

Sophie was about to say that what was going on might be a lot worse than some trespassing and vandalism, but Sabrina Hayes spoke too quickly.

"Thank you, thank you!"

And she hung up.

But Sophie smiled as she looked at Bruce. "Eight a.m."

"Excellent."

She should have been tired. She probably was. But she was also alive with adrenaline. Once they reached Bruce's room and the door was closed and locked behind them, she turned eagerly into his arms. He indulged her in a long, wet and wonderful kiss, but then he drew away.

"Old burial grounds, dirt, icky stuff…that's when a shower and time and soap and suds and cool stuff is all the better."

She smiled. "I was thinking of a bath. The hotel offers such a lovely big tub with jets and all."

"So it does!"

They both started with their holsters and guns and then they undressed one another as they made their way to the bathroom. They were touching even as Bruce fumbled for the water, kissing as the steaming water filled the tub, and they were still half kissing and half laughing as they made their way into it.

His hands were on her.

What he could do with suds was amazing.

Steam surrounded them. They were wet and slick and it seemed that their flesh was on fire, hotter than the water. They kissed and touched…his body pressed to the length of her. They laughed, kissed all over, half-drowned, and slipped and slid until they wanted more than the tub could afford.

Soaking wet, they made it to the bed.

And he touched her.

And she touched him.

He whispered that she was a fast learner, and she assured him that he was an excellent teacher.

Then there was the unbelievable feeling of his lips again, and when she thought she might explode, implode or die of pure ecstasy, he was with her, inside her, and the incredible sensations were starting all over again…

Yes, before last night, it had been a long, long time…

But she didn't remember anything like this, ever.

After, they were together, just breathing, limbs still entwined, holding on.

And there were no words.

No words, just finally…sleep, and the feeling that she had never been so cherished in her life.

Friday morning, early

Bruce wasn't sure why he had expected Sabrina Hayes to be an older woman—prim, maybe super LA slim with a soft tinge of old-fashioned old-lady blue in her otherwise white hair.

She wasn't old at all—if anything, she was pushing thirty.

She was indeed LA slim, and she showed up in yoga pants and a tank top that advertised her gym. Her hair was blond—but it did have a streak of blue. Neon blue.

She shook hands vigorously with both Sophie and Bruce, once she had opened the gates for them and led them to a patch of parking right inside.

"We've had trouble several times—I don't know what it is about people thinking that historical properties are fair game for being abused. But then, half the people in this country don't seem to think a thing about history, anyway. Hell, the schools aren't doing anything about teaching history. Well, you see, that makes us all the more important. We have all kinds of literature about the LA area available in the church." She suddenly made a face and asked, "Too much? Sorry, my dad is a history professor at UCLA. He's supported our group since I was a child. We've saved missions all up and down the coast—and a few decaying saloons, taverns, inns and theaters, too."

"Not too much," Sophie assured her. "But please, tell us what kind of trouble you've had?"

Sabrina looked surprised. "I thought you were here because of my report. I called and said that I needed the property to be patrolled, at the very least."

"I'm so sorry, I don't know about the call," Sophie said. "We're here because—"

"You can help us, right?"

"Please, tell me, what's been going on?"

"Last week, a group of kids climbed the wall, and I found beer bottles and all kinds of trash all over the graves. A few weeks before that, I'd come in and found out that some of the tomb-stones had literally been ripped out of the ground and laid up on top of each other. And then the neighbors have called us re-peatedly about all the screaming going on."

"Screaming?" Bruce asked.

"When?"

"Oh, I get calls on that almost every day. And, of course, the people reporting that the ghosts are out here partying, too."

"I didn't know that ghosts partied loudly," Bruce said lightly.

Sophie glanced his way with a serious frown.

Sabrina Hayes laughed delightedly. "Trust me, I have been here at all hours. The only danger here comes from those mor-tal creeps who like to break in."

They were looking for more than a creep.

Bruce waited to see what Sophie might have to say; it was her case.

"We're worried as well, Miss Hayes, that a murderer might be at work here," Sophie said quietly. "We need access to the grounds and the church—and whatever catacombs may lie be-neath."

"A murderer?" Sabrina Hayes said. Then she gasped. "Oh! Oh, my God, you mean that man who killed the Black Dahlia girls? Oh, no! No, no, no—nothing like that could have gone on here."

"We're following up on a lead. May we search the church?" Sophie asked.

"Of course. The first church on this property was here be-fore Felipe de Neve was governor here—Spanish governor—in 1777. In that year, Neve wanted more balance—military to bal-ance the power of the Church. The Los Angeles Pobladores was the name given the original forty-four townspeople—the name meaning townspeople! Twenty-two adults, twenty-two children. Anyway, before they came, there had been burials around the original church, but our earliest gravestones are from the Spanish period here—and, as you can see, there are numerous styles of graves now. The current church has been here since 1862. It was built in the Gothic style, and the graveyard served the people until about 1920, when it became too full to accommodate more dead—and, of course, by then, Los Angeles had many beautiful cemeteries."

As she spoke, Sabrina Hayes led them to the front of the church where richly carved double doors allowed them entry.

The church might have been something created somewhere in Norman France; it was definitely Gothic with its graceful arches and ribbed vaulting. The altar was on a raised dais; there was a high podium—reached by winding stone steps—for a priest to deliver a sermon.

"The church is Gothic—even the shape of the windows is gothic—but the windows are Tiffany stained glass, right?" Sophie asked as they entered.

"Yes! They were fashioned in New York in pieces, and then his workers came here and put them all together, installed in the church." She sighed. "Lucky thing—most scroungers who hang around here wouldn't know the value of a Tiffany window if it were to bite them in the ass. Uh…sorry."

Sophie laughed softly. "No worries."

"Well, at least they're protected—they've been reinstalled with sheets of bulletproof, earthquake proof, just about anything else proof Plexiglas on both sides." She grimaced and continued. "I was just in the church this morning," Sabrina said. "I didn't see any sign of disturbance or anything."

Bruce looked slowly and carefully around.

She was right. Nothing was out of order.

There was no blood.

It certainly didn't appear that horrible murders had taken place here.

"What about the catacombs?" Bruce asked.

"You want to go to the catacombs, too?" Sabrina asked.

"Yes. Please," Sophie said.

"Well, excuse me for a minute, then. I have to get to my car. As you saw at the gate, we use old-fashioned padlocks. Old things—old measures. Excuse me."

Bruce looked at Sophie and smiled. When she had stepped out, he said, "I want to take a loop around the church while she's opening the padlock."

"See if you can find Ann Marie?" she asked.

He nodded.

"Go."

He hurried out. Sabrina was at her car. He smiled and waved. "I'll be right there—just taking a look at the fantastic windows."

"Cool. This will take me a minute... I think I have too many keys to things!"

He waved and started around and came to the spot where he had seen the lovely young ghost the night before.

"Ann Marie?" he said softly.

No reply. Nothing at all.

He'd called Jackson while Sophie had been showering that morning; Jackson had his people back in Virginia looking up everything they could about the cemetery—including a girl named Ann Marie.

"You might have given us a last name," he said softly, aware he was speaking to nothing but air.

He started back in. As he did so, he noticed a fresh chip on an old tombstone. Pausing, he hunkered down by it.

Then he saw that there was something different—it wasn't a chip caused by a slight accident, by wind, rain or any other natural device.

Deep in the chip, there was something metallic.

Before he even dug in his jacket pocket for a knife and an evidence bag, he knew what he was going for.

There was a bullet imbedded in the stone.

It had very recently been fired.

He was suddenly chilled to the bone.

Someone had shot at Grant Vining. There just couldn't be that many shooters around—especially shooting at cops trying to ferret out the truth of a series of murders. So it would seem that same someone might have been shooting at Sophie.

If so, they didn't know the murderer.

But the murderer sure as hell knew them.

A trapdoor slightly behind the altar—created of thick heavy wood and metal—led the way down to stone steps that went to the catacombs.

Sabrina struggled with the door. Sophie hurried over to help her.

"Thank God you've got some muscles going for you," Sabrina murmured.

Sophie shrugged. "I try to keep up," she murmured.

Sabrina straightened and indicated the winding stone steps that led into the darkness below. "Oh, wait…hang on. We aren't so historically minded that we forget safety."

She walked up to the altar and found a switch. Lights suddenly flooded the catacombs.

"Excellent," Sophie assured her.

Sophie started down the steps just as Bruce returned to the church. He strode over to them swiftly. "Aha! Down to the depths of hell!" he said.

"A brightly lit hell," Sophie told him.

"All the better."

He made his way past Sophie and down the winding stone

stairs. Sabrina followed them tentatively, as though afraid of what they might find.

Sophie hoped that none of the priests had been very old. Or that they had suffered from heart disease or arthritis or any other malady that might have made the treacherous steps any worse.

The floor was rough. Stone and dirt. A large plaque on the wall noted the dead who lay beneath their feet.

There were tombs lined up along the walls, with plaques above them commemorating the dead. "Priests were buried here, in the church," Sabrina told them. "And then, of course, those who earned special favor with the priests were buried down here, as well."

The catacombs appeared to be clean and clear.

It wasn't the kind of floor that might be cleaned with a few bottles of bleach.

There were no implements that suggested they might even possibly be used to bisect a human body.

"Oh, thank God!" Sabrina breathed.

Sabrina was relieved. Sophie wasn't at all sure.

"What's beyond that wall there?" she asked Sabrina.

"Dirt. Earth. And maybe more long-dead people," Sabrina said. "This is it—the foundation, the catacombs...this is it. Look, I know that this is... I mean this is truly a horrible situation for all of Los Angeles, for all of California. We kind of all need to be terrified, with a killer like that running around. But even though you didn't find what you were looking for, you will see to it that the church is more protected?"

Sophie looked her way. "Oh, definitely. I plan to have cameras up by tonight. They'll guard the entrance to the church and take in what they can of the graveyard."

"Cameras? Oh, well, we can't afford them. I mean, if we could, our preservation company would have cameras everywhere."

"We'll see that they're put in," Bruce said. He was looking at Sophie oddly. She frowned at him. He was stone-cold serious.

"Are we done here?" Sabrina asked.

"For now," Sophie told her.

As they left the church, Sophie found it strange that Bruce stayed extremely close to her—so close that she almost tripped over him.

Almost.

He wouldn't let her fall. He steadied her and turned quickly to Sabrina Hayes. "Miss Hayes, do you know of a young woman by the name of Ann Marie who is buried here?"

"Ann Marie—do you have a last name?" Sabrina asked.

"I'm afraid not," Bruce told her.

"The archives are actually downtown at the museum."

"Great. Thank you," he said. Then he told her, "Miss Hayes, forgive me. We're going to have to get more officers down here."

"Really? But you didn't find anything."

Sophie stared at him.

He looked steadily back at her.

"Someone was firing a gun into the cemetery last night. In fact, I'm going to suggest a sniper's rifle, but then, I do have a bullet that lodged into a gravestone, so we will find out for sure."

Sophie felt a bolt of heat and an eerie sensation of fear—unlike anything she'd experienced before—sizzle through her.

The sound she had heard last night…the commotion she had heard on the road.

Someone out there had been firing at her. There had been a silencer, or something similar to a silencer, on the gun. She'd heard the sound of that bullet…

And she—who should have known much better!—hadn't even realized what it was. But then, she had been busy, searching for an opening, and seeing…

A ghost.

She pulled her phone out to call Captain, staring at Bruce all the while.

"I—I don't understand."

"Someone was shooting in here last night," Bruce said. "I hope you don't have the place rented out tonight."

"Sunday...a wedding," Sabrina said, distracted. "But are you sure—"

"Yes," Bruce said, his voice final. "Yes, we need a crew out here."

Sabrina Hayes wasn't leaving her precious property; she stayed.

Sophie wasn't leaving—not while her department was studying the stone, not while experts were working on the trajectory of the bullet.

Captain himself came out. The media frenzy on the killings was such that he was taking a hands-on interest in everything that was going on.

Henry Atkins wound up out there as well—while there were thankfully no corpses and they didn't believe they'd found a crime scene, the place had become part of the investigation, and as such, it would be photographed.

She couldn't help but wonder about Henry.

He did so love his work.

Henry appeared to be in a kind of strange, professional heaven.

He was actually working, but there were so many amazing things to photograph. He excitedly snapped pictures of the old angels and cherubs and the amazing monuments.

There with the forensic team, Lee Underwood shook his head while looking at Sophie. "So, it's you and Detective Vining. Someone is out for the two of you. Idiot. If he were to kill you both, they'd just bring on more and more detectives. And it's been announced everywhere that the FBI is in on the case, too!"

"I don't know if they were shooting at me," Sophie said. As

far as she knew, neither she nor Bruce had said anything about having actually been in the graveyard the night before.

"I thought you guys scoped the place out? Working a lead. That's why we're here, right? And you all looked at it last night and met Miss Hayes here this morning. So, last night, if you were on the outskirts by the fence, someone had to be up high, shooting... Hmm. If they were aiming at you..."

"Yes?"

He shrugged. "They have lousy aim. They shot into the cemetery. It looks like they were aiming at the pretty angel over there with the folded wings. They missed. But man, they were way wide of you or your friend. Well, we have to move onward." He made a face. "Those experts are on the bullet and trajectory," he said, pointing to more of his team. "Me? I get to explore vandalism. Beer bottles. Oh, and cigarette butts. Yep, the good stuff!"

"At least it's not blood today," Sophie said.

Lee agreed. He brushed back a lock of hair from his forehead and grinned. "And, tomorrow, it's the weekend. I'm off. But if I know you, you won't take any time. I'll think of you when I'm kicking back with a few at the beach!"

"You do that," she told him, smiling.

He moved on, hunkering down to collect a cigarette butt she'd have to admit she hadn't even seen.

She was sitting on a steplike group of tombstones. They belonged to one family. The design, she thought, was unique. The oldest tomb was up high—the others came down by six-inch increments, creating something of a pyramid effect.

A large plaque to the side of the unique configuration stated the name Johnstone, and beneath it, the several members of the family who had been buried there.

Jacob Johnstone had died in 1843. He had several sons and grandsons interred in like stone coffins on either side of him, creating the steps.

A handsome Madonna and Child stood guard across from the plaque, gentle eyes watching over all.

"That's really beautiful," Henry Atkins said, snapping away as he walked up to her.

"It's a very unique burial ground," Sophie said. She realized that she was watching Henry differently.

She couldn't help but wonder about him.

About his pictures...

His apparent fascination with the old case plagued her.

"This place is...wonderful," he said, his face alive with excitement. "Actually, I wonder that they've never done any kind of an archaeological dig here. I mean, I don't know that much, but Miss Hayes was telling us that indigenous peoples were buried here, even before the Spanish came. Oh, I'll bet that Chuck Thompson would just love to dig around in this place!"

"Chuck is an ME. I imagine he has enough dead bodies to deal with," Sophie said, studying him with a frown.

Henry Atkins was oblivious. "No, no—I mean yes, but... I guess you didn't know. Chuck was going to be an anthropologist, but then he was going to be a doctor, and somehow he wound up becoming an ME. Apparently, he was very good at it somewhere along the line in his training."

"I see," Sophie murmured.

Her phone buzzed. She looked down at it and saw that she had a message from an unknown number.

Something made her glance up. Bruce was watching her. She was by the side of the church, and he had stuck close by. She realized that he was standing as if he were her personal bodyguard.

They hadn't a chance to talk alone. She didn't know how the hell he had found the bullet.

"Check your messages," he mouthed.

She nodded and looked down, thinking that he had written something to her.

But it wasn't from him. It was from Angela Hawkins, Jackson Crow's wife—and the expert in his office who dealt with case assignment and research.

Angela didn't bother with greetings—just her name, and what she had found.

Ann Marie Beauvoir...murdered April 3, 1903. Eighteen years old at the time; she was a performer with The Follies, a group that did everything from Shakespeare to burlesque in the Los Angeles area—some of it a bit racy for the time. She headed out to meet with someone who was about to change her world...pave her way to the stages of New York City and Paris, France. Her nude body, throat slit ear to ear, was found in front of the church. She was buried there five days after her death, mourned by her family and friends.

Sophie looked up at Bruce, and knew that he had already read the message, which had been sent to both of them.

And she knew that he understood.

They needed time in the cemetery—alone.

They had to find Ann Marie. And when they did, they had to pray that she could tell them what she knew, and what she had seen of a murderer.

CHAPTER ELEVEN

Friday, noon

"We're getting out of here. For now, at least," Bruce told Sophie.

She shook her head, looking up at him. "There's something here, Bruce. I know it."

He hesitated. "Sophie, someone took a shot at you. You and Vining. They got Vining—they missed you. But they will surely try again."

"What do you suggest I do? Retire?" she asked drily.

"Okay, so only you and I know that we were in this grave-yard last night. Most of your colleagues don't know that shot was aimed at you. I do know that."

"Well, my colleague Lee, at least, figured out that you and I would have scoped it all out—and that possibly one of us was being shot at. Maybe it was aimed at you," she said.

He decided not to argue that. "Maybe. But I'm not a cop. They're after you and Vining—when Vining isn't in the field, you're the lead detective, even if the entire force is involved."

"But that's the point. I don't think the killer will keep trying—that would be stupid."

"Unless someone on the force is involved."

She shrugged.

"Well, if it is a cop—that person does know where you were."

"We don't really know. If Lee thought that we would have scoped it all out, others might, too. I just don't think it will do any good to say anything. Bruce, really—"

"Oh, hell, I'm not going to say anything. This is your call, all the way."

He took a seat next to her on the steplike tombs where she was perched. "Sophie, the thing is—you may be in danger. Serious danger."

"I'm a cop," she said. "By the very nature of my job, I'm in danger."

"I know. But—"

"Bruce, I can be careful. I know how to watch out."

"The thing is, when you go back to see people who were already interviewed, you seem to have a knack for asking the right questions—and getting leads from them that we didn't have before. Seems like somehow the killer knows this."

She hesitated. "Bruce, I was just talking to Henry Atkins. He's…too excited about the cemetery. We've both seen what he's done with the pictures from the past—and the present. There are no new clues—as if someone knows the old case and police procedure too well. Do you think…?"

"I wouldn't discount anything right now," Bruce told her. "I don't feel we're getting anywhere here."

"But we need to find Ann Marie. Bruce, she was murdered, too. She was an actress. She's apparently been hanging around a very long time seeking justice. She may have seen something. She was worried about us last night, so she does know something. Damn it! I can't believe we're getting nothing!"

"We need to come back. Alone," he said.

"And how do we manage that?"

He laughed. "Hey, you were the one ready to jump over the fence. And break into the church."

She flushed slightly and looked away.

"We'll find whatever's here. But not now," he told her.

"And what is your suggestion for the present?"

"The hospital. I know that you want to see Grant—whether you admit it or not. And I want to see my brother."

"Brodie is here?"

"Of course. I told you that he'd be here. He spelled Jackson last night, and they'll spell each other, on and off, until Grant is out of the hospital. After the hospital, we'll head to your house."

"I can't hide in my house."

"No. But we can get the lock fixed and install cameras. And then, we can set up a command center there. Jace Brown will have sent you his pictures—maybe we can find something in them. You have a large screen at the house?"

"I do."

"Okay."

He watched as Sophie went and spoke with Captain Lorne Chagall. Chagall nodded gravely as he listened to her.

And as Sophie walked back over to Bruce, Chagall nodded to him, as well. He smiled. He wouldn't dare tell Sophie—she might just be too touchy on the subject—but with Vining in the hospital, he didn't want her to be on her own.

And for some reason—most probably his association with Jackson Crow and the FBI—Chagall seemed to trust him.

As he drove to the hospital, Sophie was busy with her phone. "I can't see much of anything on the phone...too small," she murmured.

"You're looking at the pictures that Jace Brown sent you?"

"Yes."

She fell silent and studied her phone until they reached the hospital.

Brodie was there when they entered Grant Vining's hospital room. He rose, smiling to greet them.

"Hey, there, Bruce. Your brother is a hell of a guy. Nice of you to drag him all way out here," Vining said. "But you know, we do have a ton of cops."

"Someone shot you, Grant," Sophie reminded him.

Funny how she didn't tell him that someone had also tried to shoot her. But of course, she wouldn't. She didn't want to be taken off the case.

And she didn't want to admit she'd been crawling around the cemetery after-hours.

"How are you?" Sophie asked anxiously.

"They say I'll be out in a day or two."

"Don't rush it," Sophie said.

"I hear you're making headway."

"I don't know if we've made any headway or not. But I do believe that our killer scoped out his victims through the Hollywood Hooligans."

"Quite possible. But as to that church...they're still there searching, right? Have they found anything?"

"Nothing as yet, sir," Bruce said, piping in.

"We're going to head to my house and get the locks fixed," Sophie said. She was quiet a minute. "And set up for work there."

"Because you think that someone LAPD is involved?" Vining asked.

"Yes," Sophie said flatly.

"You have anyone in mind?"

"Vaguely."

"You're my partner, Sophie. Share."

"Henry Atkins."

Vining was silent. "Because he's being...ghoulish?"

"Because of what he's been doing with the old photographs and new photographs. His crime scene pictures are nearly identical to the originals."

Vining was again quiet and thoughtful.

"Henry has been with us a very long time. He's an excellent photographer. It may just be an obsession with using his work as his art, in a way."

"Maybe."

Vining shrugged. "Talk to him. As a friend. See if you can find out where he was when the murders were committed. If he doesn't have alibis, take a closer look."

"Yes, sir."

"I don't believe it, you know."

"I don't want to believe it." Sophie hesitated and then said, "Grant, someone was in my apartment. They took a page that I'd printed on the Dahlia killing, one about cops being under suspicion then. The thing is, I know you all want to believe I was careless somehow, but I wasn't. The only time my keys were not in my immediate possession was at the station."

"Do you know how many people are in that station?"

"Yes, sir."

"Keep me informed. And if you bring me anything, make it candy. No flowers. I'm not dead yet!"

Sophie tried to smile at that. She couldn't.

"Grant—"

"Stop, Sophie. I have the best guardians in the world. FBI. I'm going to be fine. You watch out for yourself."

"I will." She glanced at Bruce. "I'm working with the next best to you there is."

"Glad you figured that out," he told her. "Okay, go do what you need to do."

She nodded.

Brodie spoke to Bruce. "Jackson is coming back in an hour or so. I'll meet you at Sophie's house?"

"See you there," Bruce said.

He set his hand on the small of Sophie's back to lead her out. She didn't protest.

Because she was learning that no man or woman wasn't vulnerable?

Or because Grant Vining was watching?

He wasn't at all sure.

But he smiled. It was all right, either way.

As promised, Jace Brown had sent Sophie scores of pictures, all taken at various shows featuring Lili Montana. She was downloading them to her computer in her home office when she heard a soft "Hey."

She turned. Brodie McFadden had arrived. He was just checking in with her, she figured. Bruce was out front with the locksmith.

"Hey, Brodie."

"So," he said, "we've checked out of the hotel entirely—we figured that, now that you're in compliance with your partner, we'll all be hanging here in whatever our off hours turn out to be. Not to worry—either Jackson or I will be with Vining at all times. Unless Jackson pulls one of his Krewe members out here, and if so, you won't have to worry, no matter what. His Krewe... they'd all die before they'd fail to keep someone safe, so..."

"I do have faith in all of you!" she assured him. "I know Bryan, of course, and Jackson Crow."

He took a chair near her desk. "Bryan and Marnie think that the sun rises and sets around you, you know," he told her.

"That's really nice."

"Well, you were damned careful not to let anything happen to Marnie."

Sophie smiled at him. "Marnie is one of those people you admire all the more when you know her—she's loved as an icon, and deserves every bit of it. She's just a nice person."

"Yeah, she is," Brodie agreed.

Sophie hesitated a moment and then asked him, "So you see the dead?"

He nodded. "You get used to it."

"I wish!"

"You will. Trust me. Hey, you should have seen the three of us. My mother never had any patience with someone not seeing the truth, so she was haunting the hell out of all of us—but we didn't want to face it. I can say proudly that I was the one to just spit it out—guys, admit it, Mom and Dad are here! And while Mom is still disappointed that none of us was cut out to be an actor, she does approve of the path we've each taken. We like solving puzzles, I guess."

"Looking for justice," Sophie said softly.

Brodie shrugged. "That may be a little too lofty—although, there is no feeling in the world as great as being able to save a life."

"All three of you...so similar."

"Oh, not really. Bryan is a mountain man—loves the Blue Ridge, our cabin out there, hiking, fishing, you name it. Bruce is the sports guy—he probably could have played pro ball. Oh, but he's also a huge Lovecraft fan—and a space nut. He reads avidly about every move NASA makes."

"I didn't know that."

"Well, you all haven't had much time to chat about the mundane, huh?"

She smiled. "No. I had no idea about NASA. Does he want to be one of the first men on Mars?"

"I don't think it goes that far. I said space, but he finds the things they're learning that have to do with our Earth fascinating, too—NASA is working on predicting tsunamis and floods so that people can be warned, especially in developing nations where weather can be so devastating."

She smiled, lowering her head. In a matter of days, she had learned just about all there was to know about the man physically. And she knew that he was very easy to care for...too easy. She'd come to like him. Really like him. Crave being with him, as well.

But she knew almost nothing about his interests.

"What about you, Brodie?"

"Ah, well, I'm the one who loves the water. Beach. Surf, diving, boats, you name it. Underwater exploration. Wrecks—old wrecks. Love 'em! And you?"

The question took her by surprise.

Did she actually have interests? She'd done nothing lately but work, come home, do chores and read...yes, she'd done some reading.

"I really can't tell you just how much Marnie came to care for you and appreciate you. You've got to be a very dedicated detective."

"I guess I am that," she murmured. "Oh, and I love creature movies—you know, *The Lizard that Ate Manhattan* and that kind of thing."

He laughed. "Hey, nothing wrong with a good lizard movie."

She heard a little beep.

The pictures had downloaded.

Bruce arrived at the office door. "Ready?" he asked.

"Yep—good timing. I've got everything that he sent," Sophie said.

"Let's see what we can see," Bruce said.

Sophie hooked her laptop up to the TV in her living room, to use it as a giant screen, and starting clicking through the album she'd downloaded. The pictures struck Sophie as being almost unbearably sad; Lili Montana had been lovely, and you could feel her vivaciousness through the pictures. Most of the pictures Ian Sanders had taken centered on Lili. Some were Lili and other members of the cast.

There were pictures of Lili with Jace, and pictures of Lili with Kenneth Trent. Sometimes she was in costume.

"Hey!" Sophie said, rising from her chair to point at the large screen. "This was one of the later performances. It's at an old hotel downtown—I know the place. It's right near the alley and the studio."

"Yeah," Bruce said. He stood, too. "There, right there. Is that Brenda Sully—there in the audience?" Bruce asked.

"It is!" Sophie said.

"And look who she's with," Bruce said.

"The other woman?" Brodie asked curiously.

"It's the rather rude young actress who claimed that Kenneth Trent was completely surprised to realize that he knew Brenda Sully. And I believe Kenneth was surprised. But that is the woman who was in Kenneth's office yesterday—her name was Grace Leon," Sophie said.

"She obviously knows Brenda Sully," Bruce said. "They're there—watching the show, together."

"Did you suspect a woman was a possibility as the murderer?" Brodie asked.

Sophie glanced at Bruce, shaking her head. "In the Dahlia case, different theories suggested a woman—but I don't know. I'm not sure that Grace being rude and using the death of Lili Montana to further her own career makes her a killer."

"But she sure as hell knew who Lili was—and she knew Brenda," Brodie noted.

"I met many of Brenda's friends—I wound up at the station most of the day when her body was discovered, just dealing with all the people who knew and loved her. She and Lili... I got the feeling they were more like Marnie. This girl... Grace Leon... she is an opportunist."

"But you don't think she's a murderer?" Brodie asked.

"We can all be fooled," Bruce said. "But I don't know. She is a liar, that's for certain."

"And now we need to speak with her again," Sophie said.

She flicked to another picture, wondering if there was any more to see.

And there was something that seriously surprised her.

"Bruce!" she said.

"I see, I see."

This time, the Hollywood Hooligans had been performing in an actual theater.

The photo had been taken from the stage. The entire audience was visible.

"That is..."

"Yes," Sophie said.

"Who?" Brodie demanded.

"That's our medical examiner. One of the LA medical examiners, I mean. But he's been assigned this case...both of the victims." Sophie said.

It was Dr. Chuck Thompson. He was in a casual short-sleeved shirt and jeans, sitting in the audience and smiling away, his hands lifted as he clapped.

"Dr. Chuck Thompson was in the audience—and Lili Montana was onstage," Bruce murmured.

Sophie remembered what Henry Atkins had said that morning.

Thompson had wanted to be an anthropologist—to study people. He'd wanted to dig in the field, know more about those who had come before...

He was an ME.

He sure as hell knew how to cut up a body.

Sophie gave herself a shake and looked at Bruce. She was suspecting everyone now.

"Next," she murmured aloud, "I'll be suspecting Captain
Chagall."

"What?" Bruce said.

"No, no, I didn't mean that. I just wonder...why wouldn't
Dr. Thompson have said something when he was working on
Lili's corpse?" she asked.

"Maybe he didn't want that to make him seem like a ghoul—
or get himself thrown off of the case," Brodie suggested.

"Or," Bruce said, "maybe he just saw the show and didn't
know who all the players were—the Hollywood Hooligans are
an ensemble. They're never billed with big name stars. The players get their breaks when an agent or director is in the audience
and sees their actual work."

"I don't know. She was on his table..." Sophie said.

"And not looking much at all as she had in life," Bruce reminded her softly.

"Before we jump to conclusions, let's see what else we have
in these pictures," Bruce suggested.

Lili in costume, Lili putting her makeup on. A pretty girl who
had been loved and admired.

Just as Brenda Sully had apparently been loved and admired.

More than ever, Sophie wanted to catch the killer. "You
know," she said softly. "I'm a cop. We're trained not to feel this
way, but..."

"But?" Brodie asked.

"I don't think this killer should just be apprehended. I think
he should be boiled in oil and drawn and quartered."

"Don't look like that!" Bruce said.

"Like—vicious?"

"No, stricken. Sophie, come on. You wouldn't be human if
you didn't empathize with these girls." He moved closer and

took her hand. "And what we're feeling is natural—the way we act on it makes us what we are. Then again, no cop is asked to give up his or her own life when it comes to a draw," Bruce reminded her. "And you were threatened last night, Sophie."

"It is strange. Do you think it might be more than one person involved?"

"I don't know. But I don't think so," Bruce said.

"It's very elaborate," Brodie noted. "One corpse the first day, laid out like the Black Dahlia. And then, just one day later, another corpse. Laid out like the Black Dahlia—in almost the same place."

"I still think it's one killer—and I think that the killer has been reading up on the Dahlia and planning the murders for a long time. After he had learned everything that he thought he could and made his plans, he chose his victims. Both girls resemble Elizabeth Short. Both wanted to hit the big time. What they never discovered years ago was where Elizabeth Short was murdered. There was supposition not so long ago that if Dr. George Hodel was indeed the killer—and his own son, ex-LAPD, believed it—that she was killed in what was his home then. But, by now, there have been dozens of theories. Way too late to prove any of them. And while there's the obvious connection in the past and the present, even if we knew who killed the original Dahlia, it might not point to our current killer."

"Sophie, what do you think about the possibility of two perpetrators?" Brodie asked.

"I don't know, either, but I doubt it," Sophie said. "This whole thing—I mean, from the killer's point of view—depends on anonymity. More than one killer...you're risking more mistakes."

Her phone rang as she spoke and she picked it up. Captain Chagall was on the other end of the call.

"Captain, anything?" she asked.

"Not that we can find. But I do understand your determination that we search—it can be described as a 'weird' place, and the Hollywood Hooligans did perform there. You believe that the killer was watching the girls, and that he found them through their performances?"

"Only Lili Montana was with the company. Brenda Sully had gone in to ask for an audition. But she attended performances. I'm going over pictures now that were sent to me by Jace Brown. That's her current boyfriend, the one she started dating right after she broke up with Ian Sanders several months ago. He has a lot of pictures."

"We're living in the digital age. A zillion clicks at one time, and of course, selfies are snapped right and left. But you've already interviewed both men."

"Yes. One was with friends on the night Lili was killed, one wasn't even in the city. They're in the clear."

"We've got the studio. We are on track. Tomorrow morning, you'll run the meeting. Make sure everyone knows what we have in every direction."

"Yes, sir. Are you still at the church?"

"No, back at the station. We have more and more calls coming in. And don't worry—I'll see that you have access to them all."

She thanked him and hung up. Bruce and Brodie were both looking at her.

"General meeting, summary of progress, tomorrow morning."

"Always a good thing," Brodie murmured.

"But a little uncomfortable—when you believe one of your fellow officers or coworkers might be involved," Bruce noted.

"There is that..." Sophie said, and sighed.

"How are you going to handle that?" Brodie asked.

"Carefully," Sophie said. She hit the button on her computer to bring up the next image.

"Oh!" she said.

"Yep," Bruce murmured.

Because now the Hollywood Hooligan picture featured Lili Montana at the train station.

And there, watching the interactive performance, was another man they knew.

Police photographer Henry Atkins.

"Well, he's not hiding his presence," Bruce noted.

"What do you mean?" Sophie asked.

"Enlarge behind Henry Atkins to the left," he said.

Sophie did so. With Henry was Lee Underwood and a few other men and women Sophie knew from the forensics department.

"How did no one recognize her?" Sophie asked.

"No one would have recognized her when she was found," Bruce said flatly. "What's puzzling is that no one else mentioned the fact that they'd seen her perform."

"Yes, but as you pointed out… Hollywood Hooligans put on a different kind of theater experience," Sophie said. She shook her head.

"I can see where maybe one person didn't recognize her, but…" Bruce murmured. "Or, sorry, let me correct that. When she was found, no one—not her closest friend—would have recognized her. But once her identity was known and we were looking into the Hollywood Hooligans…well, someone should have mentioned that they'd seen her."

"So…now I'm suspicious of Henry, Lee Underwood—and even the medical examiner," Sophie said. "It's really going to be one hell of a meeting tomorrow."

"At the least, every one of them needs to explain them not mentioning the fact somewhere along in the investigation," Bruce said.

"Let's see what else shows in those pictures," Brodie said. "I'm coming in a bit late to the party—trying to catch up."

Jace Brown had not just loved Lili—he had loved photograph-

ing her. There were more pictures of Lili—in a burlesque costume, in Victorian attire, in mime whiteface.

Lili emoted. She was vibrant.

Sophie vowed silently that she would find the young woman's
killer. The monster who had stolen life and dreams and everything else from Lili and Brenda.

Another shot of an audience popped up.

"Whoa," Bruce said. "Is that...?"

Sophie couldn't have been more surprised.

"Yes. That's Captain Chagall," she said. "Captain Lorne
Chagall."

"That is going to be one hell of an interesting meeting tomorrow," Bruce said.

CHAPTER TWELVE

Friday, late afternoon

Bruce knew that Sophie wasn't going to wait; she wasn't going to lead a meeting with a hundred or so officers in a room and turn around and question the men with whom she worked most closely.

He didn't argue with her when she wanted to head straight to the station and talk with Captain Chagall.

"Do you want to go in with him alone? Do you want me to talk to one of the other men? Like Lee or Henry?"

She shook her head. "Come in with me."

"All right."

She turned to him. "I work with these people—closely. And the fact that they watched a troupe of performers doesn't mean anything. That none of them mentioned it…"

Her voice trailed.

"I'll back you up," he said.

When they reached the station, the desk sergeant—someone who also seemed to be a friend of Sophie's—told her that

Lee Underwood and others in the forensic crew were still out at the church.

Captain Chagall was in his office.

Bruce followed Sophie. The captain was on the phone. He motioned them to come in.

Sophie took a seat in front of his desk. Bruce did the same.

The captain set down the receiver. "That was Tanenbaum from forensics. They're finishing up in the burial ground." He took a breath. "Sophie, I realize it's an odd place for a performance—maybe not so odd in LA, but odder than most—and still…nothing. The Hollywood Hooligans have performed all over the city. I know that because I've seen them."

"Excuse me?" Sophie murmured.

"I was in the train station a while back and there was a piece of theater going on right in the middle of the place there. I guess the troupe was really advertising for a performance they were having somewhere else. They all gathered in the middle and were doing some silent acting. Mime-like." He shook his head. "I was thinking about it today—I might have seen her. Seen Lili Montana. Anyway, we can't tear apart every place that troupe has performed. We'd be ripping up the county."

"The Hollywood Hooligans are far more popular than I realized," Sophie said.

"Oh?"

"Jace Brown was very much so in love with Lili. He took pictures of her everywhere. You're actually in some of them—as are Henry Atkins, Lee Underwood, and even Dr. Thompson."

"Really? The only time I ever saw them was that day—the day at the train station." He shook his head. "I've been on the force since I got out of college. Thirty-three years. And, you know, we've had our share of mysteries out here. Tragedies like Marilyn Monroe, George Reeves. And mysteries all the way back to Fatty Arbuckle and the silent era. There were cases everyone pondered over and over again—but nothing like the Dahlia." He gave her a wry smile. "Okay, maybe Marilyn Monroe. But as to the past and the Dahlia, we all swore that if such a crime was to happen today, we'd be able to find the killer. Things are different now...but do you realize that we don't even have a damned suspect?"

"Sophie goes at it every waking minute," Bruce said.

Chagall looked at him and nodded. "That's our Sophie. Sophie—and dozens of other cops. However, the rest of them have dinner and go to bed."

"I've been going to bed," Sophie said.

Bruce looked at his hands, trying not to smile. She had almost choked out the words.

Sophie said softly, "Captain, hear me out on this, okay? That's the point—we have nothing. And we should be able to catch him through forensic science—or at least have found something through the crime scene. Who else would know how to get by cops better than a cop? And the one thing I do find the longer I look is that a lot of people in this department have been to some kind of performance put on by the Hollywood Hooligans."

"That's a slippery slope," Captain Chagall warned her.

"But we want the truth."

"Yes, we want the truth. Go on with your investigation the way you see fit, but I am warning you—be careful. I'm assuming you want a career with this department. And don't get me wrong—I want the truth as badly as you do. Just be careful on your way as you're trying to get to it."

"Yes, sir. I will be careful."

She rose; Bruce did likewise.

"What are your FBI associates saying, Mr. McFadden?" Chagall asked.

"So far, sir, they've been working like the police. They've gone back and questioned people. They've gotten the same information. They've gone through the rosters of the Hollywood Hooligans and gotten nothing. Like the police, they've verified alibis. I know you're in contact with the LA office, too—and if they had anything, if anyone had anything, I know that we'd all be sharing."

"Of course. So, your brother is an investigator, too. Interesting family."

"We all went in the same direction, sir."

Chagall was quiet. Watching him, Bruce couldn't help but wonder if Chagall himself had thought that, perhaps, the crimes were just too perfect.

That maybe one of his own was involved.

And that was why he, and now Brodie, had been allowed on the investigation.

Welcomed in.

"Well, get to it," Chagall said.

"Yes, sir," Sophie said.

"Watch out for my dedicated girl," Chagall said, as they headed out.

"Sir!" Sophie protested.

"You're one of my best, Sophie. That's why I'm saying that."

"Thank you," Sophie murmured.

They left the captain's office.

In the car, Bruce sat still for a minute, waiting to see what Sophie wanted to do.

"Well, it's too early to hop a graveyard fence," he eventually offered.

"I'd like to talk to Henry Atkins."

"We just left the station."

"He wasn't there. I looked."

"Then he's working."

"No." She glanced at her watch. "He's off now…probably cut out a little early." She dug out her phone.

"You're calling him?"

"I am."

"You're going to tell him you suspect him?"

She shot him a slightly evil glance. "No. I'm going to ask him to go through photos with me."

Bruce put the car into gear. "Okay. Which way?"

"He lives in Melrose. I'll put it on speaker." She had her phone out, dialing as she spoke.

"Hello?"

"Hi, Henry."

"Sophie?"

"Yeah, I know you're off, but I was hoping I could come by."

"Sophie, you need some rest."

"I know. And I will get some. But I was hoping you'd humor me and go through crime scene photos—old and new. And I have some to show you."

"Oh? Okay, I'm just pulling into my drive. I mean, I could come to you, but what isn't in the office is downloaded into my equipment. I have everything here."

"I'm on my way."

She hung up and looked at Bruce.

"Okay, I'll take us over to Melrose."

"We'll just talk to him."

"A slippery slope, remember?"

"I'll be subtle and respectful," she promised.

Traffic was LA bad. As he drove, he was surprised when she turned to him. "So, I heard you could have played pro ball."

"Who knows, maybe," he said, glancing her way. He knew that she was trying to be balanced, to be the best detective, but remember, too, that it was her career—and not her entire life. "I still love a good game."

"And reading."

"Love a good book," he agreed. "A good movie—a good play."

"We can check in to Hooligan performances ourselves, you know."

"We could."

He glanced her way. "Do you read anything other than crime manuals and ME reports?"

"Ouch!"

"Do you?"

She laughed. "Yes, historical novels, mysteries, and I love romances. And Dickens! I can reread *A Tale of Two Cities* over and over again. Okay, and then, there's a great book about H. H. Holmes and the Chicago Exhibition, and a great book on people trying to steal Lincoln's corpse—"

"That's my Sophie!"

He smiled; she did, too.

"Turn there for Henry's house," she said.

Henry seemed excited to see them.

He probably didn't get much company, Sophie thought.

Maybe his work made him an introvert—and maybe, like some, he had gotten to a point where he was restless or uncomfortable when meeting friends at a bar, or heading off to a game. Maybe he really didn't have much of a life outside of working.

She understood, because maybe she was getting that way herself. She gave herself the excuse that she'd been giving so much of her time to being a caregiver.

But that was over.

And now...

Bruce was amazing. He'd given her something more.

But she didn't want to think about it too deeply. Bruce would be leaving. She would still be here. Unless she could talk him into staying. Unless...

She couldn't think that way. Things were good between them. Excellent. He'd given her moments she hadn't even imagined. It was more than just sex; it was his laughter, waking with him, his sense of...life.

"I have tea on," Henry said, "and I made sandwiches. Simple. Ham and cheese and mayo and lettuce and tomato. I know Sophie forgets to eat."

"Henry, thank you. That's so sweet," Sophie said.

"And she makes me forget to eat," Bruce said. "Thank you, Henry. That's above and beyond."

"Have a seat in the back. I have the big screen up. I can show anything you want."

"Thank you," Sophie said. "And you can put up some pics I have on my phone?"

"For sure. I have every cable known to man," he assured them. "I'll get food."

Henry's house was amazing with art. And his taste was eclectic, to say the least. He had pictures of seascapes, mountains, children, animals—and framed shots of bizarre crime scenes, some from the gangland killings in Chicago during the height of the mob—some more contemporary and local. He had pictures from the night River Phoenix had died at the Viper Room, pictures of various cemeteries and old churches, graves and gravestones.

"Interesting," Bruce murmured, as they made their way to the back.

"Tea!" Henry announced, joining them. "Eat up, then I'll start."

She thought of herself as a fairly hardened cop—she'd seen a hell of a lot. But she was glad that she got down a sandwich and a cup of tea before he started his slide show for them.

"I've set it up," Henry said. "I have slides with the old Dahlia next to our two new victims. Well, you know that—I had them in the office. But here…several different angles. I made sure to repeat the Dahlia pictures from the files."

She glanced at Bruce.

How had he really known all of the angles when he'd first gotten to the crime scene?

"You know, this is sad, really sad," he said. "That old case always fascinated me."

"Old cases do," Bruce murmured. He glanced at Sophie. "Like this one, and Marilyn Monroe."

"Well, the CIA killed Marilyn. We all know that," Henry said.

"Or," Bruce suggested, "it was suicide. But let's see the Black Dahlia. No suicide there," he said drily.

The pictures on the screen—if seen separately—might have been mistaken for the same ones.

"They're identical except for the canvas bag with the bloody water in it," Sophie said.

"Whoever did this copied all the old details—except the one which might give away some forensic evidence," Henry said. "A bag with bloody water…he might have gotten some skin cells somewhere or something. This guy…he's good. And he likes taunting the police."

The images on the large screen were truly savage. The grotesque, bloody grins on the victims' faces were awful.

"My opinion? Of the past, I mean. It was that doctor—the surgeon. That Walter Bayley guy. Oh, you know, there is also an unnamed cop listed as a suspect. Could have been a cop. I mean, cops are people, too, right? And, hey, we all know that a murderer can put up a good front. Like Ted Bundy. Good-looking—charming!"

Henry was almost gleeful, showing them the pictures, comparing body positioning. Sophie again felt her heart bleed for the young victims.

Finally, she said, "Henry, can you set these up for me?"

"Sure. What are they?"

"Pictures that the boyfriend took. Of Hooligan performances."

"Sure. The Hooligans are great. Well, I mean, it's so sad now. But they really are up-and-coming. You know the Groundlings, right? A ton of comedians and actors and actresses cut their teeth with that group. The Hooligans are moving right in that direction!"

"You've seen them perform?"

"Sure."

"Henry, you never mentioned that."

"Oh?"

"Henry, you knew that Lili Montana was a Hooligan," Bruce said softly.

"Well, I... I guess I thought of the Hooligans as performers and Lili as a victim, and I don't think that I ever saw Lili."

He seemed intrigued, eager to see the pictures. He took Sophie's phone and hurried to find his attachments. There were many pictures to go through. He stopped when he came to the captain and laughed. "I'll bet you Chagall didn't even know what was going on at first. They do a lot of those little impromptu pieces around the city—advertisements for their real performances."

"I'm sure Captain didn't know what was going on at first, either," Sophie said.

"Look, there's our ME Chuck Thompson. Thank the Lord, the man does look at something other than a corpse!"

"And there's Lee Underwood," Bruce pointed out. "With you."

"Yeah, I told Lee about the Hooligans. Got him to go with me. But I don't think that Lili was even in that performance. Don't know where she was..."

"She was in it," Sophie said. "That's why Jace Brown took the pictures."

"Oh. I guess I didn't realize. See—when you look at the performers, they're all wearing those plague mask things. Well, they aren't really plague masks—they don't have the big noses. They're almost movie masks. Like in old Greek or Roman theater."

He flicked to the pictures of the performers.

He was right.

"I'm sorry, I wish fervently that my having seen them could help in some way. But...hey... You think that someone chose Lili because she was a Hooligan? Have you talked to other performers? The troupe's director?"

"Yes, a few times," Bruce said.

"Am I helping you any?" Henry asked anxiously.

"Sure. And the sandwich was great," Sophie told him. She smiled and rose, and took her phone back as he unattached it from his viewing screen.

He looked at them both anxiously. "Can I do anything else? Do you want to do—something else?"

He was lonely, she thought. Because of his work, maybe. Or maybe because of his dark obsessions. He didn't have many friends, she thought.

Could that lead to him being a killer?

"Henry, thank you so much. I don't know if anything helped or not. I'll have to keep thinking and trying and..."

"No pictures of the old church," Henry noted.

"Jace wasn't dating Lili when they did the performance there. She was still with her old boyfriend then, Ian Sanders."

"Ah. That place is amazing. I'm going to go back and just take more pictures of the art and the tombs and everything else. So cool. People forget history in LA. It is La La Land. They want to see Rodeo Drive and all the movie star homes. But that cemetery—it is so amazing."

"Yes, it is."

"Well, technically, it's a graveyard. Or burial ground. Attached to the church. Cemeteries really came in with the Victorian age...spend time with your deceased love ones. Have some lunch with them, sit on a bench with the angels..."

"Yes," Bruce said, smiling. "It's good to stay close to the dead."

Sophie cleared her throat. "Well, we've got to get going. Henry, I can't thank you enough. I hope you don't mind that I called—and I may call on you again, okay?"

"Of course, Sophie. Anytime."

When they were out on the street, it had finally gotten dark.

"Time to hop a wall?" Bruce asked.

They were both startled when they heard another voice.

"Absolutely. Of course, I can kind of hop right through it," Michael Thoreau said.

"Where have you been?" Sophie asked him.

"Watching Kenneth Trent," Michael said. "Hey, let's go—shall we?"

"All right," Bruce said.

"What about Kenneth Trent?" Sophie asked, sliding into the front seat. When she turned, Michael was already behind her.

"Kenneth Trent is a boring individual. He writes. And writes. And gets on the phone. And arranges rehearsals. And calls his performers. And writes. Oh, he is having a performance tomorrow night. It will be at the Dunston Inn—it's an old place in Malibu."

"Still active?" Sophie asked.

"Nope. They rent it out for parties and the like. Weddings, receptions for funerals. And, apparently, theatrical performances."

"We never have seen the Hooligans," Sophie told Bruce.

"Are you asking me out on a date?" Bruce teased, sliding out on the road.

"Cart before the horse," Michael muttered. "Ah...sorry! I think you two are adorable, really."

Bruce smiled, shaking his head, glancing over at Sophie.

She wondered who else knew that there was more than the case between them.

When they neared the old church, Michael leaned forward and spoke up again. "You can park there, across the street. That way, anyone following you around will think you're in one of the little bars over that way."

"Good idea," Bruce agreed.

He slid into public parking, but displayed his police sticker. They hopped out of the car. The stone wall surrounding the church and the graveyard was about a block down and across the street.

As they left the car, a rather inebriated couple was exiting the closest bar. The man stopped and pointed to the old church and burial ground.

"Cops were all over that place today," he said.

"Well, they should be. Do you think they got the ghosts?" the woman asked, and giggled.

"I don't think cops go after ghosts," the man said. "And why would ghosts hang out there? It's creepy. The coolest 'spirits' are over here!"

"No, no, trust me! The place is haunted," the woman said. "I heard them all...twice. They were like...like having a party or something. Screaming, going crazy. Poor things. They didn't have any good music."

The couple moved on.

"If I weren't about to trespass, I'd stop them. Maybe I should stop them anyway—neither of those two should be driving," Sophie said. She started to walk in their direction.

Bruce caught her shoulders. "No, no—"

"But, Bruce, I'm just going to suggest that they get a taxi."

"You don't need to—they're waiting for a ride. See?"

The man had his phone out and he was watching the approach of their cab.

"Sure you're ready to leave?" the man asked the woman. "We could go party with your ghosts."

The woman suddenly seemed sober. "Oh, no. No. That place is bad—really bad."

The man looked up and saw Sophie and Bruce watching them. He scowled for a minute, and then smiled. "That place there—Crusty's—makes a great crab sandwich. And amazing margaritas!"

"Thanks, we'll try them out," Bruce said.

A car drove up; the couple hopped into it.

As they drove away, Sophie was anxious. "Bruce, see? I'm telling you—there's something there!"

"Well, we're about to check it out, aren't we?"

They crossed the street. Bruce was looking up and around.

"Forensics find out anything about the bullet fired at you? Anything you heard that you're not telling me?"

"From what I did understand, they believe it came from some kind of vehicle driving by. Like a pickup truck or something else tall. They're still playing around with trajectory models."

"It wasn't a random bullet."

She realized that he was keeping himself between her and the street.

"Bruce—"

"Just in case there's another random bullet out there," he said.

"And you're as valuable as I am," she said softly.

He smiled at her. "Not to me."

"Oh, please," Michael said.

They both smiled, but quickly drew serious. They were approaching the spot in the wall where Bruce had found best to climb over.

He glanced around, looking out for anyone who might be going by, and then reached and got his hold. She well imagined that he could have played football. He was lithe and quick, with powerful arms and legs.

He pulled her up after he was on top, and helped her leap down.

Michael was already there, amidst the shrubs that grew by the wall.

They walked around the tombs where Sophie had sat earlier. Then around the front of the church.

At the side where Sophie had first seen her, they paused. And waited.

"Beautiful angel," Michael said, noting a sculpture of an angel with outspread wings, her head bowed, her hands folded in prayer.

Then he repeated his words.

"Beautiful angel!"

And she was there. Ann Marie, in white, with long blond hair flowing—as if she were, indeed, an angel.

She seemed to glide as she walked over to them. She was staring at Michael with something like awe.

"You're dead," she whispered. "And you're in the world."

"I am…do you never leave this place?" he asked her.

"I… I am hardly here!" she whispered.

She started to fade.

"No, no, you just try harder. Take my hand!" Michael said.

Sophie was amazed, and shaken. It was one thing to see ghosts. It was another to see Michael interacting with this young woman.

Ann Marie took his hand.

And she seemed to find substance again.

"I can take you from here," Michael told her. "I'm not the best, but I can show you…"

"Michael," Bruce said. "We need her help."

"Yes, yes, of course," he said. "Ann Marie, we have to know what you know. What goes on here?"

"The screams..." she whispered.

"From where?"

She shook her head. "I'm not sure... He comes... He has keys. He comes...alone. And then, he comes...with the girls."

"The girls? How many?" Sophie asked, frowning.

"There have been...several."

"Where does he go?"

Ann Marie appeared to be distressed. "I don't know. He's in the graveyard with them. He auditions them... I know... I know an audition."

"Auditions them where?" Bruce asked.

"Here. In the graveyard. And I try to warn them...warn them to run. So that it won't happen to them. So that they...so that they will not be me. Sometimes...right here. Right by the angel."

"And then?" Sophie asked, her words barely a breath.

"I don't know. I try so hard. But they don't see me. They can't hear me. And I feel myself slipping away, like dying again. And then..."

"Yes, Ann Marie, and then?" Michael asked her. "Keep my hand. Hold on to me. I will give you strength."

She smiled at him. She was still in awe of him. "You're so kind."

"And then?" Sophie couldn't help but urge.

Ann Marie shook her head. "Somehow, I hear the screams. Somehow, I hear them. And I know. I know that wherever he has them, he is killing them. And I can do nothing about it."

"But you have helped, Ann Marie!" Michael told her. "You have helped. Sophie—that's Sophie, that's Bruce, and I'm Mi-chael—Sophie has been convinced that there's something here. And she's right."

"But we were all over this place today. Forensics couldn't find anything. They searched and searched for blood, for...for anything," Sophie said. She hesitated. "The killer has ripped two girls apart, Ann Marie. How could he have done that?"

Their newfound ghost friend really appeared about to cry. "I don't know. I don't know. When I saw you... I was so afraid."

"And this has happened...more than twice?" Bruce asked.

She nodded. "Four times, no, five times...maybe. I think. The first was...long ago. I don't have...time, now, here...it just goes on."

Sophie and Bruce looked at one another.

"How the hell will I ever get cops back in here?" Sophie murmured.

"You got to be friends with the young woman running it all, right? You became really friendly with her today. Sabrina Hayes, right?" Bruce asked.

She nodded. "Fairly friendly, at least. I don't think she's going to call me for a mani-pedi date or anything."

"We'll go through her," Bruce said.

"Yes, please...it will happen again. It will happen again. First, there had been time between it all...days, maybe weeks," Ann Marie said. "And then...two nights in a row."

"He has to come by car, with his victims," Sophie said.

Ann Marie nodded. "I guess. I don't see the car. And he opens the locks, and they talk, and they laugh. And then..."

"What does he look like, Ann Marie? What does this man look like?"

Ann Marie sadly shook her head. "A ghoul," she said.

"A ghoul?"

"He comes in dark clothing...and he wears a mask. Something very strange, like an old Greek theatrical mask."

Sophie looked at Bruce. "Like the Hooligans!"

He nodded in agreement.

"Thank you, Ann Marie," Bruce said.

"Thank you," Sophie repeated.

Bruce turned away and started walking slowly. Sophie watched him as he made his way through the slanted old stones and monuments, occasionally glancing back at Michael and Ann Marie.

Sophie turned to run after Bruce, but nearly slammed into him. "What, where are you going?"

"I'm an idiot—I started off without you."

"No one can know we're here," Sophie said.

"I can't risk that. Stay with me. I wanted to see where Ann Marie can see around the graveyard, and to check the church and the locks and the windows…he might have a key to the church as well as to the gate. But hell, forensics was down in the basement area, the old catacombs, and nothing," Bruce said, frustrated.

"We check, and we check…"

And they did. They checked the church. They went through the graveyard, checking every door and gate and slab of cement on every vault.

And there was nothing new to find.

"We'd best give it up for tonight. We can go study the old plans, and come back later. We can't get caught here, Sophie, or we'll never get back in," Bruce said.

She nodded, exhausted and well aware that he was right.

"Let's get Michael," she said.

They headed back to the angel. Michael was there.

He was seated with Ann Marie, and they were speaking softly to one another.

Again, they thanked Ann Marie. They told her they'd be back.

"And I will help any way that I can."

"Michael?" Sophie said.

"Um, I'll be here a while. With Ann Marie. I can—I can definitely help her," he said.

Michael, Sophie thought, was smitten.

Looking at them there, sitting beneath the angel, she thought that, in the midst of everything that was so tragic and ugly, the two of them were very beautiful.

CHAPTER THIRTEEN

Late Friday night

Bruce was glad to find that Jackson was at Sophie's house when they arrived; Brodie was staying with Grant Vining. Jackson had stayed at Sophie's house, working on research there—and, Bruce knew, guarding the place.

Just in case.

It was late, but they sat and talked, telling Jackson the newest developments in the case.

"We think he's killing them at the church or in the graveyard, but a forensic team found nothing—nothing at all?" Jackson asked.

"Nothing," Bruce told him. "They spent the day combing the place for a drop of blood—for anything. Not a drop of blood or anything else found. The graveyard is open by day, and the church itself from ten to six. Sabrina Hayes is there during open hours, or, I'm assuming, someone else from the private organization that runs the place. Thing is, Sophie has had a feeling about it—she's certain that there is something there. Tonight, we even heard suggestions from the living—a drunk couple from the bar across the street. A woman was certain the place was haunted—ghosts partying and all. Screaming."

"And then," Sophie said, "we heard from the dead. We know the killer goes there. And when he does, he wears a mask. Something like an old Greek tragedy theater mask."

"Which we've seen being worn by the Hollywood Hooligans," Bruce said. "Or so I assume it might be the same kind of mask."

"But it's going to be hard to share that information—since you got it from a ghost," Jackson pointed out. "However, I know that we can do something."

"What?" Sophie asked.

"First, I'm going to get Angela to go deeper—find every old plan of that burial ground and church. And then, well...the police have gone in. But not the FBI."

"That will work!" Sophie said happily.

She rose. She looked tired, and tonight she might really sleep, Bruce thought. "You're comfortable here?" Sophie asked Jackson. "You're okay sleeping on the sofa?"

"Like a dream," Jackson told her.

If he knew Jackson at all, Bruce thought, he knew that the man didn't sleep much. And if he did, he'd awake at the slightest noise.

Sophie smiled and headed into her bathroom.

"I really like her," Jackson told Bruce. "She just recently realized that she has a special talent?"

"She saw someone before, in college—and mentioned it to others. And they put her in therapy. I'm so glad that Marnie noticed something was up with Sophie and made me come out here...who knows? She might have been back in therapy again. And she is one of the most dedicated detectives I've ever come across. Tough—and determined to be tough."

Jackson laughed. "Napoleon complex because she's tiny?"

"No. Determination to be the best—because she's tiny."

"Get some sleep. I've gotten the call for the eight o'clock meeting."

"Thanks."

Bruce went into the bedroom; Sophie was already in bed. Naked.

He stripped down and crawled in beside her.

He slipped an arm around her, and then smiled. She was already sound asleep.

She was standing in the burial ground; the step tombs were right behind her, and the beautiful old Gothic-style church rose before her. Angels, Madonnas, cherubs and other beautiful funerary art seemed to come alive, along with the old broken tombstones, shifting where they stood or lay. Mist seemed to cover the place, and in her dream, Sophie tried to remind herself that it was LA, not San Francisco—but then again, mist could rise anywhere, and in the movies, it always rose in a graveyard.

It was a beautiful mist, silvery in color, and in its whirl, it seemed to make the cherubs and angels and all dance, and even the stones—the chipped and broken stones—had that sway.

There seemed to be a slight shudder in the ground.

An earthquake? Maybe just a tremor. The earth shook a lot in LA, often imperceptibly. You'd hear after the event that there had been a quake.

Maybe the tremor was causing the entire graveyard to shift and dance and…

As she watched, tombs began to burst open.

Vault and mausoleum doors burst open.

And the dead began to rise.

White and ghostly, caught in mist and silvery light, they rose. Old ghosts, those who had died young, some in finery, some in period clothing she tried to place…men in suspenders, women in cute little pillbox hats…an older lady in a long, late Victorian gown, a woman wearing a Mexican mantilla…they came from their graves, stricken and harsh…coming for her.

Ann Marie stood at her side, she realized.

Ann Marie…trying to protect others from the fate that had been her own.

But ghosts didn't kill—did they?

"I'm trying," she whispered.

An old man in frock coat walked up to her. "We need to rest. We see, we hear…"

"What do you see? Help me. How does he get in? How does he get out? How does he kill—and take the bodies out?"

"We can only see what we can see," the woman in the mantilla said.

"And we see him come. In his mask. And we see him play… he reads with them. From Shakespeare," the woman in the mantilla told her.

"And from Noel Coward, from movie scripts I know not," said an old man.

"They read," Ann Marie said softly. "And then they are gone. And then there are the screams."

"You are the living," the man in suspenders said.

"The living must help the dead," another man said.

Then it seemed that they were all coming for her, one after another, all of them…in a horde! They were moving toward her in a white mass, shining silver in the bizarre mist and light. She moved backward, backward, and fell onto the lowest of the step tombs, the pyramid-like structure of tombs where she had been sitting the day before and were now behind her…

"Sophie."

She woke. Bruce was at her side, holding her. She was shaking.

"Sophie, please, don't be afraid, and don't be shaken. It's common."

"It's common?"

"Common among us—the 'gifted,'" he said. "It's common, and sometimes, it even helps. Dreams trigger things we're thinking deep in our subconscious."

She curled against his chest and she told him about the dream. "Ann Marie didn't seem to think that anyone else was hanging around the graveyard. I mean, anyone else who was dead."

"Maybe, somewhere along the line, you will think of something."

"Bruce, I still think that I'm right. It has to be someone who has something to do with law enforcement. No fingerprints. No skin cells...a million pieces of trash—okay, not a million, not so many, but at the crime scenes, and in the graveyard...between them all, gum wrappers, cigarette butts, soda cups, beer cans... and nothing that helps."

"Well, something. They have gotten DNA—just nothing that does us any good, that seems to have any affiliation. The forensic team will give a report at the meeting. Maybe there will be something new."

She was silent.

"I know what you're thinking."

"You do?"

"We're not going to get anything useful—because a cop is involved."

"Did you believe Henry today?"

"I don't know. I think he was plausible. I also think he's..."

"He's what?"

"A bit creepy."

She almost smiled. "That's an understatement. But do you think...?"

"We can get someone to follow him."

"Someone?"

"FBI."

"That's good." Again, she was quiet.

"Are you okay?"

"Of course. I'm a cop."

"Of course," he said, smiling.

She rose slightly then, looking at him. He wasn't sure what her look meant at first. Then, she came closer and kissed him. It wasn't a tender kiss; it was wild, very hot...very...

Awakening.

Then she broke from him and shrugged. "I mean, we are both up, and already naked..."

He pulled her to him.

And he realized again that it was all a bit crazy.

They hadn't known one another a full week.

And he was more than a little bit in love.

Saturday morning, 8:00 a.m.

Sophie's professional manner was excellent, Bruce thought. Captain stood by her side, Dr. Thompson as well, should there be any questions; the local FBI agents were there, as well as members of the forensic team and the forensic psychiatrist. But it was Sophie's meeting, and she took easy and competent control. She kept each department speaking on their own progress, whether they reported that they were coming up empty-handed or not. And then, in summary, and with a smile and thanks to everyone, she explained that she was talking to them all because Vining was still in the hospital. She acknowledged that everyone had been working on the case—down to working on the trajectory of the shots fired at Vining and the one into the cemetery, questioning business owners and even people on the street. She knew that the forensic teams had worked tirelessly. She appreciated everything.

She went on to make sure that everyone was informed that they needed to keep working on any connections there might be to the Hollywood Hooligans. With another smile, she assured them all that she knew many of them had seen and appreciated the performing troupe. "If you saw anyone suspicious—think back, please—report anything. Anyone who might have been too intrigued by the goings-on. We know that while Brenda Sully wasn't a member of the troupe, she did go to the offices of the Hollywood Hooligans."

She went on, going over everything they did—and didn't—know.

"Tonight, the Hollywood Hooligans are giving a performance in Malibu," she said, looking around the room. "I'll be there. We're working the theory that the killer has chosen his victims—Lili and Brenda, at least—through the Hollywood Hooligans. He's looking for young actresses who are on the trail to their dreams, but, of course, waiting for their really big shot at fame."

Jackson then reported on the FBI's efforts, combing the streets, making sure that they went back and saw the same people, that they'd gone door-to-door around the neighborhood where the bodies had been dumped, that they would continue to be tirelessly involved, as well.

Forensics reported. It was the forensic psychiatrist, Bobby Dougherty, who spoke for the teams. They had gotten DNA and prints from the trash found at various scenes: the alley before the abandoned studio, the church and graveyard, and the body dump sites.

"So far, we have no matches—no one in the system. But, of course, we have a mound of work, and, as you know, even working with this as a priority, science can take time. And, as we all believe, this killer is careful. He knows what he's doing. I do believe this killer has either worked in law enforcement or in a lab of some kind—or has purchased every book available on the subject of forensic science and possibly seen every show out there hosted by an ME or a forensic worker." He was quiet for a minute. He cleared his throat. "I don't believe the killer started with these two victims. Maybe even in a different place—he's killed before. I think he practiced to get where he did with his last two victims. Bear in mind, this is only my opinion, but it seems most likely. There is an unsolved murder of a prostitute in Pasadena, another in Santa Monica and a homeless woman up in San Francisco. All three victims had slashes across their abdomens, as if someone was testing his—or her—abilities. There may be no relationship. None of them were displayed, but still, the slashes might have been practice. Again, it's conjecture—educated but opinion only. These murders might be related, and they might not be, and other killings might be, as well."

Sophie looked at Bruce. She was pleased—Bobby had expressed an opinion she shared.

At the end, Captain spoke. But while he was speaking, the desk sergeant came hurrying in with a paper in his hands.

"Something sent in by the killer?" someone murmured. Based on the old Dahlia case, they'd all been waiting for a note or something similar to arrive at a local newspaper office.

Bruce saw Captain Chagall's face turn hard.

"All right, who the hell is responsible for this?"

He showed them the paper; it was one of the Hollywood gossip rag magazines.

And there, on the front page, were pictures of the crime scenes.

Pictures of Lili and Brenda, as they had been found. "Henry? What the hell, Henry? How in God's name did they get hold of these?"

"Not me, oh, God, not from me!" Henry cried. Everyone was staring at him. "I swear, sir. Oh, my God, how could the paper print those?"

"Freedom of the press," Captain Chagall spat out. "And, of course, they say they're printing the pictures, asking for help from the public. Henry?"

"Everyone here has access to the image files," Henry stated.

Tension was thick in the room.

Suspicion of one's coworkers was a horrible thing.

"This was not my fault, damn it," Henry swore passionately.

"When I find out who did let these pictures leak…you won't just be fired," Chagall said. He looked around the room. "Find this killer. Find this damned killer fast!" He turned to Sophie. "Get to that magazine's offices—now! I want to know how the hell they got these pictures."

He walked out of the conference room.

Everyone heard the door to his office slam.

And everyone at the meeting was dead still for a moment.

Then they were all talking at once, denying that they could have done such a thing.

Sophie turned to Bruce. "Let's get going," she said.

She was grim as she hurried out of the station.

She was tiny, but he was using long strides to keep up with her. When they were in the car, she blurted out, "I'm right. I've been right. It's someone who was in that meeting. I can't tiptoe around anymore. Chagall said to go to the paper. Well, you know what? We're going to get to these offices and the pictures are going to have arrived in an envelope, and there will be no prints on the envelope, and no saliva on the stamp. And it was probably mailed right from a box near this station."

"Here's the thing," Bruce said. "When we're done with the paper, we'll get back in touch with Jackson. He'll have had Angela searching, and really, when it comes to finding what is needed from the past, there is no one better than Angela—not to mention that they have a whole tech department that can find just about anything. Sophie, we'll keep at it until we find the truth."

She seemed to calm down a little.

Enough so that when they reached the paper's publishers, she was brusque but professional when asking for the managing editor.

His name was Jude Conner, and was under thirty. He was, apparently, expecting the police. He explained in no uncertain terms that the United States Constitution gave him every right to post the pictures. The police were getting nowhere; the public could help.

Sophie replied—in no uncertain terms—that what he had done might have hampered an ongoing police investigation, and therefore, was possibly punishable by law. She wanted to know when, where and exactly how the pictures had arrived.

She was good at intimidating.

Bruce liked to think that his towering height and bulk standing behind her might have helped as well—and the fact that the man didn't seem to realize he wasn't really FBI, he was a consultant.

At any rate, Sophie wasn't going to have to get a warrant.

He would turn the manila envelope that had delivered the pictures over to her immediately.

She slipped gloves on before taking the envelope. Still, it had been in the mailroom, it had been delivered to a secretary, it had been on his desk, not to mention the fact that it had gone through the post office.

"He mailed it from the same place he mailed Lili's license, I'm sure," Sophie said. "But we'll get this back, and then..."

"Hopefully, Jackson will have received something from Angela by now. Although, Sabrina Hayes might have what we need, too."

Sophie shook her head. "I don't think she does. Unless she's in on it, somehow. She wanted the police there—for trespassers and vandals, yes, but... Bruce, maybe—"

"We'll check on unsolved murders in the past few years." He was quiet. "Bobby Dougherty says that the man may have killed in other places. He didn't. We know through Ann Marie that he has been using the church and burial ground. Whether the bodies were found or not, he started murdering at the graveyard. Maybe, if we can find his other victims..."

"Can we get Angela started on that? Or should we try here? Here's where we would have the reports."

"Don't worry. Angela can access anything."

"In that case, can you reach Jackson?"

"Of course. We can just—"

"Stop by the hospital."

"After I drop the envelope."

"After you drop the envelope."

She hesitated. "Bruce, what do you think? Does this point toward—toward Henry again? He is the one who took the pictures."

"He's right, though—a hell of a lot of people had access to them."

"But he is...a bit off."

"Doesn't make him a murderer. But, yes, I say he remains on the list."

"A list of one," Sophie muttered.

They dropped the envelope at the police lab and headed to the hospital.

Vining was being a difficult patient; he wanted to be discharged.

When they arrived, Jackson Crow was there—and he was patiently listening as Vining grumbled.

He so wanted out.

The captain, however, wasn't clearing him for duty; the doctors had said that he needed another day or two.

"Ridiculous!" Vining announced. "And I've heard about the

rag mag posting the pictures. Deplorable! What is the matter with people? You've been to the paper, right?"

"Yes," Sophie said.

"And?"

"Came in an envelope. I already have it back with our forensic team."

Vining nodded.

"I wish to hell I could get out of here!"

"Grant, you will. I swear to God, we're working as hard as we can," Sophie told him.

"I know, I know… Special Agent Crow keeps me up-to-date…wait, you are sleeping, right?"

"I'm sleeping," Sophie assured him.

Jackson spoke up. "You'll receive plans from the church and the burial ground within the hour. Angela has managed to get them through the years—up to the last interment."

"A massive crew has already been through the church and the burial ground," Vining said.

"There was a quake that caused some damage—and some changes—in the 1920s," Jackson said. He glanced at Vining. "It may mean nothing, it may mean something," he said evenly. "Brodie is taking over from me again in a few hours. McFadden, I'll meet you at Sophie's place."

Bruce nodded. "Can you get Angela working on something else?" he asked.

"You've got something?" Vining asked.

Bruce was glad that Bobby Dougherty had spoken about other victims at the meeting. He could say what he needed—and keep Vining in on what they were doing.

"Bobby Dougherty—the forensic psychiatrist—doesn't believe that the killer started with our present two victims. I want to see what other unsolved murders might be on the books, or, maybe, missing persons."

"This is LA. Dreamers come out here…and give up, go home, move onward… We do wind up with a lot of missing person reports," Vining said.

"And we'll do what we can."

"We have a hell of a database," Jackson assured him.

Vining was quiet for a minute. "Of course," he said, "I know that Bobby Dougherty announced this to the whole force, but… keep your inquiries FBI for the moment."

"All right," Bruce said.

Vining, too, was apparently growing more and more suspicious.

It wasn't making him happy. But he was a good cop. And good cops had to face the truth, whether they liked it or not.

"People are buried on top of people, and more people are buried on top of them," Sophie murmured.

She'd printed out all the plans that Angela had sent them, spreading the pages across the surface of her desk in her home office. It was amazing to see what had been—and what was now. Over time, gravestones had been moved. People lay in the ground—but nowhere near the place where their markers stood.

A quake had hit the LA basin on June 21, 1920. It had been a 4.9, but caused some major damage in several places.

While the church had stood well enough, the foundation had been shaken. It had been shored up, partially filled in.

A number of the priests had been interred in the foundation area; their remains had been removed and reinterred beneath the altar.

Another interesting fact that Sophie hadn't realized came clear in the old plans. Many of the little mausoleums and family vaults had more extensive catacomb areas beneath. The tomb where she'd been seated, for one. Another that belonged to a Wisdom family, and several others, though they weren't quite as large.

Excited, Sophie called over to Bruce, who was working on missing person cases and unsolved murders. He walked over to where she sat at her desk, and looked over her shoulder. "Underground!" she said. "He has these plans…he's had these plans. He's using the burial ground, we know that! And if we go by the earthquake of 1920 and all the work that went on after… Bruce! We can find where he's working. We can find his torture chamber or whatever it is he uses. He doesn't care if there's blood there, he knows that not even the people who run the church know about all this!"

"We've another problem, though."

"What's that?"

"He's washing the bodies. Where is he getting the water?"

Sophie looked at him. "Um, most graveyards have a water source. They have spigots for people for the flowers they bring their loved ones."

"Did you see any?"

"No, but I wasn't looking. And there's so much foliage around—there's probably a hose, and—"

"Sophie, if he dragged a corpse out into the burial ground and washed it there, he'd be…if not seen by the living, he would have been seen by the dead."

"Then he has a way of bringing the water down. That's the only answer, Bruce. Okay, from what we know from Ann Marie, he murdered before. Up to three other women. I think they were practice victims; I think this guy has lived with the dream of repeating the Dahlia murder for a long time—and that he's ecstatic because he's managed it twice. We have all these leads, all these *things* that we can do, clues to follow…but they send us reeling in circles. That's what he's wanted. At first, he practiced getting women to the burial ground. Auditions! And sure, explain that it's going to be a project like an old Greek tragedy—or whatever—and an actress must be able to emote behind a mask. She has to be able to play off him while he's wearing a mask. Bruce, I've spent my life out here—I have so many friends who are actors... I know a lot about what's legitimate, what's just odd, and what kind of thing can be used to snare the unwary—and those who are ambitious and naive."

"I believe you. I have no problem following your theory, your methods—and the killer's madness. Jackson will get us in. We can arrange for it tomorrow. Tonight, I think we should follow through with the Hollywood Hooligan performance. Perhaps another discussion with Kenneth—and his players. We're the only ones who know about the masks at the moment, but if what Ann Marie was seeing were theatrical masks..."

"I think we should see Kenneth before the show," Sophie said. "Kenneth Trent really should know who had the masks—and if any went missing."

"I'll tell him we're coming out to the performance," Bruce said. "And that I need a minute with him. All right?"

"All right," Sophie agreed. She'd become so excited over the churchyard plans, she'd forgotten to ask how he was doing.

He walked back to his laptop, picked it up and showed Sophie a picture. It was of a pretty young woman with shoulder-length, curling dark hair.

An actress's head shot.

She looked a lot like Brenda Sully.

And a lot like Lili Montana.

And the Black Dahlia.

"Who is she?"

"Judith Lawry. She came to LA ten years ago. And disappeared into thin air."

Sophie asked him, "No body?"

"Her body was never found. She was never found. She just disappeared. Her family lives in Kansas City, Missouri—or did. Her mother passed away about eight years ago, and her father followed a year later. According to detective notes, her mother was passionate, calling constantly. But she had been in a hotel and checked out the day she disappeared. The detectives on the case had nowhere to go. She hadn't told anyone she was doing anything specific. She left the hotel, and she was seen by the counter clerk—and then never again. Her picture was posted everywhere. No one ever came forward with any information on her whatsoever."

"She might have been the first victim," Sophie said.

"Or she might have hitchhiked or hopped a bus out of town, and anything might have happened. But yes…" He hesitated. "Sadly, the LA morgue gets all kind of John and Jane Does. You have a population like this, and…" He shrugged.

"Bruce, if this guy did start ten years ago, he'd be…well, probably older now. I'm not a behavioral scientist by any mean, and yet I read a lot, and I know that such killers tend to be in their twenties or early thirties, and they're often loner types, and some with menial jobs… And yet, if he killed ten years ago, he wouldn't be twenties or early thirties now."

"He still could be fairly young. Many serial killers start at early ages. We've all heard that you have to watch out for kids who cut off lizards' tails, throw rocks at fenced dogs, and maybe graduate to killing cats. But there have also been cases of kids killing kids—and killing adults, as well."

"But he would have pretended to be a director or a producer. Could someone young have pulled that off?" Sophie wondered.

"I think he would have had to have been seventeen or so at the time. I've seen plenty of seventeen-year-olds—male and female—who can pull off appearing to be pretty mature." He paused. "Jesse Pomeroy."

"Pardon?"

"Way back—Boston 1870s. Jesse Pomeroy was twelve years old when he was first apprehended. He started out torturing a number of children, stripping them naked, binding then, cutting them—broke one's jaw. He went to a reform school. He was let out. And then he killed. Age doesn't necessarily make a kid sweet and cuddly."

"We're back to the fact that we just don't know yet."

Sophie was frustrated.

There was a knock on Sophie's front door—and a quick little buzz from the bell.

She was embarrassed that she jumped at the sudden sound.

Bruce pretended not to notice. "Jackson, I'm sure," he said. "I'll go get him."

When Bruce came back, he took up a perch on Sophie's desk. Jackson took the one other chair in the office.

"I have something for you—it will be in those files, but Vining brought it to my attention."

"What?"

"Six years ago. Stella Greenwood. She was found *in the tar pits*. Her throat had been slashed. She was from Montgomery, Alabama, just out here a week—she wanted to be a star. She was a foster child, so she went missing without anyone paying attention. A hotel manager called the cops when she didn't pay up. Her body was found before the poor girl even became a missing person case."

"So, we may have victim one—and victim two. And if so, and if that's all…he went four years between crimes," Bruce said.

"Vining had the case. You were still in patrol, Sophie," Jackson told her.

"I do remember it, though. So sad. No one cared. We took up a collection—I remember that, because I contributed," Sophie said. She gasped. "Oh! Her body was…well, she'd been in the tar. But when they got her cleaned up, death was by a hit on the head—some kind of blunt object. But…she'd also been mutilated."

"Her face had been ripped up," Jackson said. "I think our killer was practicing."

"Do we have a third?"

"I believe our third is also going to be a missing person," Bruce said, studying an email Angela had sent that was up on his phone screen. "There are a lot of maybes—but I think we have more than a maybe here. Maggie McAvoy. She was out here a year—she told everyone she was going to be in the movies. She'd call home now and then, and then she just stopped. Her roommate called the police, concerned, when she'd disappeared for a week. She'd had a fight with Maggie—over drugs. Maggie wasn't paying her share of the rent or the bills—and she was, according to the roommate—paying for drugs. She was working—she'd been able to get extra work and be paid as an audience member for a number of pilots and game shows. But according to her roommate, she'd also gotten into drugs. So police hunted down dealers and anyone else. No one could find anything at all on Maggie." He looked up at them. "She was last seen at the bar across the street from the church and the burial ground. Crusty's. And," he added, "she disappeared—according to her roommate—exactly a year ago, last Monday."

"How could anyone get away with so much?" Sophie asked. "I mean, if we're thinking it might be a cop, working every day with other cops..."

"It's possible. Bundy worked for a crisis center," Bruce reminded her.

She glanced at Jackson. "He does know his serial killers."

"Frightening, yes, but sadly, so do we all," Jackson said. "So, we think we may have found where our guy started. Do you feel that we're any closer?"

"Yes—and no," Bruce said.

"Want to see a show?" Sophie asked.

"The Hollywood Hooligans?" Jackson asked.

"We have to see Kenneth Trent again," Bruce explained. "We got a tip about masks, that the killer might wear one, but…well, the forensic psychiatrist didn't come up with that one."

"I see," Jackson murmured. "A ghost?"

Bruce nodded. "I told you about Ann Marie."

Sophie added, "I announced the performance today. I want to see exactly who does show up. I'm willing to bet that we will see Henry Atkins. And others, perhaps. Others I work with every day." She trembled slightly, not afraid, but definitely disturbed. She looked at Bruce and Jackson. "Friends," she added softly. "Friends—who may be savage psychopaths."

CHAPTER FOURTEEN

Saturday night

The Dunston Inn had been built in the 1920s to host the stars of the silent-movie era. When talkies had come in, the Dunston Inn had hosted the new stars.

The building had been designed in the Deco style, with clean, handsome arches abounding. Fixtures were elegant, chandeliers were sumptuous, and the lobby—where show-goers arrived— was large and welcoming, offering comfortable wingback chairs and numerous chesterfield sofas.

The check-in counter was for ticket sales that night; the friendly young redhead who sold Bruce the tickets to the performance told him that he was lucky—there had only been four left for the evening. "We never sell more than a hundred!" she said. "The performances are interactive. You can actually see the same show with the Hollywood Hooligans several times—and have a different experience every time. Of course, if you have friends, or want to come again, this show will last four weekends—or four Saturdays and Sundays."

Bruce thanked her and asked if he could see Kenneth Trent. The girl was surprised.

"He's here, right?" Bruce asked.

"Oh, yes, he is…he's here. He gives his performers last-minute notes before the show. Perhaps you could see him after the performance."

"I'd really love to see him now," Bruce said, producing his private investigator's license. It didn't actually grant him the same rights as other law enforcement, but it seemed to work everywhere.

"Oh!" the girl said. Then she sighed. "All right. He's in the kitchen. I can't lead you to him, I'm alone out here at the moment. But—"

"I can find my way," Bruce assured her.

She hesitated again. "Okay. The elevators over there are the first step for our guests. There are four floors, and as they arrive, guests are escorted off at different floors. You'll see. You really are here for the performance, right?" There was a slight edge to her voice then.

"Yes, we're really here for the performance."

"Sorry." She offered her hand suddenly. "I'm Madge. And I'm heartbroken about Lili, but you have to understand, Kenneth works so hard! And if she had just been…well, just been happy being a Hooligan, I think she'd still be with us."

At first, Bruce thought that Madge was cold. Very cold.

But then he saw the tears in her eyes.

Lili was dead.

But apparently, the old adage was true.

The show—this show, at least—must go on.

He realized he was being cynical. Lili Montana was dead—hardly cold. These people were her coworkers.

But they couldn't stop living. Rent would still be due; electricity and internet bills would not stop because Lili was gone.

"I'm sorry for your loss," he said softly.

"Kenneth will be making an announcement tonight. Tonight's performance is being given in honor of Lili."

"So, I take it that Lili was supposed to be in this show?" Bruce asked her.

"Yes."

"So who is taking her place?"

"An old friend of Kenneth's. The 'elevator operators' will be giving you programs. The new actress is named Grace Leon."

"Ah."

"You know of Grace? You've seen her perform before?"

"We've met," he said simply.

"Oh, well, good, anyway… I can tell Kenneth you're coming. We're on an intercom. I got distracted. Walk by the elevators and down the hall. There are some carved double doors that lead to the dining room—don't go there. Some of the guests will come back down and be with our 'Nine-days Queen' there. It's a great show—all about the death of Henry III's son, and Lady Jane Grey, the poor cousin who was supported by the Protestant masses, and queen for nine days before Mary—Henry's oldest daughter—came in with her troops. And, eventually, poor Lady Jane…well, it's all history. Kenneth wrote the script. It's great. So—go by the double doors on down the hallway. There are plain doors there—that's the working kitchen, but of course, it's not working tonight. There is a bar out in the courtyard. That's where they let people out."

"I'll find Kenneth," he said. "Thank you."

The lobby was beginning to fill up. He wove his way through the theatergoers until he came back to Jackson and Sophie.

"All set with tickets, and we walk past the elevators to get to Kenneth Trent. He's giving his performers last-minute notes."

"I really can't wait to see this," Sophie told him.

"You do like a good historic story," he said, smiling.

"I do." Her smiled faded. "But let's go ask the director some questions."

"Lead the way," Jackson said.

He did. They went down along the hallway, past the double doors to the dining room and on to the kitchen.

He tapped lightly on the door and opened it. Kenneth was at a table by a large serving station. He looked at the three of them with a bleak smile as they entered.

"No performers," Sophie murmured.

"I just sent them off to their starting places. Madge said you were coming." He inhaled, and exhaled deeply on a sigh. "What can I do for you tonight? This is the first night of this show." His voice grew raspy. "It's our first show without Lili."

Sophie found a chair across from him; Bruce slid into a chair next to her.

"Kenneth, we're not here to make you miserable in any way," Sophie started. "But we need to know about the masks the company uses."

He frowned, looking perplexed. "Masks? This show doesn't make use of any masks."

"But you did a takeoff on a Greek tragedy a while back. Your performers all wore masks," Sophie said.

"Oh, those, yes. They were Greek tragedy masks. That performance was really more of an interactive workshop—we invited guests to learn about acting—about using their voices and bodies to portray emotion when their faces weren't visible. It was…it was excellent!"

"But," Bruce asked, "did you wind up being down a mask or two?"

He laughed softly. "We were down dozens of masks. The audience members who wanted to participate in the event as a workshop all kept their masks." He looked perplexed, and then he sat up straight. "Oh, no…someone used one of my masks? How? Do you know? Have you got anything?"

"Not yet. But we do believe that the killer is disguising himself," Sophie told him.

"Or herself," Bruce murmured.

"I bought two hundred of those masks. I bought them from Hide N' Seek. It's a costume company on Vine. I'm so sorry— they could be anywhere."

"Do you have any kind of a record of people who were involved in that workshop?" Bruce asked.

"Um, mostly. A lot of tickets are bought online, and most people use credit cards. Sometimes, though, someone comes up with cash at the last minute." He cleared his throat. "The show is due to begin."

"We're going to need everything you have on the masks," Sophie told him.

"I'll call my bookkeeper first thing in the morning. We'll get you anything you need," he promised. "Are you—are you here to see the show?"

"Yes, we are, Kenneth," Bruce told him.

"I'm hoping that you'll love it. Painless history," he said. He was quiet for a minute. "It should have been Lili," he said softly.

"And, instead, it's Grace Leon—as Lady Jane?" Sophie asked.

Kenneth Trent nodded. "I—I need to open," he said. "And you all… I know we're still talking tragedy. But I believe our show is good. I hope you're able to enjoy it. In some small way."

They thanked him, and left, heading for the elevators themselves. A number of theatergoers were getting into the elevators.

Some had already gone up.

The "ushers" were there, in 1920s red-and-gold uniforms with little pillbox hats. "Enter, if you will, an old realm, where kings held sway, and power, faith and love could be punishable by death!" a young woman usher told them.

She stopped them, handing Sophie a single red rose and pinning little boutonnieres to the lapels of Bruce's and Jackson's blazers.

Their roses were red, too.

"Beauty and life," the usher said. "Delicate, and fleeting."

They entered the elevator with a group of other people. It went up and stopped on the second floor.

"You six, this is where you begin your journey into Tudor England."

Bruce was about to protest; Sophie was selected in the six. He was not.

But she looked at him, and he knew what she was thinking.

Divide and see everything we can!

She was a cop; she was armed. They were at a performance. He had to let her go.

The elevator door began to close, even as she stepped off.

Sophie wished that she had come just to see the show, that she was here only for fun purposes. Her group joined another that had just stepped off one of the other elevators.

They were greeted by Grace Leon as Lady Jane Grey.

"Dear friends, that you've supported me so beautifully is such a dear and wonderful thing. But then, of course, you are Protestants, those of the true faith of England, and initiated by our great king, Henry VIII! Such blood that ran, such blood…oh, dear friends, it breaks my heart that so many died in the flames as England found her way to holiness. I bear my dear cousins, Mary and Elizabeth, no ill will, but we all fear Mary—and her way of worshipping idols in her Catholicism!"

Grace Leon was in a spectacular costume, and she moved among the crowd, greeting them, welcoming, explaining the situation in London.

She urged them to come with her as she led them through

rooms that explained a bit about her great-grandfather, Henry VII, and then Henry VIII—and the beheadings and burning that had gone on. Henry's son, the poor child, her dear friend, who had passed so young, had sworn that she must be queen.

As the spectators moved along, Sophie noticed that Dr. Chuck Thompson was in her crowd.

He saw her.

And beamed at her.

He quietly made his way around others. As Lady Jane talked about the troubles that had rocked the country, Thompson made his way to her.

"Sophie," he whispered. "This is fantastic. I didn't know you enjoyed the theater."

"Oh, I love entertainment in any form," she whispered back. "But, of course, I'm here specifically to see the Hooligans—and the young lady taking Lili Montana's place."

"Such a sorry thing. Any headway? We don't get as much information in the morgue as you do at the station. Of course, my work on the victims is done—and I have spoken for them the best that I can."

"Come! Come and see London!" Lady Jane said.

They were ushered down the hall into a large conference room. An excellent set designer had changed it into a street in London. Actually, a lot was a backdrop—of the Tower of London.

Kenneth Trent was there himself, now in Tudor costume, a hat with a sweeping plume, leggings and a shoulder cape over a rich shirt in crimson velvet.

"Friends, countrymen! Here we are, caught in the vicious turmoil of the day! Be ye Catholic? You risk your necks beneath the reign of such as Lady Jane! And yet, be ye of Henry VIII's good English faith, you risk life and limb if Mary is proclaimed.

Ah, Bloody Mary! She has already promised a purge—a purge of blood and fire, when she regains her throne."

Sophie had managed to stay to the back. She realized that "Lady Jane" had met them, but this was the true beginning of the show.

All ticket holders were in the conference room. A hundred people.

She saw Jackson to the side. Searching, she found that Bruce was closer to the front.

Kenneth Trent went on about London and the circumstances. Sophie half listened, and half looked around.

She was no longer by Dr. Chuck Thompson.

Kenneth drew an audience member to the front with him. Sophie saw why people were so fond of the group; his story was about Tudor London. His lines and his work might have segued readily to the day—not that Catholics and Protestants were killing one another in LA. But rather, he managed to keep the play historical, and yet make comments that had a great deal to do with tolerance in their present day—accepting others for whatever their beliefs might be.

She listened...and she looked.

And there, to the far corner, was Lee Underwood. He was with a few other members of the forensic team.

And, searching, she finally saw Henry Atkins.

Watching. Gleeful.

"Well, you did get some cops out."

She almost jumped; Bruce had now come to stand with her. She nodded and whispered, "Hail, hail, the gang's all here. Henry, Dr. Thompson—and Lee Underwood."

"And two others from your precinct." He smiled at her. "And Jackson says there are two FBI members here—the two over there who look like a sweet young couple, holding hands."

"I did give a speech," she murmured.

"I'm going to try to stick with Henry Atkins," he said.

"I've already talked to Chuck Thompson."

"I'll give Jackson Lee Underwood to watch."

He moved away from her.

She looked for Thompson and moved back by him. He beamed again as she joined him. Other players suddenly came from around the backdrop. They included Jane's doomed husband, Lord Guildford Dudley; Henry VIII's last wife—the one who survived him—Catherine Parr; and the man she loved, her husband after Henry VIII's death, Thomas Seymour. They met Thomas Cranmer, the doomed Archbishop of Canterbury. Henry's only son, the poor dying Edward. Three others came forward, priests from the rivaling religions, and two more young women—a prostitute and a serving girl.

And last, the executioner.

When the players had been introduced, they began to separate the audience.

Sophie clung close to Dr. Thompson.

Their group followed Lord Dudley. She didn't see where Bruce and Jackson wound up.

They went through various scenes, Dudley—or, the fine young actor portraying him—talking about his love for his wife, and how, despite treason, Mary really had no longing to execute her. He talked about Lady Jane's rise to power, and then her imprisonment. Wyatt's Rebellion—against Mary's proposed marriage to Philip of Spain, another Catholic—doomed Jane and Dudley in the end. To her credit—while she was guilty of burning and beheading hundreds, thus earning the moniker Bloody Mary, Queen Mary had not wanted to order the execution of her cousin. Wyatt's Rebellion left her no choice.

Especially since Lady Jane would not disavow her faith.

They shifted scenes and moved throughout the inn.

And then, as the players all shifted again, Sophie found herself being whisked away, on her own, by none other than Lady Jane Grey—Grace Leon.

They went into a small inn bedroom—reset to appear to be a room in the Tower of London. Before the door closed, Grace fell to her knees in prayer. Her life on earth was nothing but flesh; she would not risk her soul and betray her faith.

Then the door closed, and she turned on Sophie, completely dropping her character.

"How dare you? How dare you harass and ridicule Kenneth? This is an abuse of police authority. I will report you! No, I'll sue you—I'll sue you and the LAPD!"

She was vehement—and nasty.

"Miss Leon, I came here to see a performance. Kenneth Trent knows that I'm here. Thus far, I had enjoyed the performance. I have the odd feeling that the rest of the Hooligans would not appreciate you attacking an LAPD officer. No one is harassing you in any way."

"You're here!"

"Yes, this is a performance open to the public."

"I'm warning you—if you continue to harass Kenneth, I will come after you."

"And I'm warning you—you continued to threaten an LAPD detective, I will see that your darling little ass is dragged downtown for questioning. There is speculation that Lili and Brenda's killer might be a woman. Brenda had been about to audition. Lili was one of the favorite players. Who might have benefited from their deaths? Oh, that would be you!"

Sophie hadn't begun to think of such a suspicion until she had said the words. Even then, she didn't believe what she was saying.

She knew the killer was a man. Ann Marie referred to the killer as "him." Then again, he wore a mask. Lili and Brenda had been told that they were meeting a man.

A woman could play a man.

She was pretty sure, though, that she had just retorted an-grily—taken a shot in the dark because she'd been so startled by the attack.

Grace Leon stared at her in pure shock, her mouth just wide-open at first, and then working. "Me?" The question was a squeak. "Oh, my God! You can't believe…oh, God, no! How horrible, I'd never… I'd never…please, tell me you don't be-lieve that?"

"Grace, we don't know what to believe as of yet. We're try-ing to find a killer, and we're working every possible angle. We know where Kenneth was during the murders. We're not ac-cusing him of anything. But he is a help to us. And we are here to see the performance."

The door to the little bedroom burst open then. The per-former playing Dudley was there, with a small group of audi-ence members.

He was perfectly in character, seeing Grace—or Lady Jane Grey—and rushing in to see her. "My love, my love…"

He pulled her into his arms.

"They've allowed us this time!" he whispered. "This pre-cious time together. My love, how will we face this…how will we die?"

"With honor, oh, my beloved, with honor. Sweet, my own sweet lord, this time on earth for any is so brief. What we do… we will be together in Paradise, together in the gentle love of our most gracious God!"

"They say that the blade will be sharp. That it will be quick."

"I will die with dignity, so I swear!"

"And, I, too, my love, and believe in sweet life after death!"

Grace had done a good job of recovering her character. The door opened again.

This time, it was the executioner.

The final scene took place back in the conference room, the

backdrop shifted slightly to show that they were on Tower Green. A scaffold had been added.

Lady Jane went up to lose her head, giving her last words—about Mary's rights, about her acceptance of her fate—and then forgiving her executioner. She asked if her head would be removed before she reached the block; she was told no. She nearly lost her calm after she blindfolded herself and then couldn't reach the block. She was helped, and spoke her final words—straight from the New Testament. "Lord, into thy hands I commend my spirit!"

There was a drumroll, and a curtain dropped all the way around the scaffolding.

The end was greeted with thunderous applause.

"Interesting," Bruce murmured.

He had come up behind her.

"Very," Sophie said.

Lee Underwood waved and came over to join them. "Hell of a performance. Of course, I don't really know a lot about British history, but my heart was bleeding for that poor girl."

"Bravo, bravo! I loved it!" Chuck Thompson came to join them as well, and, just a second later, they were joined by Henry Atkins.

Henry might have clapped a great deal. His rose boutonniere was crushed against his chest; a few of the petals had broken. His rose wasn't completely red; it must have been exceptionally pretty as its petals were a mix of red and yellow.

"Great!" he said, smiling broadly. "I thought that this might be another of their comedy skits, but, wow, fantastic. What experience did you have? Anything in a small group? I was with Mary Tudor—me, Lee and six other people. The actress was great. She was so torn. And then so righteous! Phenomenal!"

"Then we went home with the executioner," Lee said. "Met his family, and learned that he practiced with his ax constantly.

He didn't want any debacles, and, while he kept quiet, he hated that he killed so many people for being steadfast. Of course, he said that a man had to be careful, very careful, about expressing his opinion.

"Henry, how the hell could it have been a comedy?" Lee asked. "Look at your program? It's titled *So Longing, Doth Beauty Die!*"

"Hey!" Henry protested. "Come on now. *Death at a Funeral* was a comedy."

"And," Chuck said, "Remember *Death Becomes Her?* You can never judge anything by a title."

"Okay, okay—I stand chastised," Lee said. He grinned at Sophie, Bruce and Jackson. "I was planning to come even before your announcement at the meeting, Sophie," he said, then lowered his voice. "I know you were watching the audience as much as the players, but…aren't they great?"

"Very good," Sophie said.

Lee lowered his voice still further, sounding anxious. "And?"

"And it was a great performance piece—different from anything I've ever seen, certainly," Sophie said. "What about you three? Anyone you noticed who was behaving strangely?"

"Tons of people come to multiple performances," Henry said.

"Because you get a different experience every time—depending on who you follow," Chuck said.

Sophie was shaking her head.

"What?" Lee demanded.

"You guys…you saw all these shows—you had to have seen Lili Montana."

"We were talking about that when we got here," Chuck said. "That we'd been to so many, and we were all there with Lili Montana—and we never knew her name."

"And didn't recognize her," Lee said.

"How would we recognize her?" Henry asked, shaking his head. "Her mother wouldn't have recognized her."

"But when we found out who she was—" Sophie said.

Lee shrugged. "We see a lot of corpses. And you have to remember—the one show—we couldn't see their faces."

"With the masks," Henry said.

"None of us knew who anyone was," Chuck finished.

Jackson excused himself; he went over to the couple who were actually FBI, or so Bruce had said.

"You three came here together?" Bruce asked.

"Sure," Lee said. "I would have come anyway, but after Sophie talked about the performance tonight at the meeting, I asked Henry if he was coming."

"And Chuck Thompson had called me already," Henry said.

"We figured we'd see the show as we planned—and follow Sophie's instructions from the meeting."

"I didn't really give instructions," Sophie murmured.

Jackson returned to their group. "I should get back," he said.

"You guys don't want to have a drink or anything?" Lee asked.

"Not tonight," Bruce told them. "But thanks."

"That's right. Our Sophie works around the clock," Lee said.

"Our Sophie is going to go home and go to sleep," she assured them all. "But I did enjoy the show."

"Did you learn anything?" Chuck Thompson asked her.

Was he looking at her strangely? Or was she really suspicious of him, too? What if it was all crazy, and people were just being normal—getting out and having a good time when they weren't at work?

"All about Lady Jane Grey!" she said lightly.

She bid them good-night.

The room had already thinned, but the ushers were there to get them down the elevators and out to the lobby.

Kenneth Trent was thanking everyone who had come as they exited.

He looked anxiously at Sophie, then Bruce, and Jackson.

"Well?" he whispered.

Each of them told him that his show had been exceptional.

Bruce reminded him that they needed a list of all the people who had been involved in the interactive show with the masks.

"Everything I have!" he vowed.

They were out in the car before Sophie told them, "I had one hell of an interesting one-on-one interaction!"

"Oh?" Bruce asked, frowning.

"Our sweet little friend and fledgling star—Grace Leon. She can really turn it on and off. She fell on her knees in character, praying—then an instant later leaped up and attacked me. Oh, not physically! Just verbally. She was going to sue me and the entire force for harassing Kenneth Trent."

"Really? Well, she is his star now, I guess," Bruce noted. "What did you tell her?"

"I did say that there could always be the suspicion that a woman was guilty—and that we could talk at the station. Since she took over what would have been Lili Montana's part, well, at the least, she had motive."

"And?" Jackson asked.

Sophie grimaced. "She was horrified at the suggestion—and I don't think she was acting."

"Well, it's true. She did take over for Lili Montana," Bruce said.

Even on Saturday night, traffic was heavy returning from Malibu. Bruce drove; Sophie had asked for the back seat, determined to go through her phone—and the plans she had received from Angela Hawkins regarding the old church and burial ground again.

Staring at the plans, and remembering the graveyard as they had last been in it, she gasped suddenly.

"I think I've found something…and, Bruce, between my

dream, and the circumstances, and just the fact we suspected and know…"

"What?" Bruce asked, glancing at her through the rearview mirror. "You know which tomb he might be using?"

"Maybe," she said. Jackson had turned, and was studying her. She wanted to be careful. Her instinct was there; she didn't want to make a rash determination and be wrong.

"Are you going to share?" Jackson asked.

Bruce gazed back at her again quickly, and then returned his attention to the road. "The dream…and our theory. I think I can picture the place. That one family set of tombs…the ones that stack up on each side and create a pyramid effect."

"Yes!" Sophie said. "The plans show that it's dug out deep, there are more family members beneath the ground. It's not just tombs—it's catacombs."

Bruce kept his eyes on the road and spoke softly.

"Johnstone," he said. "The family name on those tombs is Johnstone. And, Sophie, I think you could easily be right. You might have found the murder site."

CHAPTER FIFTEEN

Saturday night, late

Sophie wanted to head straight to the old church and burial ground. Jackson was the one to remind her that they needed to have legal entry.

"And we can have it by tomorrow," Bruce said.

"But if we went out now—"

"We have no tools. We can't just dig around blindly," Bruce said.

"Sophie, don't forget, I did ask that my LA office have agents do sweeps around that area tonight, watching that it stays quiet," Jackson said.

"If we went prowling around and accomplished nothing—and Sabrina Hayes found out—she'd be furious. She's been cooperative," Bruce said, "but that can change. We can do it right in the morning. If you just go in and by some legal flaw get evidence thrown out when it comes to court, the DA's office would have your head. And if we're wrong, we'll have to access other tombs—and that missing part of the foundation that seems to have disappeared after the quake," Bruce reminded her.

"Sophie, I've never seen anyone with more pull than Adam Harrison—the man who is the real head of the Krewe," Jackson said. "We'll get access, bright and early."

"You don't think that the killer will have figured out that we're onto him?" Sophie asked. "Oh, stupid question. Cops flooded the place. But if there is anything there, he might get in and try to get rid of it by tomorrow."

"The cops searched—and found nothing," Bruce reminded her. "He won't think that we're going back. And the first search was LAPD. The second search will be FBI."

"Besides," Jackson said softly, "once we find his killing field... well, there will be no way for him to get rid of that much blood. He must have instruments down there. He might have been able to keep the studio and the dump sites clean, but I don't believe he could have murdered the girls with such savagery—and left nothing."

They were right, Sophie knew.

They reached her house; Jackson was heading immediately back to the hospital.

When Jackson had gone, Bruce pulled out the plans to the old burial ground and studied them, as well.

"Johnstone—they must have been an influential family. They have a huge family plot, except that the plot goes way underground. Look!"

He was sitting on the sofa, and she'd curled up comfortably next to him.

"I saw that," Sophie said. "I think that there is some kind of entry at either the foot or the head—I mean, the way the coffins are stacked... I don't think there could be an entry through one of the coffins. No room. But the way they're stacked, it looks as if there could be a doorway at either end of the pyramid stacks."

"And it could go deep." He was quiet a minute. "It could even connect."

"Connect to?"

"The missing chunk of foundation—or, what's missing when you see plans of the cemetery that were drawn up after that quake."

They heard a car, and then a knock at the door. Brodie was back from his turn on guard duty at the hospital.

He sat and listened as they told him about the Hollywood Hooligans, the performance, the fact that a slew of people might have masks, and that Jackson was arranging to get them back into the church and graveyard. He reminded them that Jackson had just come to the hospital to relieve him, so Vining was caught up as well, and still chafing to get out of the hospital.

"That's a print of the plans Angela sent? Can I see?"

"Of course," Sophie said, handing them over.

He studied the plans, and agreed with Sophie's theory. "Johnstone. I think you have something there. Of course, with anything that old, it's still a long shot," he said.

Then Brodie yawned mightily.

Sophie realized that they were sitting where he slept, and she jumped up. "We'll take this up in the morning!"

"Bright and early," Brodie said. He stretched out the minute they vacated the sofa.

"Brodie, there are sheets and pillows!" Sophie said. "They're just folded—"

"Good night. I could sleep sitting up right now," he said.

Bruce shrugged and urged Sophie down the hall.

As they went into her bedroom, it occurred to Sophie that they had already acquired a weird little ritual. First thing—guns. They went on each bedside table, snug in their little holsters.

Then...

They looked at one another. There could have been a discussion about whether they needed sleep most, or if anyone was in the mood, if...

No discussion.

Sophie practically flew across the bed into his arms. He kissed and touched her, and they were back to their other ritual, busy discarding one another's clothing, and their own clothing, and creating wild piles of fabric wherever.

Then they were tight to each other's bodies. And lips, fingertips, were everywhere on flesh, and some caresses were tender, and some were passionate, until they were fit together, locked together, rolling, whispering, laughing...and then just moving, writhing, arching...and feeling.

But that night, when she lay in his arms, she couldn't help but wonder. What was she going to do when it was over? She hadn't felt this alive in so long she couldn't remember when.

All she knew for certain was that no matter what the future brought, they had to find this killer. Tomorrow, they'd revisit the graveyard. And this time, they would find out what was going on.

She lay next to him, trying to cherish the time when they just rested, so close.

Finally she slept, and didn't dream, until her phone rang. She woke up, startled. She knew, instinctively, that it wasn't a waking-up-time of morning.

She glanced at the bedside alarm clock. Four a.m.

She fumbled for her phone.

She saw that the call was coming from Kenneth Trent and answered it immediately.

"Kenneth. What's wrong?"

"She's missing!" he said.

"Who's missing?"

"Grace—Grace Leon."

Her heart thudded, but she remained calm and logical. "Kenneth, we just saw Grace. She was in your show."

"But she didn't turn up after the performance…she wasn't where she said she'd be. What if she…what if she fell for something, auditioned after the show, *more* than auditioned for another show—for a golden opportunity."

That puzzled Sophie. It wouldn't be an unheard of thing that Grace had more than "auditioned" or that there had been more to her audition than just some line reading. It wouldn't have been with Kenneth, of course.

Kenneth Trent was gay, and he had a partner; from everything they had seen and heard, he had a sound relationship.

There really shouldn't be any kind of audition she would have gone to after the show—that late at night. True, there were so many different kinds of projects that went on in LA, and perhaps even late at night, but, at this point in time—would Grace have fallen for anything happening at odd hours?

Bruce was up, leaned on an elbow, watching as she spoke.

"Kenneth, where was she supposed to be?"

Kenneth hesitated on the other end. Then he began to talk. "She…okay, so, when I did the casting for my show, I was torn—it might have gone to Grace, but it could also have been another girl who auditioned. Except Perry—Perry Sykes, he played Dudley tonight—had a thing going with her. Grace, I mean. He talked me into taking Grace. I mean, she was good, but it was between her and the other girl, and Perry said that it should be Grace. They were meeting after the show—Grace and Perry—and with the cleanup and the wind-down…and we finished at eleven, and they were both still chatting with different people after. We had some agents there tonight, and a few directors and producers. But Perry had taken a room at a hotel back here in LA…that new boutique place on Sunset, kind of between the Mondrian and the Best Western. Something really special, something to celebrate opening night, her first role…and the two of them. But she didn't show. Perry went to her house, but she wasn't there. Oh, and she had texted him at midnight. 'I'll be right there. Can't wait.' Detective Manning, you don't write a text like that and then…don't show. Or don't be anywhere. She's missing. I know she's an adult. I know the rules are that you're not missing until twenty-four or forty-eight hours or whatever, but please! Help me…help us!"

"Okay, I'm getting up. We'll get right on it. What kind of a car does she drive? I'll get an APB out on her right away. We'll find her, Kenneth."

"After what happened to Lili, I'm so worried about Grace. Please, I'm so scared."

"I'm on it, Kenneth. Her car?"

"An old Ford…wait… I'm with Perry."

The phone was handed over.

"This is Perry. I have her license plate number."

"You do?"

He cleared his throat. "I paid a ticket for her." He rattled off the number. Sophie scrambled to the bedside table for a notepad.

Bruce saw what she was doing.

He was dialing Jackson before she finished writing.

"I'm back at the hotel. It's called Sunrise, Sunset. We'll be here, I guess. Unless we can do something else."

"Just stay where you are. We'll call the Malibu police," Sophie said. "We'll get in touch with you as soon as possible. Stay where you are. If something did happen—maybe Grace lost her phone—she might still come to you. Don't move."

Perry agreed.

Sophie didn't really think that Grace Leon was going to show up at the hotel.

She didn't want Perry Sykes—who sounded so frantic—out on the road.

Bruce was already up, reaching for his clothing, cell phone pressed to his ear with his shoulder as he dressed and spoke to Jackson at the same time.

Sophie called Captain, waking him, to report Kenneth's call. "I'll get cops in Malibu searching right away, since that's where the show was," he said. "But, Sophie...maybe this girl just decided to do something else tonight."

"Maybe. But I don't think so."

"Okay, I'll take care of official channels."

"I'm going back to the graveyard."

"Sophie, we searched."

"Yes, yes, we did. But, Captain, you won't believe it. I can already hear someone screaming from that graveyard—I can hear them all the way over here."

She quickly hung up; she wasn't going to give him a chance to argue.

She turned and looked at Bruce. He didn't try to argue with her, either.

"Let's go," he said.

She was ready.

They ran out to the living room. Brodie was already up, too. "Good thing I didn't put on my pajamas. Where are we going?"

"You—back to the hospital," Bruce told his brother and added, "Please. Jackson is the official one here, so if you don't mind."

"I live to serve!" Brodie promised.

He was out the door before them.

Both cars revved at the same time. Sophie was grateful they were all on the same page, moving at top speed.

She didn't need a ghost at the moment to tell her that they were going in the right direction. Cop's gut instinct.

Something was going to happen.

Something that would take them in the right direction, closing in on the killer.

Sunday, the wee hours

The traffic was light—still existent, of course—it was, after all, LA.

But it was an easy drive, comparatively, to leave Sophie's place in Los Feliz and head to the old church.

Bruce reckoned that he'd also gotten good at maneuvering around LA. Then again, he'd spent most of his adult life in DC and the surrounding communities; the Beltway could be a nightmare.

It was barely Sunday morning.

And, yet, like Sophie, he believed that their killer had struck again.

They were halfway to the church and graveyard when Sophie's phone rang; it was Captain, reporting that Grace Leon's car had been found.

Her car was found parked in a lot—not back in Malibu, but off Sunset.

"She must have left the inn, headed in to meet Perry Sykes as she said she was going to—and then been waylaid," Sophie said. "Bruce, Henry was at the play. He drove there with Lee Underwood and Dr. Thompson."

"And they all had plenty of time to get back here. An hour out to Malibu, maybe, maybe a bit more, maybe a bit less," he said. "Any of them might have taken Grace."

"How could she have been fooled by any of them? And why in God's name—knowing what happened to Lili Montana and Brenda Sully—would she go with anyone?"

"Maybe he's changing up his operation," Bruce suggested. "We know that Brenda and Lili were lured first to the studio. Then, they were taken for their 'audition' to the graveyard."

"How the hell does this guy have a key?" Sophie murmured.

He glanced her way. "How the hell did he have a key to your apartment?"

"Because he is someone I work with," she said.

They had reached the graveyard. He barely drew the car to a halt; Sophie was out of it.

She was already heading toward the place in the old stone wall where they had gone over before.

He had to hurry to get the key out of the ignition and run to her side. She was waiting; he hopped up and reached down for her.

They made it up on the wall and then hopped down into the graveyard. As they made their way through the shrubs and broken stones toward the church and the Johnstone set of family tombs, Sophie was whispering urgently.

"Michael! Ann Marie! Where are you?"

She stopped dead, staring at the Johnstone tomb.

"Michael!"

Bruce started studying the tomb. It was possible that there was some kind of a secret closure on one of what appeared to be cement sarcophagi—but it did seem that they were solid and aged. They had figured that the opening had to be at one of the ends.

He started to move around the tomb, but the ghost of Michael Thoreau—hand in hand with the ghost of Ann Marie—was hurrying toward Sophie.

"Hey!" Michael said.

"What's gone on here tonight?" Sophie asked.

Michael looked at Ann Marie, shrugging as he looked back at Sophie.

"Um—nothing," Michael said.

"That we know about," Ann Marie said.

"There haven't been any screams? Nothing? Did anyone open the gate?" Sophie demanded.

"Um…" Michael said.

"We didn't hear any screams. We would have heard screams," Ann Marie said.

Michael admitted, "We weren't by the gate. We were...we've been talking and working on..."

"He's been teaching me how to concentrate and appear—to those who can see us. We've been very busy," Ann Marie said.

"No screams," Sophie said, and she appeared to be perplexed. "Oh, Bruce, if I am wrong, if there's nothing out here, no one out here..."

"No screams," Bruce said. "But if Michael and Ann Marie weren't paying attention..."

"Damn, we're so sorry," Michael said, horrified. "But honestly..."

"What if he has another girl?" Ann Marie asked, stricken.

"Still, we should have heard," Michael said.

"Not if he was quick—as he would have been," Bruce said. He looked at Sophie, and she knew that she was really worried.

For Grace Leon, first.

And then, of course, if she didn't find anything here, her credibility would wind up being in question.

"We're going to find something," he said, determined. He gave her a serious nod. "We will find something. We will find Grace."

Alive! he prayed.

As he made his way around the steps, he forced himself to use logic. Grace Leon was missing—and she should have been with Perry Sykes.

But then again, they didn't know Grace.

Maybe she'd changed her mind.

Maybe she had gone to the home of a girlfriend.

But she wasn't answering her phone. She wasn't responding to texts. And her car had been abandoned.

Bruce could hear a car door opening and closing from somewhere; Jackson and the FBI or more members of the police department must have arrived.

He was at the head of the tomb. He scanned it, then began to touch it. The damned thing just appeared to be sealed cement.

"Bruce!"

Sophie called out to him from around the other end of the stacked tombs.

"Bruce!"

The last call of his name sounded...breathless.

Almost...

Strangled off.

He ran around the tomb as quickly as he could.

Well, he hadn't found the entrance. Sophie had.

She'd pushed...and the wall of "cement" had swung inward, revealing...

Steps.

Down into stygian darkness.

But...

No Sophie.

She had disappeared. Right down the flight of stone steps that led into that hellhole of black.

Sophie gasped, trying to regain her breath. She felt like an idiot; she'd pushed hard—and fallen.

The impetus of her own weight had brought her careening down the stairs.

She moved each of her limbs; she was all right. She fumbled in the darkness, finding her penlight.

Even as she did so, she was aware of an odor. It was an odor of rot and decay, an odor of the earth...and more.

It was the smell of rot. Rotting, putrid blood.

She sat up and leaped quickly to her feet, looking around. At first, her little light did little. She saw the death of decades; family members in broken, rotting coffins, the stacks inside the catacomb built to align with the steps outside and above the ground. Some had been interred and then cement closed over the coffin slots.

Some…just lay there.

A bony hand, barely connected to bony arm through mummified flesh, dangled from one. The rot had touched everything.

That was time. The ravages that time played upon human flesh.

She heard a squeal; a rat raced over her foot.

She played her flashlight more deeply into the tomb.

And then, she saw her.

A woman, alive, her clothing half ripped from her body, and tied down on what should have been a cover to a tomb. Her hands had been stretched high above her head and tied, her feet had been trussed together, and then tied to some kind of stakes that protruded from the makeshift marble bed.

"My God!" Sophie breathed. She started to race forward; she stopped, going for her gun, and then waving her light around the place.

"Sophie!"

She heard Bruce; he was calling to her frantically.

"Here! I'm here," she cried. "Hurry!"

She could hear his footsteps on the stone stairs that led down.

Having sent her light over the space and finding no one else— no one living at least—she hurried toward the woman who was tied to the slab.

It was Grace. As she reached her, Grace started to scream.

"It's all right. It's all right," Sophie said. "It's Detective Manning. You're all right."

"No, no, no, no!" Grace cried, ripping against her restraints. "Help, oh, God, help me, help me, help me!"

"I'm trying to help you!" Sophie declared.

Grace looked at Sophie. Her eyes were wild and disoriented.

Sophie dug in her pocket for a knife and slit the bindings holding Grace; she had managed to cut her arms free when Bruce reached her. He pulled his pocketknife out and freed her from the ropes about her legs.

Grace tried to sit up. Sophie reached for her; Bruce dialed for an ambulance, but of course, by then, it seemed that sirens were screaming all around the street.

"You...who...oh, God, oh, God, where am I?" She looked around, and a scream tore from her lips.

She started to fight Sophie. "No, no, no, please, God, don't hurt me, don't..."

"It's Detective Manning, Grace. I'm not going to hurt you. But who did this? Who brought you here? Please, Grace..."

"My car... Perry... I have to meet Perry... No, no, no... I don't know..."

"We're not going to get anything from her right now. Maybe later," Bruce said. "Sophie, she has to get to a hospital."

"Of course," Sophie said. She tried to help Grace. She was strong, but Grace was dead weight, barely coherent, and fighting her, though Sophie doubted that she meant to.

Bruce stepped in.

As he lifted Grace up, Sophie saw that she was covered in earth and dust and...something red.

And then she realized. It was the blood she had smelled.

Not so fresh, after a week.

Blood.

Blood...probably belonging to Lili or Brenda.

Sticky...dried, rotting...

She swallowed hard.

She had to remember that they had just found Grace alive. And finding the young woman alive...

"Let's get her up," Bruce said.

"They're coming."

The sirens were now almost deafening.

Sophie used her light to illuminate the steps first for Bruce, who made his way up carrying the wildly mumbling and flailing Grace Leon. She followed behind him, but then paused.

They'd found Grace.

Thank God, they had found her alive.

But they had found her alone.

There was no trace of the killer.

How the hell had he gotten Grace down there—and how the hell had he gotten out and gotten away so quickly?

They reached the top step and were back out in the night air—air that now seemed incredibly cool and sweet.

The police had simply used a metal cutter on the gate; cops, forensic people and others were quickly flooding the graveyard.

Luckily, paramedics were already with them. Bruce handed Grace over to one of the young men; he quickly laid her down while his partner joined him, calling in to speak with a doctor as others came forward with a gurney.

Jackson Crow stood at the no-longer hidden door to the tomb. "Anything?" he asked Bruce.

Bruce shook his head. "Sophie?"

"No. She thought I was going to hurt her."

Bruce shook his head. "Don't know with what, don't know how badly, but this time, she was drugged. She may know something, but I think that she was attacked, and didn't see whoever took her, and I think she was just coming to when Sophie went flying down into the tomb."

How did he know that she hadn't simply walked down the steps? Ah, probably the dust and grime and tomb rot that was surely covering her now.

"I'll go to the hospital with Grace," Jackson offered.

"Sophie may want—"

"No," Sophie said quickly. "I need to get back down there, Bruce."

He looked at her. "I intend to search, you know."

One paramedic was receiving instructions from the doctor who would meet them at the hospital. Sophie heard him giving details about Grace's pulse and other vital signs.

Then they were carrying her away to the waiting ambulance. Jackson hurried after.

Captain Chagall had arrived and hurried over to Sophie.

"You found her! Alive. Is the killer here?"

She shook her head. "He's got to be somewhere close. But I don't know where. I'm going to get back down there. I need a floodlight."

"Floodlight!" Chagall called out.

An officer, grim and pale, hurried over to her with a large floodlight. She turned, allowing the light to flood the tomb.

"More lights!" Chagall called out. "Sophie, careful what you touch. McFadden, will you go with her?"

"Yes, Captain, of course!" Bruce said, following Sophie down.

Someone from the forensic team, a paper mask over his nose and mouth, gloves on his hands and paper booties over his shoes, came hurrying after them.

"Detective Manning!"

It was Lee Underwood. She had a feeling that he'd just been dragged out of bed to be here.

"Gloves, Sophie, Bruce."

Sophie accepted them, sliding them on quickly.

Another light flooded the place.

Chagall was descending the stairs with his own flashlight.

Sophie began to explain. "We found her on that slab. It's been set up on broken tombstones. And there...not sure what those spikes are at each end. Her hands were tied over her head, the ropes attached to that spike. Her feet were bound together, and then attached down there, to that spike."

"Son of a bitch," Lee Underwood swore. He'd backed into an

old coffin, right at the place where an earthquake had broken up the concrete seal. The coffin bounced out and to the floor.

A skeleton, with partially mummified skin and tattered remnants of clothing, burst out of the decaying coffin.

"Underwood. What the hell?" Chagall said.

"Captain, not his fault—it's all decayed down here," Sophie said.

"There's blood all over. We need samples, tons of them," Chagall said. "We need fibers, hair, you name it. Underwood, get your boss, get everyone—and quit knocking the long-dead around, all right?"

"Yes, sir!" Underwood said.

Someone else was coming down the steps, an officer, with yet more light.

He was followed by Henry Atkins.

"Grace Leon, alive. Thank God." He saw Sophie and beamed. "You saved her—I just got the call from Captain."

"Kenneth Trent called Sophie," Bruce explained.

"But...how did he know?" Henry asked, bewildered.

"He just knew that she wasn't where she was supposed to be," Bruce explained.

He was studying Henry.

It appeared that Henry had just been awakened.

As they all had been.

"Where did he go?" Sophie murmured. "The killer...he got her here. And then...where the hell did he go?"

"Sophie, you're something. How did you find this place?" Henry asked.

"It's getting crowded down here," Chagall said, ignoring Henry. "I'm moving out. Manning, McFadden, do your looking, then let the forensic team do their jobs before we turn the whole damn thing into a pile of bone and ash."

There was really nothing else to see. Whoever had brought Grace there was gone.

Their hopes of catching him lay with the forensic team.

"Water—where did he get the water to wash the bodies?" she asked. "And his tools—where are the tools he used to slash them and bisect them?"

"I don't see anything," Underwood told her.

Henry Atkins was already busy setting up his camera.

"Let's head up. With all the commotion, he's probably long gone. He might even have left Grace here alone for hours, and been nowhere near here when we arrived. But maybe we'll find something in the graveyard," Bruce said.

She nodded. But as Bruce headed toward the stairs, he suddenly stopped and looked back at the tomb slab where Grace had been tied down.

He walked back toward Sophie and the slab.

Sophie was next to him, but he was seeing just beyond the slab. She moved slightly to manage to get to his range of vision.

And she saw what he had seen.

Tiny, and hard up against the shored-up earth wall at the rear of the large catacomb.

It was a boutonniere. A boutonniere like those worn by the "guests" who had attended the night's performance by the Hollywood Hooligans.

Its petals were smashed.

Petals could have been smashed on any of the roses worn that night.

But this rose was different.

The petals weren't just red, as most of the boutonnieres had been. They were hybrid, red and yellow. *Just like the rose she had seen on Henry Atkins.*

CHAPTER SIXTEEN

Sunday, break of dawn

Bruce straightened, letting Sophie pick up the mangled rose boutonniere with her gloved hands.

He turned to look at Henry, who was already busy shooting pictures.

Chagall was staring at Bruce; he turned, curiously, when he realized that Bruce was looking at Henry Atkins.

"What? What is it?" Captain Chagall demanded.

"This," Sophie said, her voice weak. She, too, was staring at Henry.

Lee Underwood gasped.

Henry put down his camera, interested in what was going on.

"What? What is it?" Henry asked.

"It's the rose you were wearing," Sophie said, staring at Henry.

"The rose I was wearing?" Henry Atkins appeared to be truly confused. "The rose? Oh, you mean from the show? I must have just dropped it. Can't believe it—I never contaminate a scene."

"Henry," Sophie said, and her voice was torn. "You didn't

just drop it—you're not wearing the same clothing you had on at the show." She added, "And you just got here—you were never even at this end of the tombs!"

"No. No. You all can't be serious. I mean, how do you know that's the rose I was wearing?" Henry demanded.

"I saw it when it was still on you. It was colored differently than most people's, and crushed in this peculiar way," Sophie said. Her voice remained a tight, thin stream.

"Sophie! Hey, you guys, come on! You can't be serious. I work with you every day."

He was looking from person to person as he spoke, desperate for someone to pipe in and help him out.

Everyone just stared back at him.

"Sophie, what is this thing?" Captain Chagall demanded. "What is it about the rose?"

"Everyone had one—everyone who went to that performance," Henry said. "*Everyone.* Captain—"

Chagall spun on Sophie and Bruce. "Everyone had one? You didn't drop this?" He turned to Lee Underwood. "You were at that performance, too."

"Mine is back on the jacket I was wearing," Lee said. "I can prove that right now—it's out in my car." He appeared stunned—and just as sick and disbelieving as Sophie. "Henry, sweet Jesus! We were supposed to have some drinks after the show, but you said that you were tired, that you were heading back. Oh, God, I don't believe it, Henry…"

"Don't believe it—because it isn't true!" Henry protested. "I wasn't the one who bugged out on everyone first. I was still game for drinks, remember? I said I was tired only after Chuck Thompson decided to blow off drinks!" Henry said.

To his credit, Bruce thought, Henry did look like a deer caught in the headlights—completely stunned by what he was suddenly facing.

Henry's voice grew desperate. "Listen, Captain, Sophie—
don't look at me like that. It's a rose. Every one of you had one
of those roses, too. Okay, so, Sophie, that couldn't be yours, the
women's roses were different, but… Lee, you had one. Bruce,
you had one. Some other petals might have broken. Anyone's
petals might have broken."

"Yes, they might have, Henry," Sophie said. She was barely
whispering. "But I saw yours…saw the way the petals had been
crushed on it. And yours was different. Yours had a mix in the
color of the petals. Not just red. It was red and yellow." She
paused, looking at Henry as if her heart was breaking. "I didn't
see any others like it. Yours was…just like this…"

"I know when you crushed your boutonniere. The scene we
were both in with Mary. It was when she hugged you. It crushed
when Mary Tudor hugged you!" Lee whispered. "I remember."

Henry shook his head.

"I didn't do this. I would never hurt anyone."

He appeared so completely honest. But it was true. There was
no doubt it was the rose Henry had been wearing. Crushed in
the same manner. With the little tinge of yellow in the petals.

"Henry. We're going to need to talk," Captain Chagall said.

"Captain," Henry cried. "I didn't do this thing!"

"Henry, I'm going to have to ask you to step up and out of this
catacomb—and the graveyard," Chagall said. His voice was hard.

Henry looked as if he was about to cry. "Captain! I retire
soon. How could you…how could any of you believe that I…
that I could have done anything so horrible!"

"Henry, I have to ask you to step out."

"But—"

"We'll find out, Henry. We're going to dust and fingerprint—
and we'll find out," Chagall said quietly.

"You've got to be kidding me!" Henry protested again. "I
mean, what if it is my flower? The ushers gave them to everyone.

Every man. I might have had it attached to my clothing when I got here. It might have just fallen off when I came down here. Captain, I was sound asleep. You called me and I woke up and got dressed fast as possible."

"I understand that," Chagall said.

"Captain, this is ridiculous."

"That's as it may be," Chagall said quietly. "But, Henry, one of your photos made it into the paper. You'd been to see the Hooligans—"

"Half the city has been to see the Hooligans," Henry protested.

"Henry, will you come with me, please?" Chagall said.

"Are you arresting me?" Henry demanded.

"I'm holding you—for now. I want to give you the benefit of the doubt," Chagall told him. "We're going to talk."

"You're going to interrogate me. I know the tactics."

"Under these circumstances, there is no choice but to bring you in—and investigate."

"This is all circumstantial."

"And damning, Henry. We have to work through this. You can give us your permission to search your home and your car, or I can get a warrant."

Henry stared back at him. "Search anything I own. I'm innocent, and I can't believe that you found a flower, and that you can immediately suspect me."

"Let's go," Chagall said quietly.

He indicated the stairs.

Henry looked around the little underground room of the dead, looking for help from someone.

Sophie spoke up. "Henry, if you're innocent, it will be proven. Or, I should say, you are innocent until you're proven guilty." Her tone was soft. Bruce felt a little pinch in his heart. Henry could be ghoulish. But he was her friend.

She didn't want to accept what was happening. She'd been suspicious—but being suspicious didn't mean that you wanted to believe.

Henry turned and walked heavily up the stairs.

Chagall nodded to them, and headed up after him, calling out to another member of the forensic team to pick up the camera.

"We're good here," Lee Underwood told Sophie. "We'll… keep working…"

His voice trailed.

Henry was his friend, too.

Sophie headed up the stairs. Bruce followed her.

He watched Sophie take a moment. Just breathing.

"Let's get out of here," Bruce said.

"It's not—finished," Sophie said. "It's like we got to the end… and it just wasn't right."

"Sophie, you were the first to bring up Henry as a suspect. Someone involved. Henry knows the Dahlia case. And, for now anyway, we found Grace—that's what is most important, certainly. Actually, *you* found Grace. And then… Henry's little rose," Bruce said. "Sophie, I sure as hell don't know how it got there—unless it was there before we found Grace."

She nodded, looking around.

"Bruce, he had Grace. I believe that the slab where she was tied was definitely where the killer slashed and murdered Lili and Brenda. But with what? Where are his tools?"

"I'm willing to bet that they'll find them. Stashed where a coffin should be. The forensic team will find them."

"And what about the water?"

"They'll find that, too," he told her. He looked around the burial ground. It was no longer crawling with techs and cops.

Most officers and the forensic team were below, working down in the catacombs. A few men and women could be seen, quietly watching the entrances to the cemetery and to the tomb.

And two lone techs were tracing the ground, meticulous as they did so, their pinpoint lights covering the ground inch by inch.

"There's got to be something we can do," she murmured. "We were going to search, to try to find whoever did that to her...or... Bruce, I just feel empty!"

"Home, Sophie. Let's go home." As he spoke, his phone rang. Jackson was on the other end. "Jackson—calling from the hospital," he told Sophie.

"She is going to be all right?"

He nodded, listening and conveying at the same time. "She will be fine. She has been drugged. They're working on figuring out just what kind of a cocktail she was given. He hasn't been able to see her yet, they're working with her, and she may be incoherent for some time. He's not leaving."

"What about Grant?" she asked anxiously.

More members of the forensic team moved by them, all respectfully acknowledging Sophie; in turn, she nodded sadly to the trio.

"Henry Atkins! Can you believe it?" the young woman in the group said as they passed.

"Come on, Henry is creepy," the tall young man in the group said. "I've been to his place. Have you seen all the pictures he has of crime scenes...blood and guts!"

"Oh, good! Judge him for that," the young woman said. "We're in forensics. We collect and study blood, bugs, urine... and other crap. We're all creepy as hell."

"I don't know about you, but I haven't disemboweled, cut up and murdered anyone," the tall man said.

"All for a picture," the third member of the group, a short, stout man with a receding hairline, put in, his voice a whisper.

They headed down the stone steps by the no-longer hidden door to the catacombs below.

Bruce waited until they were gone.

"I don't think that Grant is still in danger," Bruce murmured.

She shook her head. "I know that we should be... *Celebrating* isn't the right word. We should be relieved. Grateful, I guess. It seems...it seems it was Henry. There are still so many loose ends, so many explanations we need. But I just feel empty. And still afraid. I don't want Grant to be alone."

"Not to worry. Brodie is on with Grant. You know that."

"Brodie didn't get any sleep."

"That's all right. Brodie was in the army—a foot soldier who was in a few campaigns where they had to be awake and alert for hours on end. Brodie is all right for now—if he wasn't, trust me, he would tell me. For now, you need to get some sleep. You're going to want to talk to Henry Atkins tomorrow. And you're going to want to talk to Grace Leon. Sophie...this has been intense. Every waking minute for nearly a week solid."

She nodded. "We're not going to find Michael and Ann Marie," she said.

"Not with this much activity around—no, I don't believe we will."

"We may have found this killer, but we've done nothing for Michael," she murmured, "or Ann Marie."

He took her by her shoulders and met her eyes. "In the words of the great fictional Southern heroine, Miss Scarlet O'Hara— 'Tomorrow is another day!'"

She smiled weakly at that. "You've read *Gone With the Wind*?"

"Of course. My mother starred in a stage adaption. Naturally, we all read the book—and heard her emoting around the house, of course."

She smiled at that. "And your dad?"

"Oh, he was Rhett Butler, of course."

She looked at him strangely then, and quickly turned—as if afraid he would read her expression.

"You're right. Let's go."

They headed to the car.

It was morning in truth; the sun was rising over the City of Angels.

Sunday morning; traffic was coming alive, as if the city's hundreds of thousands of cars awoke to and were generated by the sun.

He had driven about half a mile when Sophie broke the silence. "Bruce, did you see his face? Henry's face. He was stunned. Absolutely stunned."

"Yes."

"You're not going to argue that? You're not going to tell me that he might be a fantastic actor himself?"

"No. He appeared stunned."

"Do you think we got it wrong somehow?"

"There's some damning—circumstantial—evidence against him. That was his rose. I didn't see another with the same coloring. Not on anyone—not all night. But then again, I wasn't studying every man's chest and boutonniere."

"What if someone planted it?" Sophie asked.

"Who? You? Me? Grace Leon?"

"Don't be sarcastic."

"I'm not. Sophie, I'm wondering, too. But it might just be that we can't believe it's over. You've got a dogged determination when you're on something—and then it's almost a letdown, as if you should still be drastically hurrying, when you get to a conclusion."

"Something just doesn't feel right yet."

He agreed with her. Tonight—or this morning—had been almost...

Too easy?

Anticlimactic?

"For now, sleep. When we wake up, we'll deal with all the questions. Sophie, there was nothing left for us to do there."

"We could have kept searching the graveyard—as we were going to do before—before we found the little rose."

"The place is crawling with cops and FBI agents."

"I know. But, Bruce, what if it isn't Henry?"

"You mean, what if he was being set up?"

"That's possible. I mean, okay, the man is a bit creepy. But I think you—and maybe others—made note of the fact that being creepy or ghoulish doesn't make you a murderer."

"No. But it does add to the possibilities."

The sun was almost bright when he parked in front of her house.

"Sleep," he said, and it sounded ironic.

"Shower," she said. "Bruce, look at me, smell me! It's horrible, that scent of blood."

He set the shower warm and steamy for her as she stripped. She stood under the spray for a long time. He was afraid for a minute that she'd fallen asleep in the water, and he helped her out, and helped her dry, and she smiled and allowed him to do so.

They slipped into bed. He held her.

He thought that she had drifted off when she said, "You'll be leaving."

He pulled her tighter to him.

It was true; LA wasn't his home. He knew that through the investigation—working as a "consultant" for Jackson—he had begun to feel, the way that Bryan surely had, that being a Krewe member might be a very interesting way of making use of his friendships with many who were dead.

And if he joined them, the Krewe worked out of Northern Virginia.

"I won't be leaving until all the questions are answered," he said. "There's a lot…seeing if Henry cracks, if he confesses. Hoping that the teams did find the killer's murder tools. The water supply. And we have Grace Leon. She may know something, remember something."

She didn't reply. A few minutes later, he realized that she was sleeping.

He held her tight.

And slept alongside her.

Sunday, noon

The day began with a sweet dream.

Sophie was resting, sweetly comfortable in cool, clean sheets. The air conditioner hummed. She felt a feather-like touch down her back, a sweet and subtle caress that seemed to tease and ever so sensually arouse.

Another touch, so light at first, bringing a liquid heat that seemed to grow. She stretched luxuriously, feeling that slow, simmering, burn.

She moved into just gradually awakening.

She was with a man. Bruce. A man she was coming to crave.

And the touch was going on and on...

That brush of fingers, stroke of hand, and those kisses, moving over her breasts, then midriff, belly, down to her knees, up to her thighs and then...

Then she was wide-awake. Body on fire. Arching, writhing, searching.

He rose above her, eyes on hers, and they were together, moving and moving.

Fire roared all around her, entered her blood, her limbs... her soul.

Beautiful. The sweetest dream, but real, flesh and blood, flesh that still lay hot and deliciously damp next to her own.

She exhaled a sigh.

He rolled and perched up on an elbow and told her with some amusement, "This is what a Sunday should look like. Okay, if you were a beat cop, you might work Sundays. But you're a detective now. You've got other cops backing you up. You don't have to work every moment."

"I've noticed just how much you don't work when you're on a case," she told him gravely.

He shrugged. "Sometimes, I'm not so bad. I have faith in my brothers—and in others when we've worked together. Now, if it were another Sunday, we could get an old-fashioned real live newspaper. I could hop up and make us coffee, and then we could sip it together in bed. Then you could hop up and make omelets, and we—"

"Oh, no. My omelets are god-awful, Bruce."

"Okay, I can make the omelets."

"However, I do prepare a really mean turkey. And—though I have no clue why—a great Hungarian goulash."

"Good. Then, I would cook breakfast, and later—when we've hung around in bed all day, reading the paper, maybe heading to a park or a museum, you could whip up dinner."

"Probably much better that way. Bruce?"

"Yes?"

"I actually do get the paper. And I can make coffee."

It might have been a cue—her phone rang. Then his phone rang.

"On a different Sunday," Bruce muttered.

He reached for his phone.

She grabbed hers.

It was Captain Chagall that Sophie said hello to.

"I thought that you'd want to know, Sophie. Grace Leon is awake and aware. And asking for you. I'm here at the hospital. I have Henry stewing in an interrogation room at the station. Anyway, come see Grace. Then you can be with me when I start on Henry."

"Yes, sir," Sophie said quickly, glancing at Bruce.

His face was strange.

She rose, ending her call.

"What is it?"

"The LA FBI office led the search of Henry's home," he said.

"And? Blood?" she asked. "Bloody clothing? Trinkets—trophies he took from his victims?"

He shook his head.

"Bruce!"

He hesitated just a moment longer. "They found a high-powered sniper's gun. Military issue. It's a USMC Hi-Lux—brand-new, really expensive. They found it under Henry's bed."

"And the bullets fired from it will match what went after Grant Vining—and me."

"They're testing it now."

She shook her head. "I've always seen Henry with a camera lens."

"Well, he knows how to focus," Bruce said drily. "That's for sure. We're going to the hospital?"

"As soon as possible."

He was up and headed for the bathroom door. He turned and stopped her—even though she hadn't followed him. "Nope, nope, gotta do this one alone, no matter how badly you want to rush in!"

She laughed. "I don't mean to stomp on any ego, but... I'll be fine."

"The problem isn't you," he told her. "It's me."

He hurried in; he was out in approximately three minutes.

They were in the car and headed to the hospital before a full ten minutes from start to finish had gone by.

She smiled, leaning back in the car.

Nice to have a guy who could move...

In so many ways.

"What?" Bruce asked.

"You're good. Really good."

"Thank you."

"No, I meant at getting ready to leave."

"Oh, well. Okay, thank you for that, too. So are you. Not many women can begin to move so quickly."

"Hey! Not just women. When we were young, Andrew..."

Her voice trailed but he cast a smile her way. "Andrew?"

"He had way more hair-care products than me!"

He smiled. Then he seemed to be serious when he asked her, "So you don't mind that I've hogged the driving."

She laughed, closing her eyes and leaning back.

"Hell, no. I spend way too much time swearing at other drivers on the expressways. Go for it!"

The general feeling seemed to be one of elation—mixed with sadness. Not a week had gone by and this case with a horrendous killer consuming the force, the media and everyone involved, was almost at a conclusion.

A suspect had been arrested.

A patrolman showed them a newspaper while they were waiting to meet up with Captain Chagall at the hospital.

"Copycat Dahlia Killer Caught!"

"How the hell do they get this stuff so fast?" Bruce wondered as he scanned the article. He looked down at Sophie; he'd been reading over her shoulder.

"I don't think Chagall wanted any of this. I mean, Henry hasn't even been questioned yet—he hasn't been officially charged!"

"They don't name him—but they do say that 'an anonymous source' has informed them that the police are holding one of their own."

"It had turned to day when we left," Sophie said. "Maybe

the media swarmed the graveyard after. God knows, there were enough people wandering around."

Chagall came into the waiting room. He saw them reading the newspaper and he shook his head with disgust. "I don't know who the hell our leak is. I'm going to have to hold a press conference because of this and tell them what we want them to know."

"You would have had to speak with reporters today no matter what, Captain," Sophie said. "What are you going to tell them?"

"That we are holding a suspect. You know about the sniper's rifle, right?"

Sophie nodded.

"Evidence is mounting up."

"But you still haven't questioned Henry?" Bruce asked.

"No—I still have hours left before we have to charge him. He spent the night at the station—behind bars. He's been raging and spitting—but hasn't asked for an attorney yet. When Sophie is finished with Grace Leon, we'll head to the station."

"Have you spoken with Grace?" Sophie asked him.

He nodded.

"And?" she pressed.

The captain shook his head. "You ask your questions. Sometimes, people word things differently, and we get different answers. This time? I don't think that will happen. But she's specifically asked to see you. She's in 407. There's a cop sitting right outside her door."

Bruce raised his eyebrows at that. Either the captain was by nature a very careful man, or he wasn't so certain that they'd caught the right person.

"Come on."

Sophie actually took his hand as she headed down the hospital hallway, looking for room 407.

There was a chair for the officer outside her door, but he was standing. He nodded to the two of them.

"Afternoon!" he said.

"Hi," Sophie replied. Before she headed in, she paused. "Officer... Bartlett." She read his name off his name tag. "You okay? Do you want coffee, or anything? Are they looking after you?"

"Nurses and LPNs here are great—I'm offered everything. But thank you, Detective Manning. Sir," he added, nodding to Bruce. Bruce nodded and smiled in turn. He knew why Sophie was admired by her fellows; she was polite to and appreciative of others. She could be caring with victims and witnesses; she could also be strong and determined—and find out what she needed to know before becoming concerned and nice.

When they walked into the room, Grace Leon was sitting up in bed.

She had makeup on and her hair had been brushed.

But she cried out to the two of them. "Detective Manning... Mr. McFadden. Thank you! Thank you from the bottom of my heart. I can never thank you enough. I'm alive. Oh, God, I'm alive. And I was so rude to you, Sophie. I was such a bitch. But you understand I was protecting Kenneth. I had to. He's a really good guy. Trying so hard. I beg you—forgive me! I was so rude—and you saved my life, anyway."

Sophie was uncomfortable, Bruce knew.

"We're very glad you're alive, Grace," he said.

"It's all right. We all act badly sometimes. Not act—you're a very good actress—behave badly," Sophie amended. "But, please, it's my job—" She glanced at Bruce "It's our job...all of us with law enforcement. It's what we do. And we're incredibly grateful when we do get somewhere in time to save an innocent victim."

"I would do anything for you guys!" Grace said. She glanced at Sophie, and then at Bruce. He really didn't like to think too much of himself, but he knew her look. She made it pretty clear. "Anything," she repeated.

"We just need to know what happened last night," Bruce said.

"The show...you saw the show. The guy who plays Dudley... Perry. Perry Sykes. He and I are... We're seeing each other."

"Yes," Sophie said. "It's thanks to Perry and Kenneth that we found you."

Grace nodded. "I owe them so much."

"Go on, Grace, please," Bruce pressed.

"Okay, so...there's not much, I'm afraid. I was talking to a lot of people after the show. So was Perry. Perry helped me get the role." She was quiet. "It had been Lili's role."

"We know," Sophie said. "Grace, please. Last night?"

"I'm getting there, I'm getting there...it's just not much," Grace said. "I parked my car in the lot off Sunset. I thought I'd be plenty safe—it was maybe near 1:00 a.m., but hey, on a Saturday night on Sunset, that's not late. I felt safe. Plenty of people. Except..."

"Except?" Bruce said, hiding his impatience and speaking quickly.

"From there, I don't know!" she whispered. "I got out of the car, I locked it—and there was a bag over my head. I don't even know what kind of a bag. But it was soaked in stuff. I don't know what. The doctors say I was drugged, but by what, I don't know. I didn't drink anything—except water at the show—and I drove to Sunset Strip from Malibu, so...anyway. The bag came over my head, and I was drugged. I think he was big... I think," she whispered. "Strong."

"You never heard him speak? Did he wear cologne, or was there anything else you noticed? Maybe he was a smoker and you could smell it on him. Anything?" Sophie asked.

"No, nothing." Grace's brow furrowed in a frown. "Except... oh, well, that could mean nothing."

"What?" Sophie managed not to shout.

"Roses. I kept smelling roses," Grace said, "but then, we give them away at the show, so that doesn't mean anything." She paused, and visibly shivered. "Oh, I'm shaking again. I barely re-member you finding me, but I remember waking...cold stone... and...blood. Oh, God, that awful scent of blood. Blood and roses."

They weren't getting anything else out of Grace Leon.

Bruce turned to go.

Sophie murmured a thank you and followed.

"Hey!" Grace called. They paused. "Thank you," she whis-pered.

It sounded sincere. Bruce almost liked the young woman.

But then, she added, "Oh, Lord! Thank you! I'm not just alive, I'm going to be really famous. Reporters are coming! I'm the one who survived. They may even buy my story...there might be a book. A play. And then a movie. I can star as myself!"

Bruce set a hand on the small of Sophie's back, urging her to-ward the door with a little bit of force.

Grace had survived, yes.

But one of them just might turn around and smack her.

CHAPTER SEVENTEEN

Sunday afternoon

Henry Atkins had pushed his hair back so many times that it was almost standing straight up on the front of his forehead.

He'd spent the night in a cell—in solitary.

And he was now under arrest.

The ballistics expert had reported that the high-powered sniper rifle found beneath his bed was the weapon that had been used to strike Grant Vining, and which had also been used to shoot a bullet into a stone in the old burial ground. Why, none of them knew.

Except, of course, Sophie and Bruce.

As yet.

Henry wasn't talking to Captain Chagall or anyone else. He had said, however, that he would talk to Sophie.

He was awaiting his attorney.

He had chosen a husband and wife team with an exceptional reputation, Esther and Nathan Holloway, and they had agreed to take his case. The couple had been, however, vacationing in

Palm Springs when Henry had called; they would be with him
when he was arraigned on Monday morning.

Sophie stood with Captain Chagall, looking through the two-
way mirror into the interrogation room.

"He looks like he might have a heart attack," Sophie murmured.

"We're watching him. It might be a mercy that he's under arrest. His blood pressure was sky-high."

"Maybe being accused of murder does that to a man."

"Whether he is or isn't guilty," Chagall said, "this arrest might
have saved his life. He saw our doctor and he was given proper
medication. Bobby Dougherty has been observing him. Henry
has refused to speak with Dougherty—along with everyone
else—until he speaks with his attorneys."

"A smart move for most criminals," Bruce murmured.

"Criminals who are police photographers—sure. They know
all the techniques that cops use. But, Sophie, he has said that he
will talk to you. You ready?"

"Of course. He'll know you're watching," Sophie said.

"Yes, he will. But maybe he thinks he can play you somehow, Sophie."

"And maybe he's innocent," she murmured.

Captain Chagall sighed deeply. "I doubt it," he said softly. "We
just got another report from the forensic team. One of Henry's
fingerprints was found on the slab underground. He was never
over where that print was found," Chagall said.

"Maybe we didn't see every move he made," Sophie said.

"One of us had eyes on him at every moment. You and Bruce
were there, at the rear of the tomb. Sophie, I don't want to accept this, either. But between the fingerprint, and the crushed
rose and the rifle found under the bed..."

Sophie looked for Bruce. He had stepped aside and was on
the phone—with Jackson, she thought.

"Are you coming in?" she asked Bruce.

"He said only you," Chagall said.

"It's all right," Bruce said. "Captain, Sophie, I'm going to go ahead and meet Jackson outside—Angela has come up with more information on the burial ground. I'm going to get back out there, Captain. Henry doesn't want me, and Sophie doesn't need me. I'll call in a report about anything that the FBI research has managed to unearth." He grimaced. "Literally."

"We still have people out there," Captain Chagall said.

"So does Jackson," Bruce said, "as I'm sure you know. We'll coordinate all our efforts."

"Of course."

"What else has Angela found?" Sophie asked.

"Looks like more underground chambers," Bruce said. "If we can find the tools that the killer used…well, we all know that Henry is going to continue to deny everything. There is no way a man could have used a saw and a knife on a person and not left something behind. None of us knows the truth yet, and we need some more hard evidence."

"All right. McFadden, go. Sophie, get in there and see what you can get him to say."

Bruce turned to leave. Sophie watched him go and then opened the door to the interrogation room. Henry looked at her. "Sophie. Finally."

"Henry," she said, drawing out the chair across the plain metal desk from him. She sat, thinking of all the times she had been at that desk before, questioning suspects, reading them the best she could, and then cajoling, threatening, sympathizing… or just listening.

This was different. This was a man she knew. A strange man.

Maybe a guilty man.

And maybe just a loner who had really longed to be an artist—but had found a good living photographing and trying to read the signs in what the lens captured.

"Chagall is back there, right?" Henry asked. "Hey, Captain!" he called, waving to the one-way window.

"Of course, he's listening," Sophie said. "You know how everything works here. And you're probably smart to wait for your attorney. So, why me, Henry?"

He leaned forward. "Because you know that I didn't do this."

"Henry, I wish I knew that you didn't do this. But there is no way your rose could have been where it was—unless you'd been there. You never walked over to the stone slab. The rose was there."

"It was planted."

"By who?"

"By whoever kidnapped Grace Leon and brought her there."

"What about the sniper rifle—the one used to put Vining in the hospital."

"It isn't mine."

"It was under your bed."

"It still isn't mine."

"What if they find your prints?"

"They won't—whoever did this is smart enough to wipe everything down." He leaned toward her, his tone desperate. "Sophie, I did not do this thing. I could not do this thing. I study a lot of crime photographs. I wanted to travel the world once, get the great pictures. War in the Middle East, kings and queens ascending their thrones, violence in the streets—good things, bad things, murder and mayhem. It turned out that I became a police photographer. No kings and queens—but I did see the drug wars and the insanity of Los Angeles. Yes, I have crime scene photographs in my house. Some of them might seem grisly. I'll bet you old Dr. Chuck Thompson reads up on other autopsies or watches some of the shows on TV that feature the cases of other medical examiners. It's a work hazard. Tell me that you don't read about crimes and criminals and how they were caught and how they got away with it? I'm telling you, I didn't drop the rose. I have never owned a sniper rifle. I wasn't the one who fed the crime scene photo to the newspaper. I have had a call with my attorneys. I know that I will be out of here soon, and I might sue the department and everyone involved. This is all ludicrous."

Sophie watched him in silence for a minute. She knew that the sniper rifle found at his place was the one used to shoot Grant—and to shoot at her. But as far as she knew, Henry's prints had not been found on it. His prints on the rifle would have damned him entirely.

"Sophie, I was set up. Subtly, and bit by bit," Henry said.

"By who?"

He leaned back, shaking his head, and staring at her balefully. "If I knew that, I'd tell you—I'd be shouting it out, obviously! Maybe Kenneth Trent—he had access to the girls."

"He had an alibi."

"Friends lie."

"Henry, he was seen by an entire movie theater."

Henry threw up his hands. "I don't know." He glanced toward the windows. He spoke loudly—making sure that he was clearly heard.

"Here you go, Sophie. You all suspected me—before last night or early this morning, or whatever it was. Why? Because you thought it was an inside job. Who better to pull off a crime than those who know what the police are searching for? Okay, so I'm what you see as a creepy guy. I have no wife, no kids, no family. Well, hell, I wasn't really attractive most of my life. But now, I'm going to retire. And you're not going to pin these awful murders on me—why? Because I didn't commit them. And, hell, I haven't been hanging around getting stupider and stupider. I have the best attorneys my saved-up-never-spent-on-a-wife-or-family money can buy. So, everyone was hoping that you'd get something out of me—why? Because, of course, I might be a creepy guy, but you're a beautiful young woman— and you've always been kind to me. Sophie, there's nothing to get out of me. The crime scene photos got out—it's the day and age when the internet rules. Anyone could have done it. Every-one involved in investigating has access to those pictures. Think of it this way—hell, even our dear Captain Chagall could have done it. Oh, and the murders. Seriously? Who has experience with crime scenes? You hear that, Captain? You want to play this game? It could have been you. So there you are with me, Sophie. I can tell you nothing. Nothing. So, take that to the bank. I think we're done for now."

"Henry... I hope you're telling the truth. I really do," Sophie said, rising.

"Actually, that's not, it," Henry said.

"Then what?"

"Keep looking. For the love of God, keep looking."

She nodded, and left the room.

Chagall was waiting for her in observation. She wondered if he'd be angry—or, at the least, irritated—by the accusation.

He wasn't, but he did tell her, "Don't worry. He wouldn't get anywhere accusing me. I was playing poker with the sheriff and a few old friends until two on Saturday night—and Mon-day night, I slept at my daughter's, watching my infant grand-daughter all through the night with my wife."

"But what do you think?" Sophie asked him. "Is he telling the truth?"

"Well, he could be."

"He could be."

"Or, he could be a very good liar. As good at getting out of the accusation as he was at imitating the Black Dahlia murders. What's your gut say?"

"I don't know," Sophie said. "Anyway, I've done what I can… I'm going to go join Bruce out at the old graveyard. Apparently, he might be onto something more. Something that can help us."

The desk sergeant opened the door to the observation room. "Captain."

"Yes?"

"Sorry, Detective Manning, I didn't mean to interrupt. But it does involve you."

"It's okay. I'm about to leave. How does it involve me?"

"They're letting Miss Leon go from the hospital. She's a nervous wreck. We told her that a police officer would watch over her."

"Yes, and we will have an officer drive her home, check out her place, and stay with her," Chagall said. "So, what's wrong?"

"She wants Sophie."

"There's already a patrolman at the hospital," Sophie said.

"She wants you," the desk sergeant told her, grimacing.

"She's going to have to wait," Sophie said flatly. "Have them tell her that I will be there—as soon as I can."

"Detective Manning is not her professional babysitter," Chagall said. "Tell her exactly what Sophie said. Except, Sophie, you don't have to watch over her."

"She knows that you have a suspect in custody, right?"

"She's more than dramatic," the desk sergeant said.

"I agree. Protect and serve, and Sophie protected her—someone else can serve," Chagall said.

"I don't mind. I'll get Bruce and we'll go see her together. Tell her I will be by," Sophie told him.

"Sure thing."

He left, and the captain turned to Sophie. "Wish they would have kept her in the hospital—it's easier for us there. Do you need a car? Didn't you get here with Bruce?"

Sophie nodded. "Yep, you're right. I did."

"Lee Underwood is heading back out. He just brought some soil samples and bits of torn fabric back to the lab. I'll have him take you."

"Fine," Sophie said.

She headed out, unsure of what she wanted to find.

Bruce stood by the Johnstone tomb in the graveyard.

Sabrina Hayes was inside the old church, making sure the cops didn't destroy her company's holding.

He'd figured she might be horrified to learn that women had been killed in her graveyard.

She hadn't been. She was a bit ghoulishly appreciative of all that had happened.

"This place will be insane now!" she'd told him. "Everyone is going to want to come here."

He didn't speak with her long.

Angela had written to tell him that she was sure there was more underground—somewhere. Also, she'd wanted him to know that the Johnstone family had owned a large portion of the nearby property at one time; some of it had been farmland.

He called her, wanting to know more.

"Well, they died out at the turn of the century—nineteenth to twentieth," Angela told him. "They donated a lot of what they had to the city of Los Angeles, to museums and, yes, to the church. Property was auctioned off, and you have the bars and restaurants and what you see that's there now. But I suggest that you keep pounding on crypt walls—or maybe go through some of the skeletons there."

"Great," he said.

"No more help from Ann Marie Beauvoir or Michael Thoreau?"

"I don't even know where they are today," Bruce said. "The tomb area is just now clearing out—forensic team is heading out, leaving just one cop to keep watch, though for how long, I don't know… They do have Henry Atkins in custody, and evidence—circumstantial, no prints on even the sniper rifle—but we were suspecting him before."

"You don't sound certain."

"I'm not. He could be the killer—he could also be the perfect scapegoat."

"Where's Jackson?"

"At the hospital. He's with Vining. Brodie is watching over Grace Leon."

"You and your brother should really think about joining us," Angela said. "No pressure."

He laughed. "No pressure."

"All three McFadden brothers would be a nice addition. Mull it over."

"I'm mulling," he assured her. "All right, if you get anything else—"

"I'll let you all know immediately," she said.

"I'm going to crawl through skeletons now."

"Enjoy."

He ended the call and headed to the pyramid structure of tombs and took the stone steps down into the catacombs below. A woman with the forensic team was heading back up.

"I swear, we have everything that could be down there," she told him.

"I'm sure you do," he said. He smiled. She waited for him to leave. He didn't. She shrugged and climbed the stairs.

For a moment, he was alone. He looked around. Forensics had left their work lights up and casting a too-bright glow around the crypt.

Some things buried should remained buried. But even the earth itself could be a brutal mistress. It wasn't like an ancient tomb where shrouded bodies lay rotting.

But a quake—or perhaps several small quakes—had definitely done damage.

Cement seals were chipped or broken almost everywhere.

Along the sides, coffins were clearly visible.

The bony, half-mummified hand still dangled from the one.

There was more underground. There had been more, at least. Maybe the shifting earth had covered it all, and it was there no more?

No. There was something. The killer had needed a very sharp knife to create the Joker's grin on his victim's faces. He had needed a saw or something as honed as a scalpel to bisect the bodies.

And they had found no such tools. Nor had they found the clothing the victims had been wearing before they had been killed.

He began tapping at the seals where the Johnstone family had been interred. The seals were so weakened they crumbled easily. There were coffins. And there were skeletons.

No tools.

He straightened, frustrated, and then turned to the slab where the girls had been tied—and brutally murdered.

Walking over to it, he hunkered down.

He began to tap under the slab. Useless—so many people had been working there.

But as he pounded on the earth, he suddenly heard a difference in the sounds his efforts were creating.

A hollow reverberation. There was something hollow here.

He began to push aside dirt and dust and found nothing. He stopped himself; he needed to be methodical.

He pushed one inch at a time.

And finally, he found it.

The opening was so smooth that it appeared to be part of the earth flooring, invisible to the naked eye.

But it was there.

It didn't open; it slid back. There was no hinge, no hook, no handle.

It just slid back and led into more darkness.

"There's more, there's definitely more," Lee Underwood said.

He brushed his surfer-blond hair from his forehead as he drove.

Sophie wished that she was at the wheel.

"You don't believe that Henry committed the murders?" Sophie asked him.

He shook his head and flashed her a smile. A beach-boy smile.

She found herself thinking of Ted Bundy: good-looking, charming.

They were in a car; he was driving. But it was growing late. It would be dark soon.

She was a cop. With a gun. She knew how to use it.

And, of course, the captain knew where she was and who she was with. Even if Lee was the killer, he wouldn't dare try anything with her right now.

How could she believe it was a friend? On the other hand, how could she not, at this point, allow for every possibility?

"Henry…he's an odd old bug, but I like him. And I've been out with him now and then. We both enjoy theater and the movies. I guess I've felt bad for him now and then. Most Friday nights, I have a date. Or I have friends that I see. We go to games…we go to concerts. I knew that Henry loved the Hollywood Hooligans, so, you know, when you mentioned at the meeting that they were having a performance on Saturday night, I thought I should ask him to go. And since Chuck Thompson had been in to bring us some of his lab reports, he wanted to go. I swear, it's hard for me to imagine that Henry went from the performance to kidnapping the leading lady."

"Then how did his rose get there?"

Lee grinned at her. "Hey, I'm just the lab rat. You're the detective."

They were nearing the graveyard gates.

The place wasn't crowded along the street with cop cars anymore.

Two cars were parked just outside the gates, though. One patrol car—and Bruce's rental with the police decal.

She wasn't sure why she felt so relieved when Lee just pulled in, right next to the cop car.

Yes, of course, she knew why. Lee was a forensic investigator. Lee had been at both crime scenes. Lee worked at the station. He had access to the crime scene photos. He could have gotten into her purse—just as easily as Henry—and made a copy of her key. He could have broken into her apartment to see what she had...to steal the page about possible police involvement in the Dahlia case.

He knew what could and couldn't be found when it came to fingerprints, DNA and anything else, and he was perfectly placed to hide any incriminating evidence.

Sophie hopped out.

She saw that an officer was sitting in the driver's seat of the patrol car. He was directly in front of the gate. He could see anyone coming or going.

If they went through the gate, Sophie thought. But she and Bruce had come into graveyard by hopping over the fence.

No one was going to hop over the fence with sharp knives and a bone saw.

She walked over to the officer. She knew him; his name was Frank Paisley. He'd been with the force about three years. She liked him. He had an easy manner about him. He was good at breaking up fights—and exceptional at crowd control.

He quickly rolled down his window. "Hey, Detective Manning."

"Hey. What's going on?"

"They've pulled out. I'm on guard duty."

"But the PI, Bruce McFadden, is still in there, right?"

"Yep. He's down in the tomb thing, catacombs—whatever you call something like that. Ugh. I was down there. You know what? I'm going to be cremated. That's—creepy."

Sophie agreed. "Yep, creepy." She realized that Lee was standing behind her. "Okay, well, I'll find Bruce."

"I'm with you," Lee said.

She turned back to him. "I thought that forensics was done here."

"Basically. I can't help thinking that we missed something. Still need to find the tools."

She felt comfort in her holstered Glock, tucked into her waistband. But she also smiled at Officer Paisley.

"Keep an eye out for us, will you?"

"Always, Detective Manning."

Lee might be making her feel uneasy, but it never hurt to be uneasy.

Alert—aware—and on guard.

"You first!" she told Lee.

He shrugged. "As you wish, Detective!"

They went through the gate and over to the steps to the catacomb.

Police floodlights still illuminated the dank space. The smell of the earth rose up to greet them as they headed down.

"Bruce?" Sophie called.

There was no answer.

"Sophie, look!" Lee called.

She could see cement seal had crumbled on the ground.

And then she saw what Lee was talking about—a hole. A

gaping hole, right beneath the slab where Grace Leon had been tied the night before.

The slab...stained with blood.

She hurried over to the hole.

"Bruce?"

There was no answer.

"Let's go down," she said.

"We'll have to jump," Lee said. "No steps. You—you tall enough to do that?"

"Yes, yes, I can do it," Sophie said.

But go first? Or after? Which would afford him less opportunity for an attack?

First. She'd go down first. She'd be ready to draw on him before he landed next to her.

"I'm pulling rank," Sophie said lightly. "Hopping on down."

She lowered herself, keeping an eye on him. Then gripping the edge of the hole, she let herself fall, muscles and limbs loose to absorb the impact.

The floodlights barely filtered through. Shadows were everywhere. She seemed to be in a maze of tunnels.

She backed away, waiting for Lee.

Ready to draw.

She looked up. "Coming down?"

"Coming!" he said, crawling to the edge, as she had done.

And it was then, as she was looking up at him, that she suddenly felt the swish of air behind her.

And felt the excruciating pain as something crashed hard against her head.

CHAPTER EIGHTEEN

Sunday night

When he'd first jumped from the chamber and hit the ground deep below, Bruce had been all but blinded.

The floodlights above shone down, but they created a small pool of light just below the now open hole, and all beyond that was shadow, moving into a darkness that was so deep in pitch, it seemed that no light could penetrate its shade.

He'd entered an obsidian pit. That was his initial assessment. But Bruce carried a small flashlight on his key chain that was actually brighter than the one on his phone, and while it couldn't illuminate far, it provided a path before him.

As he looked at the construction of what had once been a giant foundation, Bruce was sure that an enterprising priest or engineer had seen to it that the web of tunnels that stretched from the church and out to the Johnstone catacomb had been sealed—they must have become increasingly dangerous, after the quake of 1920, and perhaps even some of the smaller ones that had followed.

He was equally sure that come Prohibition, some equally enterprising person—mob connected, perhaps?—had seen to it that some of them became useful again. Walls were shored up here and there with large planks of wood; some areas that had caved in had been left.

He squatted low to the ground, shining the light over it.

Someone had been there. Recently.

Bruce pulled out his phone, determined to report his find immediately.

A blinking light informed him that he had no service. He pocketed his phone. He'd just go back up and call in a minute, but he needed to know one more thing.

The answers were here. He shone his light down the hall. He stood and kept moving, slowly, closely scanning all around.

A low arch off the hallway led to another little room. Bruce ducked in.

Boxes that had stored liquor decades ago remained in the little chamber.

They were right next to a number of tombs.

Liquor box, corpse, liquor box…corpse.

But that was just one of the rooms that led off from the first tunnel where he had come down, deep into the earth. There were many more.

The main tunnel veered off in a few directions. Bruce, however, followed it in what he was certain was the direction of the old church.

He reached a larger chamber. The side walls were lined with tombs. There were massive old containers made of some kind of metal; Bruce thought that they might well have had something to do with the storage and movement of alcohol—they were covered with dust and spiderwebs, as if they might well go back to those days when speakeasies hid from the law and even the average working Joe was willing to pay a high price now and then for a drink.

One of the round cylinders had no top of any kind. Bruce moved over and looked into it; there, at the bottom of the rusted and decaying cylinder, was a cache.

A cache of knives.

He trained his little light down and saw that they were encrusted in red.

Blood. He moved a little closer, shining his light downward.

Among the objects was a bone saw.

He took out his phone again. Still no service. But he quickly snapped a few photographs of his find. He'd located almost everything.

The water to wash the bodies… Where had the killer washed the bodies?

He kept moving and hit a wall. He searched for an opening. It was no easy task with just the small light, but he was convinced that the wall he'd hit was a divider—after the earthquakes, whoever had decided that the underground should just be cut off had walled up what were the most important graves belonging to the church. Someone had long ago decided that it just wasn't necessary for people to crawl below the ground to visit the dead.

He pushed, pressed and prodded.

There didn't seem to be an entry.

He ducked down, feeling something under his feet give.

Touching the ground, he saw that it was wet. And the water had to be coming from somewhere.

He followed the wetness on his hand to the wall. And there, finally, he found the break.

Once upon a time, a flap door had been made by men who were bootleggers. They might have been cold and calculating; they might have been gangsters or mob men.

He doubted if any of them could have imagined that in their

drive to provide a commodity and make money, they had provided a killing ground for an incredibly sick psychopath.

He opened the sliding door flap.

It led into a small chamber.

Once upon a time, the "chamber" had been a wall of crypts for interment of the dead.

The dead were no longer neatly aligned in their coffins; they had become a pile of bones and scrap, all but crushed into a pile in a corner.

Water dripped from a converted pipe; looking up and trying to figure his position beneath the church, Bruce reckoned that he was near the back, where the office area would be above—along with the kitchenette and bathroom.

As long as water moved smoothly—and a toilet didn't back up—no one would investigate.

Only a plumber might one day find the diversion of the pipes.

Their killer hadn't just known about forensic detail and the Dahlia's death. He had known about the historic church and graveyard here, and the history of the underground after the 1920s quake—and the history of gangsters or desperate parishioners using the underground for bootleg booze.

He threw his light over the whole of the corridor. It glanced off something shiny.

A large metal tub.

Still filled with putrid, bloody water.

He walked to the other side of the tub. There was another set of the sliding doors there—one that seemed to blend right with the earth and stone of foundation.

There was darkness beyond. He threw his light on it and saw that the opening was right into the church catacomb. He was in a tomb—where the dead had been tossed aside for expediency's sake. To all appearances he was standing in the final resting place of five of the church's deacons and priests, including, at chest height, "Father Sebastian McDonald, beloved by his flock."

He pulled out his phone again, forgetting he had no signal. He dropped the phone, swearing at himself, and reached down to get it. To his surprise, over here—far beneath the church itself—he suddenly had coverage.

He called Sophie's number; it rang, and then went to voice mail.

The ringing seemed to echo strangely. As if her phone weren't far away.

No great mystery there; she might have come to the graveyard; she might be there now already.

Then, he heard a strange laugh. In the eerie underworld, he couldn't tell if it was male or female, or where it had originated.

The tunnels were a twisted web.

The laugh came again.

Diabolical.

A ghostly laugh in the realm of the dead.

He turned quickly toward the exit to the main tunnel, putting out his light, casting himself into pitch darkness.

Someone was out there.

It must be another cop or someone from forensics—or even Sophie. She might well have come here if she'd finished at the station.

Bull. He didn't even believe himself.

Sophie didn't laugh like that. Everyone was gone, except for the patrolman out at the gate. And he didn't know about the deep underground, or that there was more than one way to enter the catacombs, that the kingdom of the dead stretched farther than they had ever imagined.

He needed to call Jackson and get him or Brodie there, fast.

He tried to adjust to the total darkness as he felt in his pocket for his phone.

"No! Bruce...no, you need to come now. Now!"

The sudden ghostly voice at his ear caused him to jump. He thought of himself as a pretty tough guy, but the urgent whisper in the dark was alarming.

"Bruce, no...he could panic, kill her... God, help me, I know why I'm here! He's going to kill her, and I have to help you stop it!"

He realized that it was the ghost of Michael Thoreau at his side.

And the "her" to whom he referred was Sophie.

Despite himself, he felt a shudder streak through his body, and fear tear into his heart.

Sophie awoke.

It was a slow awakening; she had a thudding headache. She was awake, she realized, because she had heard laughter. It seemed such a strange sound.

Like a witch's cackle.

Then someone started speaking.

"They really are such idiots. To be honest, I think it's better this way. If it had worked as you wanted it to...they'd have figured it out eventually. As it was... I just slipped out the back. Right out the back, with no one having any idea!"

The voice seemed close, and yet far away.

It seemed to echo, and yet...

She tried to move—and realized that she could not. She was stretched out, arms pulled high over her head, feet tied together, tied down. She felt as if she was on a medieval rack...

A torturer's rack. An executioner's rack.

A light suddenly shone, straight into her eyes.

"Sophie, you're awake."

This voice was male; the first had been female.

She was blinded; she couldn't see a thing.

Lee Underwood! He had followed her down, but…

He'd been behind her; he couldn't have struck her out of the darkness.

An accomplice?

"Even you! Beautiful, smart Sophie. A tough detective, but such a nice girl. Always, though, a nice girl…it's really not with maliciousness that I'm doing this. It's to prove a point, you see. The LAPD, the FBI—all of them talk a tough trade. But they know nothing. They still know nothing."

Her head was still hurting; she couldn't place the voice. And then, with a bit of a twist of the light, she realized that the voice was off because the speaker was wearing a mask.

A Greek theater mask.

Like the ones used by the Hollywood Hooligans.

Her mouth wouldn't work; she was trying to talk. It took a moment.

"They'll find you. They'll find everything now. I'm not the one who discovered that there was another level down here," she managed to say at last.

It occurred to her that she was going to die. In a horrible way. He was going to put her into ungodly agony, slashing her face, cutting into her again and again…

And when she was dead, cutting her in half, leaving her to be found in a barren field. And the Black Dahlia copycat killer would be gleeful.

See? I can even kill a cop, and you can't find me!

"Sophie, come on. I saw you slip through the opening on your own."

It was the female voice. Sophie gritted her teeth, feeling fury tear through her.

She knew the voice.

"And I thought I'd saved your life, Grace. Hmm. Well, this isn't very original—one of the theories about the Dahlia suggested a female killer. And a cover-up. Nothing so elaborate as this, but... Well, this is just not original."

Was this wise, she wondered blearily, taunting Grace? She tried to remember all the classes she had taken on the psychology of killers, how to keep them talking, and how to disarm them.

She didn't know if she was saying the right words or not—foolish, but she was even more angry than scared.

"Oh, Sophie, I'm not going to kill you. Ugh. I don't do the killing. I just...well, okay, I did do a little cutting on their faces, and I may do yours. But honestly, none of this was my idea."

"I didn't think so. You're not that bright. Oh, and you're not that good an actress, either."

"I fooled you last night."

"So you did," Sophie admitted.

"Great show, don't you think?" Grace asked her. "I got to be exactly where I wanted to be, thanks to the killings," she said.

"You're just as culpable. You'll go to prison for just as long," Sophie said. The light was still in her eyes. She knew now that Grace Leon had struck her on the head.

"I'm not going to prison. I'm going to be a big star. You saw—it will happen."

It would happen. Sophie thought—*I will die, and this little witch will get away with all, and yes, become a star.*

She tried to move; the ties really weren't that good. If she could free just a bit of herself...

She managed to adjust her position a little. And she could feel that her Glock was still in its holster; they hadn't thought to look for or take her gun.

How the hell had she let this happen? She would be dead...

And Grace would have what she had wanted so badly; what she had become involved in murder to achieve.

No, that wouldn't happen. Because she hadn't been the one to find the opening in the catacombs.

Bruce was there. Bruce had found it. And he had to be there...
somewhere.

But who was the man above her? Lee Underwood? Maybe Bruce wasn't there; maybe Grace had set it up so that she would only think that Bruce was there. Maybe Bruce was there somewhere lying dead or injured. And if the man above her wasn't Lee Underwood, then who the hell was it?

"I'm sorry, Sophie, but it really is time to get started. There really is a great deal to do. I can't wait until you're found, until I'm called to the crime scene!"

There was absolute glee in the voice.

Grace Leon spoke up again. "I hear something."

"Don't be ridiculous. I stopped by and saw the cop in the car. He can't hear anything. I brought him coffee. He'll sleep like the dead for three hours now."

"No. I hear something!"

The man swore. The light was suddenly gone. "All right, all right. I'll show you—the entry is closed. No one knows this is here. Even if her screams carry out a bit, the stupid bar patrons think there are ghosts."

"There is something wrong," Grace insisted.

Sophie opened her mouth and took a breath to scream.

"Shut up—shut up—or I'll put my knife through your heart right now," her tormentor said. "Call for help? Whoever hears you will die, too. Oh, Sophie, live on hope for the next few minutes. We're such tragic creatures—always grasping at any hope!"

The light disappeared.

Sophie heard movement.

Her captors were moving away.

Bruce knew that he had to keep to the wall, and keep to the dark. There were chambers and niches and holes everywhere.

The long dead, the smell of the earth.

The smell of blood.

All seemed to haunt him.

"Michael, where?" he whispered.

"Shh! I'm trying! Ann Marie is here…she's going to find the right place. We just have to move carefully. It's a maze down here. One tunnel leads to another and to another. We just found it ourselves."

Bruce froze; he heard a scuffling down the hall.

It could have been rats.

It could also be human rats.

He flattened against the wall, and a crumpled piece of coffin fell.

Little pieces of old bone seemed to dissolve and follow.

It was nothing much, but he'd made a noise.

He ducked into the next room.

Then he heard a scream.

Sophie.

"Bruce, they're coming for you, they're coming for you! Two of them! Grace Leon, and someone in a mask!"

He drew his gun and felt every muscle in his body tighten.

He would follow her voice.

They might be ready for him. But he was ready for them.

Sophie screamed again. And he ran.

"Sophie, oh, man, Sophie!"

She'd screamed—they weren't going to kill her and get away with it. At least, they wouldn't take Bruce by surprise.

They would go down.

But even as she clenched and prayed, she heard that voice.

"Oh, jeez, Sophie… I'm trying, I'm trying…"

It wasn't the person in the mask. She realized, incredulously, that it was Lee Underwood at her side, trying to help her.

It was dark. So dark…

And yet his face came closer.

She saw that it was bloody and bashed. He didn't look much like the studly beach boy at all at the moment, but it was Lee Underwood, trying to untie her.

"Oh, Sophie, they hit me so hard...and I think my leg is broken," Lee said. "These knots, there's blood in my eyes..."

There might be blood in his eyes, but he had done something. It had loosed one hand enough that she could squiggle and squirm it and feel it loosening.

"Who is it, Lee? Who the hell is it?" she demanded.

"Don't know, Sophie...just..."

He'd halfway freed her.

Then he collapsed.

Someone was ahead of him. And there were two of them.

And one was Grace Leon. Their supposed victim from the night before. That had all been done to get the police and the forensic team to search and search...

And then leave the place the hell alone.

Had the killer always wanted Sophie—just to prove how good he was?

How the hell had he involved Grace Leon? Or was she the instigator?

Sophie had screamed, but now he didn't hear her.

There was a scuffling along the hallway. He thought that the two killers had ducked into another room.

He moved forward more carefully himself.

Then, out of the darkness, out of a corridor he had nearly missed, a man came lunging at him. A massive, gleaming, sharp butcher knife held high in his hands.

The mask and bone dust about him made him appear more eerie than anything the tomb could offer.

"Bruce," Michael warned.

"I see him."

And Bruce swung around. "Stop, or I'll shoot!"

The man didn't stop.

Bruce took aim and fired.

Sophie struggled hard, trying not to move in panic, but rather let the rope burns and agony she was enduring pay, at the very least.

Bruce was out there.

And the killer was out there, and Grace Leon was out there.

She kept at it, fearing for Lee Underwood. He had tried so hard to help, to free her.

Now he was down. She didn't know if he was alive or dead. They would have intended to kill him.

Maybe they thought that he was already dead.

"Bruce!"

How had Grace gotten there, and gotten in? And how had the killer come?

She couldn't worry about that now; she had to keep warning Bruce.

And she had to free herself.

Before they came back.

Suddenly, her heart seemed to leap. Gunfire. Not far.

Surely, Bruce had fired. There had just been one shot.

"Bruce!" she screamed. "Be careful, there are two of them. Grace Leon is out there—she's in on this!"

Sophie worked on her bindings.

Then she saw a flood of light. A brilliant light beamed from the doorway.

"Bruce!"

"No, Sophie, you bitch, you've ruined my life!"

Grace was back.

With a knife in her hands.

"Let me tell you, Sophie, you're going to die with one hell of a grin!"

★ ★ ★

The man was dead.

Bruce knew how to aim; he'd caught him center of the forehead, even through the mask.

He knelt down quickly to be certain, checking for a pulse, and pulling the mask from the man's face.

He stared, pursing his lips.

Yes, they'd known it was someone close to the department. "Bruce!"

Sophie, screaming again, crying out with warning. He could hear her fear for him. They had to have threatened her. And he knew Sophie; she wasn't going down without a fight.

He stood quickly, trying to race for the sound of her voice.

Light!

There was light ahead, gleaming from around a curve in the catacomb tunnel, down in one of the spiderweb-covered directions he hadn't chosen.

He sprinted, his heart and lungs on fire. The ghost Michael Thoreau came along at his side. Down the hall, he saw Ann Marie, beckoning to him from an archway.

He burst through it.

And there, tied down upon an old tomb, was Sophie. There was a crumpled body just to the side of it. A bloody, crumpled body.

And, racing toward Sophie now, her own knife held high, was Grace Leon.

He took aim.

He never had to fire.

Sophie broke free from her bounds at that moment and reached back.

Her attackers had finally made a terrible mistake; they had left her armed.

Sophie fired.

Grace seemed to freeze for a minute, as if it were a performance. As if she were a great, mythical heroine, dying with dramatic throes.

Then she fell flat to the floor.

He'd suspected that Sophie was a crack shot, too.

She turned to him, tears flooding her eyes. "Bruce, oh, thank God, Bruce, you're all right!"

He rushed to her side. She threw her arms around him and he felt her terror, felt the fierce pounding of her heart.

"They're down, Sophie, they're both down."

"Oh, God, they were going to cut me. Bruce, I can't imagine what they went through, Lili and Brenda, and even Elizabeth Short...oh, Bruce! I've killed her. We need to call an ambulance. That's Lee. He tried to help me. Henry is innocent. And so is Lee. And if so... Oh, God, please tell me that it isn't...isn't Captain Chagall?"

"No. It was the man who really did know how to cut up a body, Sophie. Dr. Chuck Thompson."

EPILOGUE

Monday morning

"Wow. You thought…you thought it was me," Lee Underwood said bleakly. He winced as he spoke to them from his hospital bed.

Sophie was at his side. Grant Vining—finally checking out of the hospital himself—had joined her, along with Bruce, Brodie, Jackson Crow, Henry Atkins and Captain Chagall.

They were a bit of a horde, and they weren't allowed to stay long; Lee was going to go into surgery for his leg.

He was going to need some serious care as he had many broken bones. And while Dr. Thompson had done the killing when it came to Lili and Brenda, Grace Leon had been the one to smash Lee over and over again with a broken piece of tombstone. He hadn't been the target for the night, but he'd been there. And, therefore, he'd needed to die.

Sophie couldn't help but feel a little guilty for having put him high on her suspect list; he'd been trying to help her while he had to have been thinking he was most likely going to be murdered himself.

"We suspected Henry, too," Sophie said, glancing at Henry.

"They had me locked up," Henry said. "Scary."

"It had to be someone connected," Grant Vining explained.

"But, Sophie, you thought it was me?" Lee repeated.

"I'm sorry!" Sophie said.

"It's because I'm so good-looking, right?" Lee asked. "Charming—the kind who could get away with it all."

"It's because you're a forensic investigator who was everywhere, had every opportunity—and could have copied Sophie's key," Bruce told him, grinning.

"And you are charming, of course," Sophie assured him.

"Dr. Thompson. Unbelievable. Do you think…do you think he just spent too much time with corpses? Or by himself? How the hell did he and Grace become involved?" Lee asked, shaking his head with confusion.

"Grace's mother died home alone—that meant that she needed an autopsy," Bruce explained. "Best we can put it together, Sophie met Thompson when her mother was at the morgue. Who knows who started talking about what they wanted—and how to get it. They were definitely an odd couple."

"Grace Leon wanted to be famous, more than anything. She needed to become lead actress for the Hollywood Hooligans. She saw it as a launchpad for fame. And she…well, they're going to exhume her mother. It's likely Grace had already killed—matricide. Maybe she even became involved with Chuck as a way to keep him from reporting the truth of her mother's death. Apparently, her mother had the money Grace needed to keep from having to take a day job," Sophie told him.

"Thompson was always at the station. And he was wary of Vining—which is why he shot Grant," Captain Chagall explained. "And," he said sternly, looking at Sophie, "I believe he tried to get Sophie with his sniper rifle, too. I knew that he'd served in Desert Storm. I had never known that he was a sniper."

"I thought we were friends. And he was making me a patsy for murder," Henry said.

"I believe he wanted to leave us all guessing forever," Chagall offered. "You were in jail when he went after Sophie. He must have wanted Grace to lure Sophie to her apartment—that's what it was all about when Grace called the station and demanded Sophie be her police protection—and then sneak her out somehow. But Sophie told Grace she'd have to wait. Chuck was calling the station, too—keeping tabs on everyone. He knew that Sophie was going back to the church. Where he made his first mistake was believing that the police and forensic crew had all pulled out. He must not have had any idea that Bruce had found the door beneath the slab on the first level of the catacombs."

"But how was Chuck getting in?" Lee asked.

"It turns out that he had a connection to the church—and the burial ground," Jackson said. "And he knew about all the things we had to discover—and that Bruce stumbled upon."

"Don't tell me—his ancestor was a Johnstone?" Lee asked.

"No, he had an ancestor who was a bootlegger, and—we're assuming—someone in the family told tales about the old days when Chuck was growing up. We found a few family tree books in his home, along with all kinds of bloody clothes. Somehow, somewhere, he combined his fascination with the Dahlia case and his own lineage. Oh, and every book ever written on the Black Dahlia is in his bookcase, along with newspaper reports, copies of police ledgers, and more. Oh, and notes. He did believe that Elizabeth Short was killed by someone in Bugsy Siegel's employ. Maybe a couple of people, including a man who was a doctor—until gambling debts and a drug habit got him into trouble and he wound up being one of Siegel's lackeys. That's what Thompson seemed to think."

"Could that be real?" Lee asked.

Bruce grimaced. "I don't think we'll ever know what really happened," he said. "I guess what mattered to Thompson is what drove him."

"He's dead, and Grace is dead," Lee said, and shuddered fiercely. "And we had just watched her...act. I guess we were really always watching her act."

"I've heard actors saying that they'd die for a role...just never knew one who would actually kill for one!" Vining said.

The nurse came in and sweetly ushered them all out. She had to start to prep Lee for surgery.

Lee grinned behind her back.

She was a pretty nurse.

"Down to the station now," Chagall told Bruce and Sophie. "You have to be cleared on the shootings. It won't take too long. And, of course, you're going to need a few sessions with one of our therapists, Sophie, before reporting for duty again. Not that we want you reporting back for a while—don't show your face for a week, and I mean that. And, Bruce...well, just for yourself, you should talk to someone, you know."

"Yes, sir," Bruce said. "I'll talk to someone."

Sophie had a feeling that the someone he would talk to just might be dead.

But as she now knew, that was all right.

Captain Chagall and Henry Atkins were heading into the station. Henry was going to work his last few weeks—at his own insistence—and then take his retirement.

Jackson and Brodie were going to the airport in Burbank; they had to head back to Virginia. Sophie gave them a lift.

Bruce had begged out of that first trip back; for one, he still had to go through a few more interviews regarding the shooting and everything that had happened at the old graveyard.

Sophie hugged them both fiercely before they headed to their gate.

Jackson smiled and told her that he knew a good place for her to work—if the L thing ever drove her too crazy.

She smiled. She loved LA. It was her home.

But then again...

She didn't mind traveling.

"And you, Bruce," Jackson said. "You know where you could really work with ease, lots of honesty—and tackle more tough cases. I'll be twisting Brodie's arm on the way back."

"You may not have to twist too hard," Brodie said, waving and hugging Sophie again. He winked at her before releasing her.

"You really have to meet the folks!"

Sophie smiled at that.

"And come out to see Marnie and Bryan."

"Sure," she told him.

She and Bruce saw the two of them off, and went back to the car.

Sophie slid into the passenger seat, happy to let Bruce deal with traffic. "Where to now? We don't have to be to the station—"

"Hawaii. As soon as we can. Great vacation spot—and we both need a vacation." Bruce grinned at her.

She smiled back at him. "Okay, so we have to arrange that. At this moment... I know that the graveyard is being ripped apart. But I think we need to move over to the section with the really beautiful angel."

"You want to see Michael?"

"Yes."

"I feel bad—we never solved his murder."

"Actually, we might have."

"Really?"

"Well, not the two of us—as in we. But yes, we—as in Angela is truly amazing and found what might be an answer."

"And that is…?"

"Even after all this—we haven't solved the Black Dahlia murder, either. Really, there are so many theories. But one is gangster related. Elizabeth Short was killed on January 15, 1947. Bugsy Siegel was shot and killed on June 29, 1947, just about six months later. But before he pushed too hard and some of the bigger guys pushed back, he was like a king in LA. He was a true godfather when it came to the creation of Las Vegas, but he had power out here, too. Friends at the top—and others as dirty and slimy as they come. Anyway, if it was true that Siegel was involved, he had a lot of people in his employ he could dispatch to get rid of an annoying reporter. There was one fellow who another mobster pinpointed in a letter to a friend when he was on death row himself, that said the man's name was Harry Lester Pierpont. He went down in a hail of gunfire in Chicago. We can tell Michael that…well, that his killer, we believe, met his just reward."

It was strange to return the graveyard—even if they weren't going belowground.

And it wasn't a quick affair.

Every cop and tech there wanted to tell Sophie how grateful they were that she had come out of it okay. And wanted to commiserate over how unbelievable it was that the murderer was Dr. Thompson!

Finally, they were able to wander away from the Johnstone tombs and over to the beautiful sculpture of the angel with the spread wings.

They sat at the base of the statue and waited, and, soon enough, hand in hand, Michael and Ann Marie came to them.

Sophie immediately thanked them.

Bruce did the same.

Michael beamed and said, "Thank you! Thank you for allow-ing us to make a difference."

Bruce went on to tell Michael what Angela had been able to learn. He listened gravely.

"So, I was getting too close to the truth."

"Yes."

"I was a good reporter. I'd have only ever reported the truth, not all the wild speculation that went on!"

Sophie looked over at Ann Marie. "We can do more research. We can see what we can find out for you."

Ann Marie smiled. "It doesn't matter now. I have Michael."

"Excellent," Bruce murmured. "And are you…thinking of moving on?" Bruce asked.

Michael smiled. "No, not yet. They're expecting this to be-come an exceptional attraction. You know…they'll do another Hollywood tour here. It will be very, very busy."

"We want to keep an eye on things for a while," Ann Marie said.

"And maybe torment a few tourists. Just a bit!" Michael said. "But despite what happened, you will be back to see us?

Sophie assured them both that she and Bruce would be back.

They left the church and graveyard and headed back to So-phie's house. They were finally alone; the night had been for-ever. They'd had just a few minutes sleep.

But now…

They didn't talk about it.

They just came together, both grateful to be alive.

Grateful to be together.

And then, when they lay, very sleepy and yet very contented, it was time to talk.

"Sophie. I want you to come back with me. I want you and me to think about the Krewe together. You're a cop. You're al-ways going to have that desire to serve and protect. But…you see the dead. Okay, we've known each other a week. I should go home alone and give you time. But I'm serious about Hawaii. I love Hawaii. Or another island. Another place you might love. I want to give you time."

She rolled over and kissed his lips.

"I need just one thing from you," she said.

"And that is?"

"You!" she said.

He smiled, and drew her to him.

"So, me, after five years...we have to make sure that I'm not just better than nothing."

Sophie kissed him again.

"I believe that you're actually better than—anything. And I'd just love to get to Hawaii and keep testing that theory."

"Really? You'd like to go away with me?"

"Hawaii sounds lovely. And then..."

"Then?"

She laughed softly. "Home with you. I do have to meet the folks," she told him.

"Ah, mercy!" Bruce said.

He pulled her close. For the moment, they did have time.

And one another.

And...life.

It was everything they needed.

★ ★ ★ ★ ★